MW01241824

HILLTOP CHRISTMAS

KATHLEEN D. BAILEY

ELK LAKE PUBLISHING INC.
PUBLISHING THE POSITIVE
Plymouth, Massachusetts
A Christian Company
ElkLakePublishingInc.com

COPYRIGHT NOTICE

Hilltop Christmas

First edition. Copyright © 2023 by Kathleen D. Bailey. The information contained in this book is the intellectual property of Kathleen D. Bailey and is governed by United States and International copyright laws. All rights reserved. No part of this publication, either text or image, may be used for any purpose other than personal use. Therefore, reproduction, modification, storage in a retrieval system, or retransmission, in any form or by any means, electronic, mechanical, or otherwise, for reasons other than personal use, except for brief quotations for reviews or articles and promotions, is strictly prohibited without prior written permission by the publisher.

This is a work of fiction. Names, characters, businesses, places, events, locales, and incidents are either the products of the author's imagination or used in a fictitious manner. Any resemblance to actual persons, living or dead, or actual events is purely coincidental.

Daniel Webster. "The Old Man of the Mountain Memorial: Remembering a Legend." *New England Magazine*

John 1:5 is taken from THE HOLY BIBLE, NEW INTERNATIONAL VERSION®, NIV® Copyright © 1973, 1978, 1984, 2011 by Biblica, Inc.™ Used by permission. All rights reserved worldwide.

Psalm 121:1-2 taken from the KING JAMES VERSION (KJV): KING JAMES VERSION, public domain.

Robert Frost. "Stopping by Woods on a Snowy Evening." *The Poetry of Robert Frost,* edited by Edward Connery Lathem. Copyright 1923, © 1969 by Henry Holt and Company, Inc., renewed 1951, by Robert Frost. Reprinted with the permission of Henry Holt and Company, LLC. Source: *Collected Poems, Prose, & Plays* (Library of America, 1995.

William Cowper. "Light Shining Out of Darkness." 1774, *Bartleby. com.* Olney Hymns, 1779. public domain.

Author's photograph taken by Sheila R. Bailey
Cover and Interior Design: Kelly Artieri, Deb Haggerty
Editor(s): Kelsey Renae Budd; Deb Haggerty

PUBLISHED BY: Elk Lake Publishing, Inc., 35 Dogwood Drive, Plymouth, MA 02360, 2023

Library Cataloging Data

Names: Bailey, Kathleen D. ()

Hilltop Christmas / Kathleen D. Bailey.

306 p. 23cm × 15cm (9in × 6in.)

ISBN-13: 9798891340718 (paperback) | 9798891340725 (trade paperback) | 9798891340732 (e-book)

Key Words: small town; childhood abuse; Christmas; forgiveness; family relationships; salvation; mystery

Library of Congress Control Number 2023947124 Fiction

DEDICATION

For many years, my family and I attended two special Christmas festivals. One, "Lights on the Hill," was held in the next town over from ours. The other, "Festival of Lights," took place in a mountain town several hours away at a Catholic shrine and monastery. While different in many ways, both exalted Christ over commercialism. "Lights on the Hill" fell victim to a lack of volunteers, "Festival of Lights" to a lack of vocations. Both furnished me with memories for a lifetime and were crucial to the concept of "Hilltop." This book is dedicated to "Lights on the Hill" and the "Festival of Lights."

ACKNOWLEDGEMENTS

This is my first book with Elk Lake Publishing. I'd like to thank publisher Deb Haggerty for taking a chance on me. Thanks to Kelsey Renae Budd for helping me make *Hilltop* into something somebody would actually want to read, and to Kelly Artieri for the perfect cover.

I'd like to thank my launch team: Glynis Becker, Laura Ritter-Cox, Kelly Criste Goshorn, Carol James, Clarice G. James, Susan Rice Patton, Clare Revell, Sandy Smith and Sarah Soon.

Thanks to my church family at Journey Church, Derry, New Hampshire, for their unconditional love and support.

And as always, thanks to my family: David, my biggest cheerleader, and our daughters, Sheila R. Bailey and Autumn Kent. (Autumn also doubles as tech support.)

Most of all, I thank my risen Lord for allowing me to tell the old, old story one more time, based out of my beloved New Hampshire.

CHAPTER ONE

"You want me to what?" Jane Archer stared at her grandmother.

Was Gram getting addled like older people sometimes did? No. Alice Merrill said what she meant and meant what she said even while recovering from a hip replacement. And what she meant now bore no good tidings for Jane.

"I want you to direct the Christmas Festival for me." Gram sounded as though her request were perfectly logical. "You have the time, and a lot of the work is already done."

Well, it would be. Gram's festival prep was legendary—at least in Hilltop.

But if Jane wanted to get out, now was the time. "Gram, I'm not sure I'm the right person to do this."

"Oh, honey, you cut your teeth on the festival. And you're so organized."

"I'll be taking care of you." It wasn't much of a gauntlet to throw down, and Jane knew it, but she threw it anyway.

And Gram tossed it back. "The visiting nurse comes every day, I've signed up for Meals on Wheels, and I have my books and my DVDs. I'm perfectly capable of amusing myself." She waved a graceful hand toward her desk. "You have the notebook."

The notebook. The two-inch-thick loose-leaf binder that helped a busy widowed schoolteacher run the legendary Hilltop Christmas Festival. That was before a hip replacement sidelined Gram, as much as Gram could be sidelined, and brought Jane home to Hilltop. Not kicking, not screaming, but also hoping not to engage any more than she had to. Especially with the festival.

"I'm not much for Christmas," she said. "I'm not, well, religious." There was more, a lot more, but Gram didn't need to know.

Gram sighed. She had always been the cool grandmother, wearing jeans and hiking boots on her weekends, keeping up with the granddaughter she hadn't expected to raise, keeping current with the fifth graders she taught, serving as a stalwart member of the Hilltop Community Church. She was still slender, her silver hair in a pixie cut, her skin unwrinkled except for the laugh lines.

But for the first time in Jane's memory, she looked fragile. "Janie, Janie. What happened to you?"

That was a valid enough question from the woman who had shepherded her to Sunday School, worship service, youth group. Jane had gone with Gram every Sunday until she left for Cornell University and stopped the week she moved into her dorm room.

But it wasn't Gram's fault, wasn't even Hilltop Church's fault. They had done their best. Jane had been damaged before she came to Hilltop.

Would Gram understand? Probably. Could Jane bear to open that box? No. She'd sealed it the day Gram met her at the bus and took her home.

Gram had done so much for her—everything, really. Taken her in, provided for her every need, inspired Jane toward her own teaching career. She owed Gram. Owed her for things even Gram didn't know about. Could anything she asked, even the Hilltop Festival, be too much?

Jane was organized. She could run a festival, couldn't she? Even if she no longer believed in what it celebrated. Faith in anyone but herself was no longer an option.

But *Gram* had asked her.

Jane heaved herself out of the wing chair and headed for the desk. The notebook was heavier than it looked, with color-coordinated tabs. Well, Jane liked tabs. "Where do I start?"

Gram smiled. "Meet with the pastor. Well, old Reverend Clarke retired, so we got a new one. You should be able to catch him at the church."

Noah Hastings shaded his eyes from the sun-dazzled snow on the church lawn. So much snow, blinding white mounds of it, like the icing their housekeeper Graziella used to slather on birthday cakes. Still, didn't it feel good to be outdoors? Noah had never been a desk kind of guy. But the love of God and his people was making him one. He could still hear the crashing ocean waves calling him back to California and a lifestyle a younger and more worldly version of himself had left behind long before he traded his surfboard in for a Bible.

He could prove himself here. In Hilltop, New Hampshire, among these reserved Yankees, with their thin, sharp faces and sharper wit. Even if he didn't get half their jokes.

His shovel scraped against the sidewalk, and he lifted another flat piece of ice and flung it on top of the powdery snow from yesterday's storm.

"Excuse me? I'd like to—"

Noah turned too sharply, and the shovel he barely knew how to wield hit the young woman at the knees. She lost her balance and tumbled into a snowbank as he tumbled down beside her, all flailing arms and kicking legs. He fought for purchase. There was none. The ice scraped against his cheek, colder than anything he'd ever felt, and stung his bare hands. Gloves. *That's* what he forgot.

What must she be thinking? In his first month on the job, would he put someone in the hospital?

The woman struggled to her feet first, a blur of color that sorted itself out to a pair of high black boots and a fitted red coat. She looked too slim to lift more than a bag of groceries, but her gloved hand gripped his.

"Hang on, and I'll pull you up." she said. "I've got some footing now."

He gripped her hands, heaved himself out of the snowbank—and looked down at the prettiest face he'd seen all day, maybe since coming to Hilltop. Creamy skin with a hint of pink from the cold, delicate features, and big green eyes framed by a tumble of dark brown hair under a red knit cap. Who was she? Why hadn't he seen her before? Was she a Christmas angel?

"Listen, I'm sorry. Really. Are you okay?"

The woman probed at one knee, then another. "I don't think you broke the skin. It's just a bruise. But you should put some ice melt down." She had a sweet voice, laced with irritation. "Anyone knows that. Talk to your boss, I'm sure the church has an account down at Gregson's. Someone could get seriously hurt, and I doubt the church wants a lawsuit."

Not quite an angel but still pretty. Noah retrieved his shovel. "Can I help you?"

"May I, and yes." The woman shook ice crystals from the ends of her hair. "I'm looking for your pastor."

Noah leaned on his shovel, sighed inwardly, and gave the response he'd already used too many times in Hilltop. "You found him."

He has to be joking. Jane looked up, past the broad shoulders to ice-blue eyes and a sculpted face crowned by too-long blond hair and a fading but natural-looking tan. Reverend Clarke, who had pastored the church in her childhood, had retired. But she hadn't expected the church board would have picked this surfer dude.

She looked him up and down. "*You're* the pastor?"

He smiled. "Yeah, I get that a lot."

"When did you—how long—"

"I took over in mid-October. Been here a month. And yes, I'm from California. Long Beach specifically."

"I'm sorry. I thought you were—"

"The gardener. That's one of my favorites. Better than pool boy."

It wasn't funny. Not really. She worked to keep her lips straight. "I'm Jane Archer," she said. "I'm here to talk about the Hilltop Festival."

"Noah Hastings. The *Reverend* Noah Hastings." He rested the shovel in a bank of snow. "I'll take a break from this, and we can talk. In my study. The pastor's study." He held the side door open for her.

Wherever Jane stood with God, she had always admired Hilltop Community Church. The gray stone building had been constructed before the turn of the twentieth century by sturdy mountain people who built it to last. Over the years, they added on an office wing, a Christian education wing, and a function room with a kitchen and small stage in the basement. Dozens of ministries fanned out from here. She remembered sorting used clothing, assembling Thanksgiving baskets, and packing boxes for missionaries back when she believed in things like missions.

Today, the cold sun shone through the stained-glass windows, casting colored shadows over the gleaming golden-oak pews. The room smelled of lemon furniture polish and a faint tinge of candle wax.

"Dazzling, isn't it?" Hastings said at her side.

Jane shrugged. "It's a church." She turned away, but not before she saw his expression tighten.

He led her down the office wing to the first door on the right and motioned her inside. Jane wove her way through crates of books and stubbed one booted toe on a duffel bag before she reached a folding metal chair. One small diploma graced the wall behind a chaotic desk. How could the man work like this?

Her fingers fairly itched to straighten the pile of papers near the edge of the desk. She sat on her hands. "Maybe I should wait till you're settled."

As he eased his long frame into his desk chair, Hastings shoved another teetering pile of correspondence to one side. "I *am* settled. You're here about Hilltop?"

"I'm Alice's granddaughter. She asked me to—" Jane swallowed. She could never replace Gram as chair. Or anything else. "To *help* her coordinate the festival this year."

The pastor leaned back, testing the strength of the chair. "I'm glad she found someone and glad it's someone close at hand. We think a great deal of Alice around here. We're all praying for her swift recovery."

"Yes, well, I'm happy to help. She's amazing. She's done so much for me."

Noah nodded. "She's done a lot for this town." He returned his chair to all four legs and steepled his fingers. "So, I understand the Hilltop Festival started in the fifties as a place for families to go to experience the true Christmas spirit."

Jane forced herself to look at him, and an unexpected heat flushed her cheeks. So what if he was attractive? She cleared her throat. "Hilltop incorporated as a separate entity in 1985, making all sales go into a separate festival account to fund the next year's event. And by the nineties, it was drawing people from all over New England."

"Fine with me." He nodded. "The town lets us use the old library, the new library, the town hall, and the school. The elementary chorus performs in my sanctuary. Are there really no issues with church and state?"

He was sharper than he looked. "Not really. Half the kids in school go to your church. It's really a community festival with everyone involved."

Noah Hastings homed in on her with those clear blue eyes. She looked away, scanning the titles on a randomly-stuffed bookshelf.

"It all ramps up Christmas Eve afternoon with the big parade. Then, there's a free community supper at the American Legion, choirs, a children's pageant, and you. The Christmas Eve service is the culmination of everything Hilltop."

Noah nodded soberly. "I'm told we can expect a crowd."

"Up to five hundred. They can pack everyone in, though it's standing room only."

Noah Hastings shook, muttering something she couldn't hear. "But we're just a little country church."

Jane shrugged. "There's a—a feeling to Hilltop. People I grew up with bring their children, people Gram knew bring their grandchildren. For those three days, it's not like any other place on earth. It's community."

"Alice and some others have told me they sense a real presence of God."

Under her coat and sweater, Jane's heart hammered. "I really wouldn't know." She flipped through Gram's voluminous notebook. Better than looking at him.

Her pretty face was closed, locked tighter than a bank vault. So, Alice's granddaughter wasn't a believer. What had happened to this Jane Archer?

But she was devoted to Alice and willing to work. That would have to do.

And she was beautiful, with that waterfall of dark curls and green eyes like the inside of a wave off Big Sur. She must get her tall stature from her father. Might be fun to get to know her better.

But he had a festival to run.

No place in his life for a woman. He was on enough of a learning curve without that. But surfing in competitions and being son to his stoic father had made him to be resilient under pressure. In a little over a month, he'd made a few friends and a dozen mistakes.

Noah seriously contemplated the old, retired Reverend Clarke's offer to call him with any problems.

This polished Ms. Archer could probably run the church better than he could. There she was with a loose-leaf notebook thick enough to use as a weapon. One of *those*. Probably had lists for everything, planned her wardrobe with an Excel spreadsheet.

Could he preach to five hundred people? Should he have stayed in California? There were churches there. He could have just kept trying till someone took a chance on him. But there was also his reputation as a party boy, surfer dude—and his Dad. He'd wanted to get away, as far away as possible.

Hilltop, New Hampshire, was probably it.Hilltop's people had been kind in his first month, overlooking or gently correcting his mistakes, everything from how to pronounce the Native American name of a hill town to how to run a meeting. He would return their kindness.

Noah smiled at Jane. "So, we meet on Wednesdays. We'll see you at the next meeting?"

"You're quiet tonight." Gram's voice broke the silence at dinner.

Jane swallowed a bite of chicken, moist and redolent with herbs. "I'm tired, I guess. A lot to take in. But this is delicious!"

"It's Anne Gregson's. She makes it for every potluck."

Gram had insisted on wheeling herself to the dining room table rather than eating dinner on a TV tray. The polished oak floors made it easier. Comfort filled the room with two lamps casting a soft glow from a nineteenth-century sideboard. Jane remembered when Gram had found the piece and refinished it.

Gram glanced at the kitchen where a dozen other foil-covered casseroles waited in the freezer. "The girls did well by us. And we've got Joe Colarusso's lasagna in there."

Jane smiled. "Your friends have been good to us."

"That's Hilltop. We help each other." Gram shrugged. "What do you think of our new pastor?"

Jane kept her gaze on her plate, sensing her cheeks flush. "He's all right. Younger than I'd expected."

"Not as young as he seems. He told us he got a bachelor's in engineering before he went to Bible college. But this is his first church." Gram chuckled. "And his first time in the Northeast. I had to take him out to buy snow boots."

Jane tried to push past the image of the tall, blond pastor. But oh, what a smile he had. Made a girl feel—well, she had no business feeling anything.

"I imagine he has his hands full." Jane took a bite of perfectly seasoned green beans. She could get used to this.

Gram nodded. "Well, he'll have you to help him. I have faith in you, Janie."

Hadn't she always?

Gram's silver charm bracelet tinkled against her water goblet. She wore it with everything. Each charm depicted some aspect of the Hilltop Christmas Festival—a gingerbread man, a snowflake, a miniscule pair of skates, a sleigh, and a sled. Jane's grandfather died before she ever got to meet him, but ever since Gram explained the charms were his gift, Jane felt connected to him.

"Any new charms?"

"Last year on vacation, I picked one up for myself. Couldn't resist." She swiveled her wrist, and Jane squinted at an exquisite, tiny rendition of the Holy Family.

"Oh. It's perfect craftsmanship."

Gram beamed. "It reminds me of why we do this."

"It's a *festival*, Gram."

"A festival where we show Christ's love to the world." Gram scraped up the last of Anne's savory mashed potatoes. "Anyway, Pastor Noah is excited about the festival. He says it's a great outreach."

Noah again. Jane couldn't stop thinking about him. She didn't need Gram's help. "I'm surprised he isn't married."

She stabbed at a piece of chicken and hoped her voice didn't betray her. Could Gram still read her every nuance?

If Gram could, she didn't let on. "We all were. He's too young for the casserole brigade—the women who chase after widowers—but he attracted a lot of attention from the younger crowd. A couple of girls made a play for him but didn't get anywhere. Noah treats everyone the same."

Yes, a Noah Hastings could dazzle the single women of Hilltop. A hunk, her roommates would have called him.

But he was a pastor.

If he knew who Jane Archer really was, he'd bolt. Sometimes *she* wanted to bolt. But she had a good life now.

She looked at Gram. "Well, I love my job. The board members, teachers, and parents are so supportive. Private school is a whole different world. I live in a town house, and my roommates are great."

"You've done well for yourself, my Janie. I couldn't be prouder." Gram took a deliberate sip of water, and her voice changed. "Do you hear from your mother?"

Jane sighed. "I'd tell you if I did."

"Yes." Gram cleared her throat. "Are you seeing anyone?"

"Now, Gram." Jane bit her lip. "I'm too busy, and I don't meet that many men."

Generations of corralling fifth graders had only strengthened Gram to never retreat. "Jane. You're in *Boston*. The city is teeming with men."

"Gram—"

"You're a bright, attractive girl. You're twenty-eight years old. You have so much to give." Gram looked down. "I know you don't like it when I quote Scripture, but the Bible says it's not good for us to be alone. I'd feel better if you had someone to share your life with."

Of course, she would. She was Jane's only living relative, except for an on-the-lam mother. And the hip replacement marked Alice Merrill's first sign of aging.

Life without Gram.

Jane couldn't bear it, husband or no husband.

She had been too glad to land in Hilltop and build a life with Gram to have had a rebellious phase. But her voice held a tinge of defiance as she cleared the plates. "What about you? You're still gorgeous, and even I can't keep up with you. Why didn't you remarry?"

Gram fingered the different charms on her bracelet. "If you'd known your grandfather better, you wouldn't have to ask."

A love that lasted beyond the grave. Gram proved that such a love could exist.

A love that would spread through Jane's hollow places, the ones she couldn't fill with a job she loved, even after lesson plans and field trips and tenure track. A love that would make it all mean something, pull it all together.

A love that lasted beyond the grave? Maybe. Problem was, she was no longer sure what else happened beyond the grave.

CHAPTER TWO

Jane woke early the next morning, determined to get her festival duties done as soon as possible. "So where do I start?" She stood in the hallway tugging on her gloves.

Gram looked up from the sofa, a compact space with books, a laptop, a phone, and remote. "Talk to Greg Gregson first. He can give you an overview of where we're at. He's at the main store most days."

"Okay. I'll be back on time to let in Meals on Wheels." Jane held her house key.

"Oh, honey, nobody locks their doors in Hilltop. I'll be fine. The delivery driver is Barbara from church. She can let herself in."

Hilltop. Someday, the outside world would seep in, and they'd learn the hard way to lock their doors, windows, and cars. But not on Gram's watch.

The snow crunched under Jane's boots as she headed out from Gram's. Snow before Thanksgiving. She hoped the handsome, wet-behind-the-ears pastor could cope with a Hilltop winter.

Main Street, a strip of red brick buildings, hadn't changed. The Two French Hens Bakery and Café had its usual dazzling display of pies in the gleaming window.

The Rexall Pharmacy staunchly resisted being more than a drugstore. The Five and Dime had always been a beloved place to spend her childhood dollars. County Bank and Trust broke the pattern of brick with its façade of good New Hampshire granite.

Gregson's Hardware's plate-glass windows brimmed with shovels and sleds against a fake snow backdrop. She opened the door and breathed in the eternal smell of sawdust and paint.

Mitchell "Greg" Gregson hefted a sack of ice melt for an older man. "I'll get this into your trunk, Ralph, and send somebody over later to spread it for you. On the house."

When he spotted Jane, Greg stopped in mid-stride. "Is that our Janie Archer? What brings you to Gregson's?"

A valid question. Her visits since college had been few and fleeting. "I'm helping Gram run the festival."

"Then we need to talk." He held the door open for Ralph with one shoulder, still balancing the ice melt on the other. Although he owned this flagship store and three others and was one of the wealthiest people in Hilltop, Greg Gregson wasn't above any task in his stores—or for the Hilltop Festival.

When Greg returned, he gave Jane a bear hug. "How long are you here for?"

"Till Gram can get around again."

"Sure you wouldn't stay and teach for us? I'm still on the School Board." His blue-gray eyes crinkled at the corners.

Really, Greg Gregson was the nicest man, always had been. With his jeans, plaid shirt, and cropped silver hair, he reminded her of an actor in a life insurance commercial.

She could come back, but could a small mountain town compete with Boston?

"How's Alice?" Greg asked.

"On the mend. Doing physical therapy with the visiting nurse. I thought it'd be hard to keep her down, but she hasn't tried to rush it. So far."

They exchanged sympathetic grins.

"How's *your* family?"

"Anne still has the boutique. She does better in the tourist season. Stephanie's flourishing—good job at the bank, decent boyfriend, and she's doing a fine job with our granddaughter." A shadow passed over Greg's pleasant face. "And Ryan is—Ryan."

"Oh, Greg." Ryan *would* be Ryan. "What's he up to now?"

"I've got him managing the Littleton store. Time he took life seriously. But he's still doing *the music* on weekends."

"Are they any good?" But Jane already knew the answer.

Greg's lips quirked upwards. "If you'd only gone to prom with him ..."

Jane couldn't help laughing. "Paul McKee had already asked me. Anyway, Paul was valedictorian, and I was salutatorian. We couldn't resist going together. Remember? It made the state newspapers."

"Yes, we were all so proud. Those were good times, Janie."

Jane smiled at the memory of summer visits to the Gregson family camp on a lake, fall harvest parties for the youth group in their big back yard, and Anne Gregson inviting her and Gram to sumptuous Sunday dinners, just because.

Jane checked her notebook and saw Greg's name under "chairman of the festival board." "Looks like Gram has you down for float building."

Greg nodded. "Just got the foundations down."

And he wouldn't charge a dime for supplies.

"We've already started committee meetings. Alice took notes from those, but I can fill in any gaps."

"Thank you." She flipped through Gram's latest notes.

"Of course. Wednesday okay with you?"

Jane gulped. "Sure. I'll be there."

"Six-thirty. Church conference room. Same as always."

"Have the venues changed?"

"Nope. Mainstage is in the sanctuary, the soup café in the church basement, cookie walk in the Masonic Temple, Beverly's Nativities in the old library, coffee house in the new library, and Santa Shop in the town hall foyer. Cookie decorating and kids' crafts are still in the school. Skating and sledding are in the park. And Charlie still lends his barn for the living nativity. He still oversees the sleigh rides, though he's using his grandsons for drivers. If there's snow on the ground, Charlie will run the sleigh rides right off the Town Common. If it's dry, he'll run them from the farm."

"Same as always."

"Yeah, why mess with what's worked for half a century?" The bell over the door tinkled, and Greg looked past her. "Back to work. Hey, I'm sure Steph would like to see you. Stop by the bank. She's the first teller on the left."

Jane exchanged one more smile with the man who, as much as anyone, had been a surrogate father for her. "I'll do that, then. See you Wednesday."

She headed for the door and almost bumped into a tall man, parka'd, hatted, and scarved within an inch of his life.

Hastings grinned down at her. "Ms. Archer! Didn't expect to see you today."

"It's a small town, Reverend. Not that many places to go." She maneuvered around him in the narrow aisle. "I must get going. It was nice to see you."

As she opened the door, she heard him say, "Morning, Greg. What do you recommend for ice melt?"

When she stepped into the vast lobby of the granite bank, she blinked a few times. The marble floors and mahogany counters had kept their old-world ambience. The interior was as Hilltop as a sunrise over snow. Was that Stephanie, that polished woman with the smooth cap of blonde hair, subtle makeup, and tailored suit?

Jane hadn't seen Stephanie Gregson since high school. Steph barely made it to her junior year before dropping out to have a baby. Steph had been wild by any town's standards, a disaster by Hilltop's. She was the kind of girl Jane hadn't dared get too close to, but perhaps now they could be friends.

As Stephanie concluded the transaction with her customer, her eyes widened at the sight of Jane. "Oh, Janie. It's so good to see you! How is Mrs. Merrill?"

Her former students were Gram's biggest fans. "Comfortable. I'm her surrogate for Hilltop."

"Mrs. Merrill says you're still teaching. That's what you always wanted, right? How's Boston?"

"I love it. My students are amazing. How are *you?*"

"Fantastic. Finished high school at night, got a job here, and found I'm good at it. I'm taking business courses at the community college. And my daughter is—well, she's everything to me. To us." Stephanie whipped out a phone to show her a picture of a flaxen-haired little girl, the perfect image of the young Stephanie. "Hayley was my wake-up call. Reverend Clarke and I had a talk, and I gave my life to Jesus. It's been five years now."

"Um, good for you."

"And I'm dating a really nice guy. We met at a Christian singles' retreat. He lives in Conway. We're taking it slow."

The "old" Stephanie had never taken anything slow. But there had always been a sweetness to her that had attracted the wrong kind of men. She still had the looks and the sweetness, but God—or something—had helped her to grow up.

Steph craned her neck to see if there was a line behind Jane. Not that it would have mattered, people in Hilltop took all the time they needed to say what they had to say. "You must be here to talk about the festival."

"I came to see you," Jane said.

"Really?" Stephanie's blue eyes widened again. "I didn't think you liked me all that much. A lot of people didn't after I … dropped out of school."

Jane looked into her unjudgmental gaze. "More like I didn't really like myself."

"Then we should get together sometime. As for the festival, I'm sewing costumes for the parade and the living nativity and helping with the floats. I'm also a parade elf. Pastor Noah says I should grow another pair of arms."

Pastor Noah again. "What's his deal?"

Stephanie shrugged. "Came here from California, that's about all I know. He had some trouble getting used to our climate and our ways. You should hear him try to say 'Passaconaway' or 'Wonolancet.' It's hysterical. But, his messages are good, and he's always willing to lend a hand. And, it doesn't hurt that he's hot."

Jane blushed. "Stephanie, really."

Steph's laugh bubbled over again. "Hey, I can still look."

Jane rolled her eyes and smiled. But there was no room in her life for blond pastors.

Or their God.

Noah's gaze followed Ms. Archer as she left the store. Nice, the way her dark curls tumbled down her back. She was ... something. She could hold her own with any beach beauty or Hollywood starlet. From across the street, he'd seen the red coat pop into the hardware store.

Well, she obviously wasn't interested. Given her aversion to spiritual matters, he shouldn't be either. How could Alice Merrill, of all people, have a grandchild with so little interest in God?

Well, Hilltop people liked to talk. Maybe he'd learn something from Greg. Gregson's Hardware was a hangout and not just for handymen.

Greg rang up his order and tucked the slip into a cigar box. "I'll just put it on the church's tab," he told Noah. "Coffee? Stay for a few?"

"Thanks." Noah lingered until Greg brought him a cup of instant coffee from the hot plate behind the register. "Ms. Archer, she seems like a nice person."

Greg leaned against the counter. "She's come a long way. I'll never forget when Alice first got her. Took six months for that kid to crack a smile."

"Alice—got her?" Noah stirred powdered creamer into his coffee.

"Alice took over raising her when Jane was ten. We all did, really. Hilltop takes care of its own."

Greg was in storytelling mode now, and Noah leaned back and let him spin it out.

"Janie blossomed here. In every club, clarinet in the school band, Student Council. salutatorian. Did well in college too. We're all real proud of her."

Noah waited. One thing he'd learned about pastoring was they'd talk if you let them. Especially in Hilltop. Since he was always the talkative one, he really had to work on being the listener.

"I'll never forget the first time I saw her—the Sunday after she came to live with Alice. Tall girl, all arms and legs, with long braids and those big dark green eyes. She wouldn't leave Alice's side. I've never seen a kid so scared."

"Her parents?"

"Jimmy Archer was seventeen. Shotgun wedding. Walter Merrill could be forceful, even more than Alice. Jimmy was gone in under a year. Carly?" Greg shrugged. "A sweet girl, but wild. Kind of like my Stephanie used to be. Should they have had children? Probably not. Are we grateful to God for Jane? Yup. The Lord works in mysterious ways—"

"His wonders to perform," Noah chorused. "Any idea why her mother gave her up?"

"That," Greg said, "would be gossip."

That was the best thing about Hilltop. He quickly learned after every church service and gathering they talked—a lot—but they knew when to shut it down.

So that's where some of her sadness came from. Jane's mother had surrendered her.

Noah knew that kind of pain.

Maybe he could help her toward Christ. He'd have to earn her trust. Maybe the festival would help. They had to spend time together, didn't they? They could be friends, couldn't they?

"I'm a fair carpenter," he told Greg. "Do you need any help with the floats?"

CHAPTER THREE

Whatever he'd expected, it wasn't this.

Noah stopped short as he opened the sliding door on the metal warehouse behind Gregson's Hardware. He took the last gulp of his takeout coffee, swallowed the last bite of his Saturday morning breakfast sandwich, and tossed them both in a trash bin already half-full.

Boxes and crates lined the walls. A flatbed trailer occupied the center of the room with a couple of forklifts parked in the corners. In the center, men, women, and older teens hammered, sawed, and stained the framework for the Santa float. Other people worked on smaller floats on the backs of pickup trucks.

This looked like half the community.

Noah stalled in the doorway. What was wrong with him? He'd never been shy before, always owned any room he was in.

Maybe because Hilltop mattered.

Miss Archer. *Jane.* Would she be at the float workshop?

He slipped in a pool of sawdust. Nobody noticed as they shouted over the screech of the electric saws and sanders.

He scanned the room, looking for Greg to give him some directions but saw something much more appealing. A tall and slender form, her denim shirt tucked neatly into a pair of faded jeans, her dark hair smoothed into a French braid. Her back was turned to him as she guided a two-by-four through the whining saw. She turned to place the board on a pile of similarly sized lumber. He saw her face, unguarded for once, and drew in a breath at the sorrow he glimpsed.

Noah crossed the room to stand in front of her. Well, he had to say hello, didn't he? She chaired the festival his church sponsored. It was the polite thing to do.

Jane Archer shut off the saw. She looked at him, straightened, and the mask of cool control dropped over her face like the gate of a medieval castle. She pulled off her safety glasses. "Reverend Hastings."

Not "pastor." Not even just "Noah" as Alice called him. Even "Pastor Noah" would do since they were about the same age. Well, he could be formal too.

"Ms. Archer." He willed his heart to stop hammering. "I didn't know you were a carpenter."

She smiled, although it was a cool smile.

"Oh, anyone can prep boards for the float. I've been doing it for years. Mr. Gregson can be ... persuasive."

"Yes." He scratched the back of his neck, shuffled his feet. Like the shy kid he'd never been.

He couldn't tear his gaze away. Cute. How would she look dressed up, hair piled on top of her head, with one of those black dresses and something sparkly at her throat?

Easy. You've barely met the woman.

And, there was the fact she didn't seem to especially like him.

Ms. Archer waited, but he could see her politeness thinning.

Noah scrambled for an answer. "I was looking for Greg."

She gestured toward the far end of the room. "He's sanding and repainting Santa's throne. He doesn't trust anyone else with it." She put her safety glasses back on and bent over toward the power switch.

Jane hid behind her earplugs and safety glasses as she finished her stack of two-by-fours. Well, of course, Greg would include his pastor.

But she had work to do.

She'd been on the float crew since she was fourteen, running the power tools since she turned sixteen. She loved the feel of the wood under her hands, watching the floats come to life, listening to the banter. Hilltop came together over hammers and saws.

They worked steadily for most of the afternoon, Jane diverting her gaze from Reverend Hastings, who looked better in a plaid shirt and jeans than any man had a right to. He ambled by from time to time, flashing that smile at everyone. Especially her. If her roommates were here, they'd be nudging her to go talk to him.

The two dozen or so volunteers worked until three-thirty when Greg mounted the flatbed and motioned for them to shut down their machines. "I'm going to send someone out for sandwiches. It's on Gregson's," he said to scattered applause. "We've got an account at the Bonhomie. Who wants to go?"

Jane could use some air. "I'll do it," she said to another smattering of applause.

A tall figure cast its shadow over her, and a deep voice spoke. "I'll help," Noah Hastings said.

She turned to face him. "I can manage. It's only sandwiches."

"Some of us may want dessert." He smiled *that* smile again.

Jane only made her way toward the pile of shipping pallets where they'd all thrown their coats. She picked out her olive-green down jacket. Noah Hastings held it for her, still smiling. She sighed, turned her back to him, shoved her arms in the sleeves, and preceded him out the door.

Oh yes, my roommates would be losing their minds over this.

They walked to the Bonhomie Market in grim silence, Jane a few steps ahead. Why was he pestering her? Was it just because they were on the board together?

Maybe he's just trying to win over everyone. For a moment, she wondered what it would be like to see him preach, see how the town responded to their young preacher from California.

She could admire that, the comfort Gram and others found in their faith. Jane would rather never get in a position where you'd need comfort.

Hastings caught up to her with those long legs of his. She watched him out of the corner of her eye. He was genial enough, waving to drivers and people across the street.

Hilltop-ites crowded the store, anxious to get their weekend shopping done. Unlike the chain markets in nearby towns, the Bonhomie stayed dark on Sundays, honoring the Sabbath whether the rest of the world did or not.

Reverend Hastings looked around the narrow aisles. "I'm amazed they can keep going. An independent grocery store in this day and age."

"I'm not." Jane nodded to one of Gram's friends. "It's close by, and everyone knows everyone." She lowered her voice. "And Dick Marcoux, the owner, has been known to extend credit for people down on their luck."

"Really?"

"Gram's known for years. Some of the families of the kids she taught needed help after the mill closed."

"What mill?"

"Whatever mill was closing at the time." Jane stopped at a large, glass-fronted cooler. "Dick *also* makes the best grinders between here and Concord."

"Grinders?"

"You know. *Sandwiches.*" She pantomimed stuffing food in a roll.

Hastings' forehead unclenched. "Oh. *Subs.*"

How had Noah not known about Dick Marcoux's secret credit program? Could any of his families use it? Probably. He hadn't seen a lot of poverty, not like in California, but that didn't mean it wasn't there. He'd glimpsed the shuttered mills, the empty storefronts, the rusted trailer homes on the back roads.

What else did this Ms. Archer know?

Jane inhaled. "Smell the cheese. Mr. Marcoux has a huge wheel of it."

The way her hair gleamed under the store's harsh fluorescent lights distracted him from coherent thoughts. "Cheese," he repeated.

"He gets it from a farm up north."

Could anything be "norther" than Hilltop?

Jane's mood seemed to thaw a little as Noah helped her choose a variety of sandwiches, throw in six-packs of cola, root beer, ginger ale, iced tea, and managed to talk her into two dozen brownies. She was wheeling their full cart toward the register when a voice came from the next aisle. "Shaddup, I told you! We ain't gettin' that!"

Jane locked eyes with him. Noah put a finger to his lips and swerved toward the sound. They turned a corner to find a man in soiled work clothes looking down at two preschool age children, dressed in jackets too light for November, huddled in the cart sobbing.

"You think I'm made of money? Just like your tramp of a Ma does."

No kid should have to put up with this. Or any woman, even an absent one. It reminded Noah far too much of his own upbringing—that is, when his father bothered to pay attention to him and his brothers.

The man reached down into the shopping cart, grabbed a handful of scruffy hair on each boy, and knocked their heads together, Three Stooges-style.

The boys' sobs escalated to howls, and Noah rushed forward as his own heart pounded. "Sir, do you think that was necessary?"

The man turned on him. "Ain't your business," he said in a rusty voice.

"It may be Police Chief McKee's business. I'm Reverend Noah Hastings, and the chief is a good friend of mine." Noah fished for a business card and found a tattered one in his jacket pocket. "Parenting is tough these days. If you ever want to talk—"

The man shoved the card in his pocket. "Leave me be."

Noah towered over him. Sometimes his sheer size did the job. "Don't beat on your kids, and I will leave you alone." He rummaged for four brownies and crouched before the two little boys. "Here's a snack for you guys. But you have to eat your supper first. Okay?" He willed them to smile, but they just stared at him.

The man gave him a look that could kill and wheeled his cart and offspring toward the checkout.

26

Noah tamped down his anger before turning back to Jane. "I'm going to get his license plate, just in case. I—"

Jane's mouth hung open, her eyes wide with terror and glistening with unshed tears.

What *had* this woman been through?

He'd have to ease the situation with a joke, one of the few tools in his pastoral toolbox. "Hey, I could have taken him."

She shook her head with a bleak look and headed toward the checkout.

Well, he was brave enough. Jane had no doubt if Hastings saw the man acting up again, there would be a report to Police Chief Paul McKee. She had glimpsed concern in Hastings' face, and selfless love. He was a good pastor.

Good thing he had been there. Child abuse always paralyzed Jane. If only she could scoop up those boys, and a dozen like them, and haul them off to a farmhouse in the country where they could grow up as tall and strong as a North Country fir tree.

At one time she'd dreamed of saving children the way she'd been saved, by Gram first and later, Hilltop. But this kind of dream would be better with a husband. Kids needed a dad. She knew because she hadn't had one. She only knew her father's name, Jimmy, but neither Gram nor her mom would ever speak about him.

Marriage was a risk she couldn't take. She would save children through her teaching and volunteer work.

Dusk had fallen and the temperature plunged when she and Hastings hurried back to the warehouse. When they set out the luncheon on a makeshift table of sawhorses and planks, the float workers fell on the spread. Jane waited her turn, helping herself to a turkey-and-Havarti sandwich and a root beer.

She perched on a low stack of pallets and spread out her lunch on a napkin. Steph and two other women she knew from school spotted her. Jane grinned a welcome. They started toward her but stopped as funny little smiles spread over their faces before they backed away.

"You don't mind if I join you?"

The reason for her friends' withdrawal was right next to her, lounging on the next stack of pallets. Reverend Hastings, in all his six-foot-whatever glory. He unwrapped one of Dick's steak tip grinders and took a bite.

Well, he'd tried to help those poor children in the market. Maybe there's more to this Noah Hastings than a pushy personality. A pastor's heart under all the flashiness.

She might as well be polite. "How do you like your tonic?"

Hastings screwed up his face and put the glass bottle down. "This is medicine?"

She rolled her eyes. She should have known to pick a better word. Her school, St. Hildegarde's, drew girls from all over the country. "Soda. Pop. We call it 'tonic' here."

"Oh, it's really good." He took another sip.

"They brew and bottle it down South in a little town called Newfields. It's a family business. Been using the same recipes for a hundred years. Dick orders truckloads. It always sells out in tourist season, but he holds some back for us."

She took another bite and washed it down. If he wasn't going to go away, she might as well get some of her questions answered. "So. How'd you become a pastor?"

He leaned back on his elbows. "I grew up in California. Middle son of three boys. I was always at the beach, always surfing. I loved that life, maybe a little too much. My dad ... My dad owns a prominent real estate company in Orange County. He always wanted us on staff. My brother Ted became an architect and joined the firm." Hastings cleared his throat. "He wanted me in engineering. Forced me into a program. I went to college for two years, but my grades were lousy. Finally, I dropped out, he cut me off, and I went to work for a board maker in Venice Beach."

Jane pushed her sandwich aside when his tone changed, became more remote.

If there's one thing I've learned in preaching, people won't open up to you unless you open up first. And Noah wanted Jane to feel safe with him. To experience the freedom and acceptance he received.

"I worked just enough to get by and learned some carpentry. Surfed in my free time and partied when it was too dark to surf."

He could have had any woman he wanted, and some of them came with booze and pot. Noah couldn't remember much about that year. Something about Jane Archer made him try.

"I stayed out of school for over a year. I was angry with my father, angry with the world. One night I left a bar, sicker than I usually got, and I wandered the streets. Until I wandered into a little storefront church."

Noah smiled at the memory. The people of the Venice Beach Mission had wrapped their arms around him, literally and figuratively. Poured hot coffee into him, cocooned him in a blanket, let him sleep in the pastor's office. And when he'd sobered up, they had told him the old, old story.

God had restored that kind of love in Venice Beach.

"I accepted Jesus, accepted His forgiveness for my sins." He saw her face closing up and hurried on. "It changed me. I went back to college and my father. I studied engineering, worked harder than I ever had at anything, made the Dean's List and graduated summa. God wants us to honor our fathers, so I thought this was how to do it."

Jane shrugged. "I'll take your word for it. I didn't have one. A father, I mean."

Noah stared at her. *So, she never got to meet him.*

He swallowed hard. "But another dream kept growing inside me."

Noah had always been good with people. He evolved into the leader of several campus Christian groups. He'd used his people skills to build bridges with other students, to win them to his Lord. When he crossed the stage to receive his diploma, he already knew where it would take him.

"I felt a call to the ministry. So, I told my father I couldn't work for him and enrolled in Bible college. Went back to making surfboards to support myself and graduated last year with an associate degree."

"Was your father okay with that?"

"No." He weighed how much to tell her. "Dad doesn't like it when his plans are thwarted. My younger brother Jeff is in college now. Engineering. He really wants to teach high-school English, but ..."

He wouldn't tell her how Dad expressed his disappointment. Or how long it had been since Noah had given him the chance.

Jane took another bite of her food. "How did you come to Hilltop?"

Of dozens of résumés to dozens of churches, nobody else had wanted him. People thought he was too young. "It seemed like a good chance to make a change," he said.

And You made a path here, God, didn't you?

Noah shivered. With its metal walls and high ceiling, the room felt cold. He was always cold these days. The parsonage had a wood stove, but he'd never gotten the hang of it. He kept the old-fashioned iron radiators running full tilt. The trustees would have something to say about the heating bill. On Monday, he was going down to Gregson's to look for an electric blanket.

I bet Jane Archer knows how to run a wood stove.

Still, he knew better than to seek companionship with any of the single women in the congregation. His Bible college professors had been clear on that. Crystal clear.

The next time he got close to a woman, it would be for life. He'd seen enough of real marriage, God-centered marriage, to know what he wanted. He'd definitely heard enough from Alice about hers with her sweet Walter.

For now, it was best to keep busy.

He crumpled his sandwich wrapping and took a last swig of root beer. He flashed a smile at Jane. How did she make even eating a sandwich on a shipping pallet look classy? "See you around."

Did she look disappointed?

If only.

CHAPTER FOUR

The following Monday, Jane headed over to get a head start on one of the most time-consuming tasks of the festival. The cookies.

"A *hundred dozen* cookies?" Jane's pen clattered to the weathered pine tabletop.

Monique Dumont Desrochers, co-owner of Two French Hens Bakery and Café, nodded. "And they'll eat every crumb."

Visions of sugarplums, or nightmares thereof, danced in Jane's mind.

Monique's twin sister Michelle Dumont Desrosiers reached for the sugar bowl. "The festival has really grown, Janie."

Monique counted off on her fingers. "There's the cookie walk itself. Nobody ever stops at buying a dozen. We always use the leftovers as dessert for the Legion potluck supper. The coffee house serves cakes and pies, but we've always given them a couple dozen cookies. And we also put some out in the soup café if anyone wants dessert."

Michelle ran a hand through her hair. "We drew fifteen thousand last year."

"That's over the full three days," Monique added.

"It's mostly by word-of-mouth," Michelle finished.

Sleepy little Hilltop, only coming alive for three days of the year, like Brigadoon. What had Gram gotten Jane into? Could she even do this?

Well, the Dumonts would do their part, and then some. Although Monique and Michelle had been married to Bob Desrochers and Bill Desrosiers since their twenties, they were, in Hilltop at least, forever "the Dumont Twins." Monique was known as the more formal twin, clad even on a workday in a crisp oxford shirt and dress pants under her floury apron. Michelle dressed more casually, in jeans and a well-worn concert T-shirt. Monique wore her hair in a French twist, while Michelle had a stylish spiky cut. But their shining dark hair, high cheekbones, and slender figures were a perfect match, and the look in their coffee-bean eyes beamed a welcome to Jane.

Jane rubbed her forehead. "Do *I* have to find bakers?"

Monique waved a graceful hand. "We do all the recruiting. But if you want to spread the word on your own, that will help. And if you want to bake, that will help even more."

"I'll see what I can do." Jane marked "cookies" off her working list. "I'll check back with you in a week."

Monique flashed a smile. "My Bob is on the Hilltop board. You'll see him at the meeting."

"The shop's doing really well," Michelle said. "The tourists love us. We had to expand to the storefront next door and hire more staff."

"Our French toast was on the Food Network," Monique said.

If anyone deserved success, it was the Dumonts, Desrosiers, and Desrochers. "Have you ever considered a branch store?"

The twins exchanged glances.

Michelle lowered her voice. "We're thinking of opening a second place. We're so blessed."

Blessed? They'd worked hard all their lives, inheriting the shop from their French-Canadian grandmother, expanding the menu, offering breakfast and light lunches, and doing everything to perfection with the best of local ingredients. Hard work could make anything happen.

The Dumonts left her, eager to get back to their baking. Jane sipped her coffee and browsed through the notebook. If everyone knew their jobs as well as the twins did, the festival could succeed, even under her reluctant leadership. Or it could be a train wreck. Fifteen thousand people, an average of five thousand a night. No, that wasn't right. There would be even more on Christmas Eve. Did Paul McKee assign extra officers? Was there a first-aid tent? And who put down the ice melt?

Jane put her head in her hands.

"His name is Fred Parker." A deep voice interrupted her brooding. Noah Hastings slid his big form into the seat across from her. "He moved up here from Nashua because he thought he had a job lead. It didn't pan out. Wife's name is Melissa. She cleans hotel rooms over in Lincoln. They're barely making it. And the two boys are Danny and Dougie."

She eyed him. "You found out fast."

"A pastor has his ways." Hastings plopped his elbows on the tabletop. "There's still no excuse for what Fred did in the store, but I understand him better now. And the church will be looking for ways to help the Parkers."

Jane looked pleased, although not necessarily with Noah. Why did it matter what she thought? She'd be gone after the Hilltop Festival. He probably wouldn't stay here long either. Just until he'd proven himself.

She did look interested in the Parkers and bestowed one of her rare smiles on him. Rare for *him*, anyway.

"Hilltop Church is good that way." she said. "So is St. Dominic's. And Gram's always looking for a family to adopt for the holidays."

He didn't know how to bring it up. But he should try. "You seemed ... That day in the store. The kids."

Jane raised one slender shoulder. "Child abuse always upsets me."

But her reaction had been out of proportion, even for a woman who loved children. There was more. Something she hid behind that seawall of activity. Jane had been hurt. Deeply. By someone she trusted.

Well, she said she never had a dad.

Alice? *Never.*

The mother? Probably.

He could and would pray for her.

She didn't look lost today, dressed in that red coat and a plaid scarf, her cheeks still pink from the cold, a glowing pink like the inside of a shell. She dropped her eyes for a moment, the long lashes feathering out over her perfect cheeks.

She met his gaze head on. "How did you find out? Really?"

"He has friends in high places." Police Chief Paul McKee smiled down at them. "Hi, Noah. Hello, Jane."

Jane half-rose from the booth and gave Paul a quick hug. "It's so nice to see you!"

"And you. Janie, you look great."

She moved over, gladly making room for him. "You look good too."

She had only kept up with him somewhat on social media over the years. His slenderness had evolved into broad shoulders and a muscled chest under his blue uniform. He wore his dark hair cropped, and horn-rimmed glasses gave him a Clark Kentish appeal. He was almost as tall as Hastings. Tentative and rather shy in high school, Paul wore a new air of confidence as he squeezed in beside her.

"Jane and I went through school together," Paul told the pastor. "We competed for grades. I edged her out by half a point for valedictorian. She was salutatorian. First time two Hilltop kids got the top honors at Regional High School."

"We figured we might as well go to prom together," Jane said.

"And Jane here is partly responsible for my career choice." Paul smiled at her.

"Really?" Hastings' glance bounced from one to another.

"It happened at prom." Paul's gaze softened with memory. "You know my parents, Noah. Mom is a physician. Dad's an attorney. They had big plans for me. I was accepted at Dartmouth with a pretty decent financial package. The prom was held in the ballroom of a resort in Lincoln. Janie and I just wanted to eat and dance and have fun. But one of the kids brought booze."

"*Ryan.*" All through school, turn over a rock, and there was Ryan Gregson.

"Yeah, Ryan." Paul's expression mirrored Jane's thoughts. "Greg Gregson doesn't drink, but Ryan must have gotten it somewhere. Half the class got drunk, and Jane and I spent the evening ferrying sick kids back to Hilltop."

She remembered that night—cramming classmates into Paul's father's van, driving through the still-chilly May darkness, wiping vomit from the girls' taffeta dresses. Helping them up the steps to their family homes, seeing the blend of anger and concern in the parents' faces. They knew being a good kid was good enough.

"By the time prom was over, I knew I wanted to help kids," Paul told Noah. "And people. The parents' looks when we dropped off their children were all the reward I needed. I told Dartmouth 'no thanks' and studied criminal justice at the University of New Hampshire."

"Your parents?"

"They're fine with it. They just wanted me to use my brain, and believe me, I use it every day as police chief."

Hastings shook his head. "Do you think they'd adopt me?"

Was there something behind the light remark, a hurt even this extrovert couldn't mask? Jane had seen it when he had spoken of his father. At least, Gram had let her make her own choices, even if they ended up being the same as Gram's.

And Mom hadn't been around to care.

She was aware of Hastings. Aware of something powerful and male and focused on her. If only he'd go away, then she could catch up with Paul in peace.

Jane searched her memory for Hilltop news. "I was sorry to hear about Sarah," she said in a low voice.

"Thanks. You would have liked her." Paul cleared his throat. "The girls are beautiful. They're four and two. I'll bring them by some time."

"Gram would be thrilled."

Hastings had apparently had enough of being left out of the conversation. "You come here a lot?" he asked Paul. "Being a cop and all."

"I don't come for the doughnuts." Paul paused theatrically.

"I come for the cupcakes." Jane smiled.

He was the same Paul—witty, self-deprecating, caring. He must have been a good husband to Sarah. Not fair she'd been struck by a hit-and-run driver. Not fair Paul was left with an infant and a toddler to raise and a town to police.

Not fair of Hastings's God.

Not fair for her.

Gram had tried to explain God's will to Jane. If Gram couldn't explain it in a way that made sense, no pastor could.

This Pastor Noah was sincere. What would it be like to have his faith or Gram's?

Jane had better get herself on firmer ground, and theology wasn't it. She reached for the notebook. "Let's talk Hilltop. Paul, what's your traffic plan?"

Noah didn't like the way Paul McKee looked at Jane—with far more interest than an old classmate should. Probably the way *Noah* was looking at her. What would it be like to try to make this woman happy, to pour himself into making things better for her? To give joy to that solemn, scared little girl inside the woman?

He looked away. He had hoped sharing his story would draw them closer together, but she had yet to open up to him.

The late-teens waitress, a dark-eyed Dumont niece, brought coffee for him and Paul and refilled Jane's cup. Jane reached for the cream pitcher, and her hand brushed his, like the tendrils of seaweed. A touch she drew back from.

But when she started chatting with Paul again, she looked so at home. He'd seen her chatting with the Dumont sisters, seen her greet people at the float workshop. She had a whole community of people who loved her, whether she realized it or not.

And she had Alice.

What am I doing here? Noah asked himself that every morning, before he went on his hospital rounds or called on the elderly or headed to the study to wrangle a sermon from thoughts he didn't have. Why did doubt have to plague his mind? He had read Scriptures, watched sermons, and prayed to God about his struggles, focusing on God's love that casts out all fear. In the back of his mind, his father's negative words would stir up waves of fear into a storm even he couldn't ride out.

Should he call Dad? Noah was the Christian in the family. He preached forgiveness and reconciliation, didn't he? It wouldn't mean anything to Dad, but it would to Noah.

God was God, but Dad was Dad.

The dad who had laughed at the Father's Day birdhouse Noah made him. Sure, it was middle-school shop class, but Dad could at least have hung it somewhere. After that, Noah learned to "forget" his projects at school.

The dad who had never shown up for any of his games, or Ted's or Jeff's, but sponsored every team, his business logo on every shirt. The dad who handed out ultimatums like candy.

With no Mom to intercede, to maybe say, "Richard, isn't that a little harsh?"

He could still remember their last meeting, summoned to Dad's office in the LA high-rise, down the carpeted corridor, as silent in its way as a church.

Dad, seated at his glossy mahogany desk, bare except for a computer. He was always on Noah about being disorganized. Just one more area where Noah didn't measure up.

"When can you start? I've put you in the Pasadena office for now, overseeing the Summerfields development." Dad's opening salvo.

Richard Hastings could make even Noah feel small, and Noah was six-four. "Dad, we talked about this. I got my degree like you wanted, but now I'm going to Bible college. I'm going to be a pastor."

"You can be religious and still work for me."

"It's not a 'religion,' Dad. It's my life."

Richard Hastings shook his close-cropped head. "Not what I raised you for."

He hadn't raised Noah, not exactly, but this wasn't the time to bring that up.

"Do you know how disappointed I am in you?"

Every day.

"I'm sorry, Dad." And Noah had been. "But this is where I belong."

Richard Hastings slapped his palm, like a gunshot, on the smooth surface of his desk. "What makes you think you'd even be good at it? You're just a big stupid oaf. You probably cheated to get those engineering grades."

He worked hard. To please Dad. But it didn't matter in the end.

No, not a phone call. He couldn't face that yet. Maybe a card? *At least I can call Ted and Jeff for support.*

But would they try to talk him out of staying here too?

What was he doing in New Hampshire, where snow got dumped on the ground two weeks *before* Thanksgiving? The stuff got in his boots, in his hair, inside his mittens.

When he first got accepted at Hilltop, he joked he'd trade his surfboard for a snowboard, but he didn't think that was happening any time soon. With him always running from building to car and from car to building, waving to townspeople who chatted happily on the sidewalk.

Were they insane?

Yet, the people of Hilltop always treated him with warm kindness in their old-timey, laidback ways. Reminding him of the parishioners from the church who saved his life, physically and spiritually.

There was more to Hilltop than its climate, but was there more to him? Sure, he had snuffed out the Parkers' child abuse and their whole dismal situation, but God always had someone to be his hands and feet. By the time Noah got to it, there was already a tidy pile of little boys' clothing in the church storage room and crates of canned food. Hilltop had woven a web of caring that went back generations. What could a raw recruit of a preacher bring to that?

Hilltop was like those childhood games where you linked hands and made a line or a circle, and someone had to break in. Noah had always been able to break through. Would he this time? What would he do when he'd broken through?

What am I doing here, God? You led me here, right?

Then there was Jane Archer, hunched over a phone with Paul as the chief showed her photo after photo of his daughters. They chattered away, scattering names of people he didn't know like confetti. Paul made her laugh. She looked happy.

For him, there was no breaking through with Jane Archer.

Not without God's help.

CHAPTER FIVE

"No! Oh, please, no!"

She tried to shrink herself, pulling the quilt right up to her chin. Was that a footstep in the hallway? Would he pass her door? Could she wait him out this time?

She reached up, her thin childish arms stretched toward the salvation that lurked just out of sight. She could sense someone. Was it her grandmother come at last to take her to the big old house in the tiny town where everyone was so nice? Or would it be the father she'd never known come to take his little girl home?

The footsteps came closer. Jane wanted to scream. What good would it do? No one to hear. She tried anyway, but no sound came out.

He was coming. Closer and closer. No place to hide.

And he wasn't.

The nights were the worst.

Jane could deal with the days, order her life to the penny, set all the parameters needed to keep out the darkness. But she couldn't control the nightmares.

Jane hadn't known the name for it until she was an adult. "Child sexual abuse." Her mother hadn't had any kind of talk with her about sex, and by the time it was over, Jane didn't care.

The abuse began after her mother, Carly, got a job at the convenience store. Larry, her mother's boyfriend at the time, didn't want her to take it.

She could remember that day, even after all these years.

He'd whined and said, "What am I gonna do in the evenings? We can't afford cable."

Carly had sat on his lap, kissed him, and teased him a little in that way she had. "All the more fun for you to welcome me home."

If only they had been able to afford cable.

He had never paid much attention to Jane. He'd given the impression he didn't much like kids. Jane had just part of a package deal.

But a week into Carly's new job, Larry began coming upstairs. Well before his bedtime. She remembered the door squeaking open that first time, his tall form silhouetted against the light from the hall, the flyspecked light bulb. Remembered his hoarse smoker's voice, the rush of his words as if even he didn't believe he was doing this when he said, "Kid, you're gonna have to keep me company."

He made her touch him, made her look at him, and he touched her. Jane writhed away from him, struggled in his big hands, until he pinned her back on her pillow.

"Don't fight this, baby. This is gonna be our secret."

"No!" She started to scream, and he covered her mouth.

"Unh-unh. Neighbors won't hear you anyway. They got the TV on loud. And you're not going to tell your mama. Who do you think she'd believe?"

Even at nine, Jane had known her mother would believe Larry over Jane, unless Carly actually walked in on whatever this was.

Larry had then detailed exactly what he'd do if she told.

That's why he hadn't penetrated, she realized later. Carly would have found out, would have noticed somehow her daughter was no longer a virgin.

She only had to wait it out, wait for the inevitable, which finally came: Carly's announcement over cold cereal, "We're movin'." And move they had, pulling out even faster than they did when the rent was late, packing while Larry was at work.

Carly had had one or two more boyfriends before she sent Jane to Gram. They had been faceless men who ignored Jane, which was what Jane wanted and then some. And, by the fall of that year, she was on the bus to Hilltop.

Gram's love and Hilltop's care had fixed her on the outside. Why hadn't it been enough? Why hadn't her real dad been there all along to protect her? Why was she still scared to tell this part of her story even now?

Jane opened her eyes to see a flowered wing chair, a white stone fireplace, and a gilded mirror flanked by framed photos, all visible in the faint streetlights.

She was at Gram's house, sprawled on the sofa. She was safe.

And Gram was coming, the wheelchair squeaking softly across the polished pine boards. How had she managed to heave herself out of bed? The pink sweats she'd slept in were rumpled, her silver hair in spikes, her face brimming with love.

"Nightmare, honey?"

If only that was all. Jane struggled to a sitting position and blotted her eyes with the tissue Gram offered. "I'm—okay." She was as good as she ever got, and she masked her fading terror with a laugh. "Gram, I'm supposed to be taking care of *you*, remember?"

"We take care of each other." Gram smoothed Jane's tumbled hair and waited a heartbeat. "You never talk about it. The *before*."

A branch groaned under the weight of the snow. Somewhere, an owl hooted. Jane shivered, though her sheets were drenched in sweat. "Not much to talk about. Mom, men, and motels. Nine schools in four years. Every school was at a different place in the curriculum, and I didn't want to be left behind."

Gram's lips thinned. "I tried to bring you here. More than once. And your grandfather tried to talk to Carly."

Jane covered Gram's small hand with her own. "It wasn't time. She had to be ready to give me up."

And give her up Carly had, placed her on the Greyhound bus after a terse phone call to Gram. A ten-year-old girl, crossing three states on a bus by herself, lugging a canvas suitcase filled with threadbare clothes and second-hand paperbacks. Gram's lips had thinned that time too.

"Do you want to talk about it?" Gram had asked, then and now.

Gram knew something, on some level. But the full story would destroy them both.

"I'll be fine," Jane said instead. "I've got you. But Gram, could you stay a while?"

Gram grasped her hand. "Of course, I will, Janie."

Jane woke to a savory smell wafting from the kitchen. She pulled on her robe and wandered into the sun-filled room to find scrambled eggs, half a grapefruit for each, and reheated muffins one of the twins had dropped off. "You shouldn't have."

Gram shrugged. "There's nothing wrong with my hands, and I can reach the counters. Walter and I put in low ones because we knew one of us was likely to be in a wheelchair at some point. You can make the coffee."

Would they speak about last night? Not unless Jane started it. Which she wouldn't.

The sun glinted off the snow outside the kitchen windows. Jane poured the coffee, took a seat opposite her grandmother, and watched a cardinal alight at the bird feeder.

"Let's do something fun today," Gram said, her voice brisk. "I need to get out, and you've been working really hard."

Jane hadn't, really, thanks to the notebook. Gram had Hilltop planned down to the last candy cane. But as she looked at her grandmother's eager face, she knew who the outing would benefit. "Okay. What would you like to do?"

Gram's blue eyes sparkled. "I need a new outfit for the parade."

"Are you sure you're up for it?"

"I am always up for clothes shopping."

Gram wasn't vain, but she liked to look good and knew what looked good on her. She had shaped Jane's taste away from Carly's flamboyant style of tight jeans and miniskirts to clothes that brought out the best in her.

"Want to go to Anne's?"

Jane had gone shopping with her roommates but missed shopping with Gram. "Sure, sounds fun."

On Main Street, fresh snow frosted the eaves of the buildings. Town workers balanced on ladders as they hung holiday banners from the lampposts. In the shop windows, glass balls on the decorative trees glittered in the sunlight. Even without a festival, Hilltop did Christmas well.

Anne's Mountain Boutique stood a little apart from the other buildings on Main, a white chalet-style house with a brick sidewalk and three stone steps. In summer, blazing annuals lined the walkway and hung from the porch roof. Today, a large fresh wreath adorned the door, and white electric candles glowed from the windows. Anne's white SUV with its "MRSGREG" license plate was parked a few spaces down from her shop. Greg had a matching "MRGREG" on his truck.

The sidewalk in front of Anne's was shoveled and sanded and had a ramp. The bell tinkled as Jane braced the door with one shoulder and pushed Gram in with her free arm. They were the only customers today—in the lull between fall foliage and ski season—and Anne was the only person on duty. She stood at the glass-topped jewelry counter, flipping through catalogs and making notes on a pad.

When she saw who her customers were, she beamed. "Alice! What can I do for you? And Janie! What a nice surprise!"

Anne Harriman Gregson had aged well. Tall and slender, she wore her still-blonde hair in a French twist and a Scandinavian-style short wool jacket over a creamy turtleneck and black pencil skirt.

"You look wonderful," Jane said. "I love your outfit."

"Newbury Street," Anne said with a shrug. "I still buy my own clothes in Boston, but I don't charge those prices here."

The Boston Brahmin who'd met Greg when he migrated South for college knew about clothes. The items in her boutique might be priced less than her own wardrobe, but they still targeted the better-heeled tourist crowd. But Gram, a strong believer in patronizing local businesses, bought several items a year from her old friend.

"I need an outfit for the parade," Gram said. "I'll be on the reviewing stand this year."

"It will seem funny not to have you walking the route, barking orders at everyone." Anne gazed with affection at her longtime fellow volunteer.

"I'll be back out there next year, and in between, I'll practice my barking. Anyway, I'd like a heavy sweater and a pair of nice wool slacks. It'll be cold, but I still want to look good. Obviously, I can't try the slacks on here."

"I've had your size on file for years," Anne said. "I knew you'd be in at some point. Let's look." She turned toward a behemoth of a brass cash register, which wasn't entirely for show since she didn't do computers.

She led the way to a rack of pants, and Gram followed, wheeling herself over the pine floor. Jane studied the cozy shop. Such a reflection of the woman and her taste, the style that was always a step ahead of Hilltop. Anne had made clever use of antique and vintage items—scarves folded on the shelves of an old China cabinet, costume jewelry spilling from a pirate-like trunk. The floors slanted like all the older buildings in Hilltop, but that was part of its charm. Family photos redone in black and white in old, chipped frames covered the walls. Jane smiled at an old holiday portrait of the four Gregsons—Ryan a preteen in a suit and tie, Steph in an organdy dress and a gargantuan bow in her hair.

Finally, Gram held a pair of tweed pants against her, studying her reflection in a vintage pier glass. "I like these. I'll take them home and try them on."

Gram wheeled herself over to an antique sleigh piled high with sweaters. How had Anne gotten a sleigh inside her boutique? The woman's will was a Hilltop legend.

"Anne, these are gorgeous," Gram said.

Anne pulled out a bright red turtleneck. "Why don't you try this one on? It's Christmas-y." She gestured toward her tiny dressing room. "No jewelry, please, as always. It snags the fabric."

Gram dropped her rings and charm bracelet into the Limoges China dish on the counter and disappeared behind the curtain.

Jane poked around the shop. There were some items she could afford, even on a teacher's salary. She fingered a jacket in a crazy-quilt mélange of velvet and satin. It would look sharp on Gram with black dress pants.

Well, I haven't bought Gram's Christmas present yet.

"Nice of you to take over the festival."

Jane turned to see Anne, her hands encased in lilac plastic gloves, wiping down the glass countertop.

"Gram makes it easy. She's so organized."

"She's a blessing to this town. The Lord sent her to us."

The Gregsons were blessings too. If one believed in that sort of thing.

Anne squirted more pine-scented cleaner. "Ryan's band will be playing for the parade, of course."

"How are they doing?" Jane hoped she didn't sound condescending.

"Still the lounges, the ski areas on weekends." Anne's smooth forehead creased a little. "He's *so* talented. I'd love to see him catch a break."

Anne always had a tin ear when it came to any criticism of her son.

Jane managed a smile, wishing her own mother was as invested in her life. "Maybe he could go to Nashville or Los Angeles, get work as a session musician," Jane said. "That's how a lot of performers start out."

Anne shuddered. "Ryan playing backup for someone else?"

She refrained from rolling her eyes. *Guess not.*

No mention of Stephanie who had turned her own life around.

Gram's return saved Jane from responding.

Gram eyed herself in the mirror with her parka draped over her bare shoulders. "Too tomato-y. Do you have something more cherry?"

"I do." Anne set the bright red sweater aside for refolding and looked through the pile again. With a triumphant gesture, she held out a cable-knit turtleneck in a softer red, and Gram disappeared into the dressing room.

"She's picky," Anne said in a stage whisper.

Jane shrugged. "Clothes are the only vice she has."

Jane sifted through the sweaters—soft mohair, sturdy wool, silky blends. It would be nice to have something new for the parade, maybe even the Christmas Eve service, or even just as a Christmas gift for herself.

Anne's Mountain Boutique carried a selection of prom gowns, cocktail dresses, and other special-occasion gowns, though Hilltop got too cold for much dressing up. Jane paged through the dresses anyway, admiring the jewel-like colors. Anne did have an eye.

What had it been like for this woman to leave her Beacon Hill townhouse, the restaurants and museums, the theater and symphony, for a small, remote mountain village? Anne had plunged into town life—PTA, 4-H, church committees, and of course, the festival. Did she ever look back?

Anne was the only person in Hilltop who had a cleaning woman. But like Greg, she gave back to Hilltop more than she got.

Jane's attention snagged on one dress, a single-shouldered column of emerald-green satin. She held it in front of her. As she swiveled toward the mirror, the dress shimmered in the soft lighting. Were her eyes really that green? She held the gown with one hand, fumbled her hair into a makeshift up-do with the other. When had she ever looked this good? Where would she ever wear it? Who would she ever wear it *for*?

A man, head and shoulders above the crowd whose laughing blue eyes teased her, came to mind. Noah Hastings. What would he think of her in this? She could picture him turning to see her, his eyes darkening in surprise and wonder ...

Pastor Noah Hastings. Jane had no business thinking of him thinking of her.

Trembling, she returned the gown to the rack.

"Cherry it is." Gram's cheerful voice preceded her from the dressing room. "Anne, do you take credit?"

Anne made a whimsical face. "The staff showed me how. The tourists don't like to carry cash." She whipped Gram's credit card through the machine and handed her the receipt. "Send the pants back after you're sure they fit, and we'll hem them. You know you'll need to because—"

"I'm short," Gram finished with a grin.

Jane smiled at the two friends' banter. Some things never changed, especially in Hilltop.

CHAPTER SIX

Wednesday had come at last. Jane balanced the notebook and everything else on one hip and wedged the church's side door open. She'd probably brought too much, but she'd never been to a festival meeting as chair. But she would do this right. For Gram.

Greg sat at the head of the long, polished table. Jane plunked her belongings down next to him. Reverend Hastings pulled out the chair across from her and gave her one of his big grins.

She sighed. It *was* his church.

He looked good tonight, dressed in a pullover sweater the color of his eyes over a crisp white shirt, comb marks in his longish blond hair. The picture of handsome. And she had imagined herself in an emerald evening gown and its effect on him.

Jane looked away. She would *not* let him distract her. Besides, there were more than a dozen other people to talk to. Greg, of course, was lending his time and considerable resources to make the festival what it was.

"He lives and breathes Hilltop and hardware," Anne often joked.

Bob Desrochers, husband of Dumont Twin Monique, was a cheerful man with a round face and round glasses who owned an accounting firm. Paul McKee was dressed in a plaid shirt and jeans and checked his phone before he settled in. Father Donovan of St. Dominic's greeted her with a wink. The heads of every department were here—the twins for the cookie walk, Joe Colarusso for the soup café, Lucy Palmer whose Girl Scout troops would lead crafts and cookie decorating, white-bearded Charlie Wenholm with his sleigh rides and barn for the living nativity, and school board member and longtime treasurer Beverly Smith who was famous for balancing Hilltop's books to the penny before the group bought her a computer.

Beverly wasn't a hugger, but she flashed Jane an "I'm glad you're here" smile.

Well, Jane didn't want to talk to Noah. And the group showed no signs of settling down. Who *could* he visit with?

Beverly, now there was a woman with a load to carry. Her husband Mark had brain cancer again. She worked full-time at the pharmacy, took care of Mark, and managed to serve her community through the school board and festival. Always with a smile on her face.

Noah slipped around to Bev's side of the table. "How's Mark?"

"Not great." Bev, a private person even by mountain standards, kept her own voice low. "He refused chemo. He's sixty-seven. How much time would that buy him?"

"I'm so sorry." Noah gave her hand a reassuring squeeze.

Bev nodded. "He's tired and forgets things, but we keep him comfortable. My sister is with him now." She gave her head a little shake, and her short salt-and-pepper hair settled back into its bob. "Well. We bear what the Lord gives us. Right, pastor?"

Well, Beverly did, anyway. He felt blessed to have her in his congregation.

"I'll be over next week, take him out for coffee."

"He'd love that."

Bev turned away as Greg Gregson called her name.

The fire chief chatted with Father Donovan, the Dumonts compared notes with Lucy, and Charlie told Wayne some anecdote. Noah came close enough to learn the story was about a local farmer, a backhoe, and "a feller from away." Since he was a "feller from away," he'd either not get it at all or get it too well.

Jane and Paul had their heads together and were laughing. He sidled closer. Jane angled her shoulder so that her back was to him and went on chatting with Paul.

So much for that.

He spotted another newcomer, tall with short dark hair and an olive complexion. The only man at the table in a suit.

"I don't think I've met you yet," Noah said.

The young man held out a hand. "Brad King, member at large. I'm an attorney. I started a practice here last year."

"Noah Hastings. Why did you choose Hilltop?"

"My grandparents had a summer place up at Lake Winnipesaukee. I always wanted to get back. I'm from Long Island, but New York has enough attorneys." He gave a self-deprecating laugh. "And there's not a lot of competition up here."

With its miniscule crime rate, Hilltop didn't *need* a lot of lawyers. Even Paul's father had established his practice over in Lincoln.

Brad, in his suit and tasseled loafers. Maybe Alice should take *him* out to buy snow boots. But Noah bet even Brad knew how to shovel a sidewalk.

And to pronounce "Winnipesaukee."

Jane leaned in, ready for another funny anecdote about Paul's daughters, but he stopped in mid-sentence.

"Looks like Greg wants to start. Catch up with you later, okay?"

"I'd like that," she said as she returned to her seat.

Greg introduced everyone and nodded to his pastor. "Pastor Noah, thanks for hosting us. Anything you want to say?"

"We'll start with prayer," he said. "I'll open, and, Father Phil, if you would close."

Jane shot him a look. It wasn't *his* meeting, but the pastor's eyes were already closed. She squeezed her eyes shut and tried to tune him out.

The nerve ...

As soon as Hastings finished, Jane took control of her meeting, working her way down the master list in the notebook.

"How are we on cookies?" she asked the Dumonts.

"We're getting there." Michelle answered. "We have about fifty bakers signed up, plus what we're donating."

The numbers rose for children's crafts, gingerbread men to decorate, and small gifts for the children's shop. Charlie voiced he'd have to add another run to the sleigh rides, and someone said the coffee house was outgrowing its venue.

Jane tried to keep track of it all, annotating her lists and missing the smart tablet her school let her use. Yes, Hilltop was bigger. The world had found her town, at least in December.

Beverly went last with her treasurer's report. "It's tight right now. We have five thousand dollars. That's from the interest on the stocks and private donations. We broke even last year. The stocks are doing well, though." She rattled off a list of the Hilltop corporation's investments.

Brad King, the young attorney, leaned forward. "What about charging for more things? Tourists have money. We could turn a profit."

"We're not about profit," Father Donovan said.

"We're not in the red yet," Beverly said. "It's barely November. People *always* come through. The ski areas donate, the larger businesses give money, and the smaller ones offer in-kind goods or services."

Brad shrugged. "How about getting one of the Boston stations to come and shoot some footage? Or hiring an ad agency, doing some branding, or advertising on social media?"

Jane sucked in a breath. She knew what Greg was thinking when he lowered his reading glasses and eyed Brad King.

"That's an interesting concept, Mr. King. We can consider it. But Hilltop is Hilltop."

"We were in *Yankee Magazine*." Wayne said. "Full spread. *They* called *us*. 'Bout ten years ago."

Jane recalled that festival, her last before she went off to college.

"That reporter was everywhere," Monique said. "We couldn't get our work done."

Charlie nodded. "Spooked my horses."

"There was a restraining order at some point," Wayne said. "But I think they got it straightened out."

If Greg had had a gavel, he would have banged it. "Anyone else have anything?"

After the meeting, Jane caught up with Hastings in the parking lot. She stamped her feet against the cold and willed him to look at her.

Hastings rolled down his car window. "Something we forgot?"

"You high-jacked my meeting."

"Interesting." He drawled the word into five syllables. "How so?"

"I didn't ask you to pray. Or assign prayer to Father Donovan."

The teasing look faded from Hastings' eyes. "You've got to be kidding."

"It's a festival, Reverend Hastings. Not a church service."

"A festival that exalts the name of Christ. A Christmas festival, whose main sponsor is *my* church. I don't see how I couldn't help but pray."

"Well—don't." Jane's teeth chattered in the cold.

Hastings rested his arm on the windowsill, and she backed away. "Ms. Archer, I will continue to pray before these and any other meetings, and Phil Donovan is welcome to close. Your grandmother would support the practice if she were here. From what I've seen, we always pray before the meetings. If you want to drop the prayer, you'll have to run it by Greg. Good night, Ms. Archer.

Noah watched Jane Archer get into Alice's car and spin out of the driveway, scattering snow and ice in her wake. He remained with his hands on the steering wheel, his engine dead. For once he didn't feel the cold.

Was that why he felt drawn to her? Because Noah was lost too.

No, he knew his purpose. To do justice, love mercy, and walk humbly with God. Despite his feelings, he knew God had found him, had placed him here.

Although he had never been a cruel man, even before Christ, Noah knew he wasn't especially insightful. Talkative, yes. It was one of the things he'd used to battle his call. But God had won that round, just as he'd won the battle to get Noah to New Hampshire.

But Noah had insight into Jane Archer. Insight from God.

What had caused her to hide behind that wall of bluster, behind the lists and clipboards and that irritating notebook? To reject the God of her youth? Jane's attitude must hurt Alice, but it hurt God even more.

It was his job to find out. Not to heal her but to point her toward healing.

And all the others. Who knew what went on inside these prim white houses?

Poor Brad. He just wanted to help, in his own way. Since he was also a newcomer, Noah made a plan to grab coffee with him sometime.

Maybe Hilltop could use someone like him after all.

He bowed his head right there in the church parking lot. *"Father, help me to see you and only you. Help me to work with these people, to be what you want me to be. Help me to want to be here. Help the people to want me here. Soften their hearts. Please help Ms. Archer. She needs you, and she doesn't even know it."*

Jane showered, brushed her teeth, and banked the wood stove and fireplace. She checked on Gram, who slept soundly in the first-floor bedroom. Sleep wouldn't come to Jane. Her head still pounded from the meeting, from sparring with Noah. As soon as she got back, she'd told Gram how it went, but that didn't make her feel any better.

Jane went to one of the long parlor windows and placed her forehead against the cold glass. The stars wheeled high over the town buildings. Although most people waited till Thanksgiving weekend to decorate, the family across the street had already strung their outdoor lights. The red, green, yellow, and blue bulbs cast colored shadows against the snow.

She heaved a sigh. *How dare he!* Even the narrow sliver of committee members who didn't attend any church wouldn't have minded the prayer.

It wasn't him. It was her.

What had she expected? Jane knew what made Hilltop tick and work. The organizers had never tried to hide what it was—a family festival that exalted Christ. There was a Santa, played for years by Charlie Wenholm, who barely needed a costume. Charlie's Santa didn't take gift requests but performed a couple of shifts at the living nativity explaining the true meaning of Christmas. Christmas hymns were sung in the sanctuary along with ditties about Frosty and Rudolph.

As Jane learned more about the world and of civics, she had wondered how long it could last. How long would church and state be allowed to come together for three days in December? It was only a matter of time till the inevitable question—why did the town participate in a festival sponsored by a church? They were one newcomer away from an ACLU suit. As a social studies teacher, Jane knew all about those.

She wrapped her arms around herself as the chill from outside sneaked through the windowpane. Not praying before a meeting was one thing. Closing the festival down, another.

The fond memories there had made a home in her heart. A bright spot to shine during her darkest times.

She knew why the town participated. Hilltop Festival brought business into town and helped it fend off the fate of those other dying mill villages. The community came together to serve others, young and old, and the poorest residents.

She recalled the stories Gram would tell around their own fire during marathon costume-sewing sessions. How estranged children had come back to parents over the festival, how longtime enemies mended metaphorical fences over Joe's soup tureen. How even a few marriages had been healed.

It was something bigger than all of them. But she wasn't yet ready to credit God.

She sighed deep within her soul. She had tried. She'd liked the kids in Sunday School and youth group and enjoyed the sociability of church. Hilltop Church's people were the nicest people in a town of nice people. As nice as her roommates and fellow teachers were, she could tell the difference between Boston and Hilltop.

But the faith beneath it all never took root.

Oh, she'd learned to talk the talk. Been in church every time the doors were open, participated in every service project, and added Bible memorization ribbons to her shelf of trophies. All the while, she'd known she could turn it off. And did.

Only Gram hadn't been fooled. Neither had old Reverend Clarke who had taken her aside at the church's high school graduation party. He'd been her pastor for eight years, since she landed in town at the age of ten.

"Jane, are you sure you're all right?" he'd asked, his kind eyes behind thick glasses.

"Of course, I am." She'd thrown him her most brilliant smile and escaped to join a couple of classmates giggling over the yearbook.

Of course, she hadn't been.

What if she had told them everything? Would things be different? Better? Worse? Church and psychologists agree confession is good for the soul, but would it be good for hers? Or would it unravel everything?

Jane skimmed up the stairs, careful not to wake Gram. She paused in the door of her old room. What a sanctuary it had been, with the high white iron bed and window seat looking out at a maple tree. Trophies and certificates sat on a shelf with Girl Scout badges and 4-H ribbons. A few of her childhood dolls still lined the shelves, though she'd been too old for dolls when she arrived. She remembered reading on that window seat, watching the leaves turn and snow fall. A safe place at last.

A good dream for a little girl. A better life than her mother had given her.

But all dreams had to come to an end.

If she stayed here, she would split open. She couldn't last under their kindness, their questioning gazes. Their litany of *"Is anything wrong, Janie?"* She would come open at the seams, and they'd see her for who and what she was.

The *who and what* Gram's God couldn't fix.

The *who and what* He didn't prevent from happening.

No charming cleric, no matter how handsome, could make up for that or make it right.

Hilltop hadn't made it right, not fully, and *they'd* loved her, fiercely and unconditionally.

She'd put the conditions on herself. And they would stay there.

CHAPTER SEVEN

The next day, she slipped into the Limelighter Grill.

Joe, the proprietor, turned toward her when the bell over the door clanged a welcome. "Janie! Wondered when you was going to pay me a visit."

Jane couldn't help smiling at Joe Colarusso whose voice reminded her of an East River foghorn, his round face already flushed from cooking.

"Have some caw-fee."

From the outside, The Limelighter Grill didn't look like much. A brick storefront broken up by plate-glass windows where diners could look out at Main Street and a sputtering neon sign. There was one single, scarred wooden door to the left, opening to a community bulletin board and a row of gumball machines. Plain booths and chairs stood among the Formica tabletops. The booths were covered in a depressing maroon vinyl that probably dated from the restaurant's founding.

But it had Joe.

As she settled on a counter stool, he set a thick white mug in front of her.

She sniffed the spicy air. "What's the soup today?"

"Cream of broccoli, tomato bisque, and Italian wedding. Plus, the usual clam chowder and chili. What'll you have? On the house."

"Um, it's a bit early, but I'm going to bring Gram down for the fish fry tomorrow. If she's up to it."

He beamed. "That's Alice's favorite."

Jane flipped the notebook open to the tabbed section for the Hilltop Café. "Joe, I got you some help. The Knights of Columbus aren't doing their hot dog stand this year, so they'll help work the café. Count on five to ten men for each night."

"Will do. You're a good girl, Janie."

He still pronounced it "goil" after all these years.

Jane sipped her coffee and relaxed. The Limelighter was like that.

"Joe, I've got to know. How did a boy from Brooklyn end up in Hilltop?"

Joe laughed his rumbling laugh. "You mean, how did I leave a place that has decent bagels for one where they eat moose?"

"Something like that."

Joe settled his bulk against the counter. "I'm seventeen and headed for reform school. Social worker snags me a scholarship for basketball camp. In *New Hampshire*, wherever that was. Anyway, I go, and I kind of like it here. So, I miss the bus home. I scrounge food, I sleep in sheds. And old Petey Marcoux, he was Dick's uncle, he finds me sleepin' in the pantry here. He don't say nothing, just hands me an apron and points me to the sink. Next day, he brings in a cot an' shows me how to fill out a timecard. Before I know it, he's teaching me the restaurant business from the ground up. When Petey's had enough, I buy him out."

Joe had married a Hilltop girl, a Dumont cousin, and thrown himself into small-town life, cooking for the ill, the bereaved, and the burned-out. First on the scene with his covered dishes and huge laugh.

"Do you ever miss New York?"

Joe gazed around his domain—the shelf full of trophies and plaques from the sports teams he'd sponsored, the signed photos of presidential candidates who'd stopped here to chat up his customers, and pictures of his four sons grinning on the ski slopes or holding up strings of freshly-caught fish. "Not enough."

How often had she hung out at this counter or in these booths, studying with Paul or another Hilltop kid, drinking coffee? Joe Junior squeezing into the booth to talk about Regional's sports teams. Friday night fish fries with Gram. A quick bite after an out-of-town game or movie. Taking a shift at the festival café, serving soup alongside the Colarussos. Listening to Joe's banter and bluster, cleverly shot down by Marie or one of his boys.

Would the Limelighter host another generation of Hilltop kids in those scarred wooden booths with the cracked vinyl upholstery? She'd seen other towns on her drive up here, hill country towns now with empty storefronts like eyes that had been poked out and empty brick mills with broken windows and silenced machinery.

Hilltop hadn't died yet. Was it the tourists who came for the festival and spilled over into the other three seasons? Or was it the heart of its people who supported the Limelighter over a chain restaurant and the Bonhomie over driving to a supermarket, making sure their money and goodwill stayed in town?

But would even Hilltop have its day?

Not on her watch.

Would Pastor Noah Hastings even realize what he had in this place?

Did she? She had friends in Boston and cordial business associates at the school. She had a place there. But nobody knew how she took her "caw-fee."

There would be no hiding from Hilltop.

And she'd worked too hard building her defenses.

Jane drained her cup. "I should be going. I have more people to see. Thanks, Joe."

"Come in again. I don't do breakfast no more. Joe Junior heads that up, but I'm in here for lunch and supper."

Jane nodded. "I'll see you Friday."

The Limelighter. Although the food never disappointed, the secret ingredient was Joe.

She was almost to the door when she heard a, "Hey, stranger. Thought that was you."

She turned to see Ryan Gregson rise from a corner booth. "Ryan."

At six feet, Greg and Anne's son moved with a lithe grace. He had his mother's narrow face and blue eyes and wore his dark brown hair a little longer than most men in mountain towns. Today his charcoal-gray suit was tapered and tailored to fit his frame.

Jane remembered his smile the most, the smile that could convince a girl she was the only person on earth he wanted to talk to. It hadn't worked on Jane, but she had spent hours consoling female friends taken in by that smile. It was a smile like Noah Hastings had. No, even the flirtatious preacher wasn't in Ryan's league.

"How are you doing?" She tried to infuse some warmth into the question.

Ryan gestured expansively. "Great. Just great." Ryan was always "just great."

"Do you like running the hardware store?"

Ryan shrugged. "All right. I'm not really hands-on. I have people who do it for me."

It was the only time Jane had ever heard the words "I have people" spoken in Hilltop. Or anywhere else.

"I'm more interested in my band," Ryan said. "I got a whole new group of guys. They're amazing. We're writing our own stuff. We're booked every weekend."

Jane had heard variations of this spiel since high school.

"A record scout from Boston was at our last gig. He's going to be in touch."

Of course, he was.

Ryan at least had a dream. But how did it feel to find the years slipping away, to see his friends established in careers and families, to see his band mates become younger and younger?

Jane had hitched her own wagon to a more reasonable star. She loved teaching, enjoyed caring for the townhouse, and relished being close to the history and culture of Boston only a few hours from Gram.

"That's wonderful, Ryan." As she had said every time. "Where are you living?"

"Got an apartment in Littleton, but I spend a lot of time here. Mom does my laundry. Or her housekeeper does, I don't know."

Ryan. Jane looked toward the door to freedom.

"You should come hear the band," Ryan was saying. "We're at a brew pub in North Conway weekends, now through Thanksgiving."

"You know I don't go in bars." One of Gram's lessons had stuck with her.

Ryan shrugged, unfazed. "Well, we'll be in the parade. It's really good exposure for the group."

Why did his crassness cause even her to squirm? Should she point out the real value of the Hilltop Festival, how it brought the community together, the hospitality shown to strangers, uniting for the greater good? It was more than "exposure" for a business, even Ryan's.

No. If he hadn't learned that growing up in Greg and Anne's household, he wasn't about to learn it from her.

"I have to go, Ryan. Hilltop business. It was nice seeing you." She waved to Joe and escaped.

Ryan Gregson was a sight best seen in a rearview mirror.

As much as Gram enjoyed the fish fry, Jane was more excited to hear from Gram's doctor that if she kept up with her home exercise, Gram would be well on her way to graduate to a walker. Even better, Hastings hadn't bothered her this week. Was he hanging back because of her anger over his prayer? Or had he simply found someone else to harass? She didn't miss him. Did she?

"Hey, Jane, a bunch of us are going out for coffee. Wanna come?"

It was another Saturday, another float-building workshop to check off her list in Gram's festival notebook. As she settled the lid firmly on a can of paint, Jane looked for the source of the voice. A high-school classmate, not a close friend but a friend because Hilltop was too small even for cliques.

"Thanks, Megan. I've got to get back to Gram. Maybe next Saturday?"

"Sure. Plan on it."

Jane stripped off her gloves, slipped on her coat, and slid the metal door shut on Greg's warehouse. The laughter of her fellow builders was the last thing she heard. The session had been productive, with a dozen floats taking shape under the hands of skilled veterans and eager novices.

She pulled her coat collar close as she walked down Main Street, already dark at four p.m. The outlines of the buildings receded into the night, but the colored lights strung on eaves and display windows more than made up for it. She'd started a beef stew in the crock pot. Maybe she and Gram would eat by the fire.

"Janie!"

She turned to see Paul McKee loping toward her with a preschooler by the hand and a toddler on his shoulders.

"Wait up!"

She waited.

He stopped and grinned down at her. "Hey, you finally get to meet my girls! Girls, this is Ms. Jane, a friend of mine. Ms. Jane, this is Madelyn." He slanted a glance upward at the well-bundled child clinging to his neck, with wisps of blonde hair poking out from her stocking cap and her blue eyes wide with curiosity. "And this is Emma." The older girl, more dignified, bore a tiny smile and eyes like a little adult.

The one who had known her mother.

Jane took a deep breath and crouched before Emma. She put out a hand, and Emma placed her mittened on it. "Emma, I'm so glad to meet you. Your daddy and I were friends all through school."

Emma nodded. "Did you go to Hilltop Elementary? I'm going there next year. I'm going to kindergarten!"

"Yes. Well, I was here from fifth grade on. You'll love Hilltop Elementary."

"Are you Missus Merrill's girl?"

"Granddaughter."

Emma nodded, as if all the pieces were in place. "Missus Merrill is nice. I like her."

The smaller girl squirmed until Paul placed her on the pavement. "Don't run away, Maddy."

"Me no run." She pulled a small candy cane from her jacket pocket and offered it to Jane as if it were the Holy Grail.

"Maddy, you already licked that. And is that fur?" Paul snatched it away and dropped it on the sidewalk.

"I wanna give Ms. Jane something." Maddy's lips formed into a two-year-old pout.

"Well, we'll find something better." He sighed and shifted on his feet, like the boy she had known, the first guy who had ever been so nice to her. The boy who was now a man. Someone who had seen his fair share of heartache. Someone who might understand her.

She flushed at the thought.

But Paul McKee would never leave Hilltop, and she could never stay.

CHAPTER EIGHT

As Jane exited Gram's car, she looked up at the stars, mentally preparing herself for another Wednesday night festival meeting. So many stars, extra-bright in the cold November sky. She'd forgotten what these northern stars looked like.

Hilltop's pristine beauty. What would it be like with someone, well, special?

Paul joined her as she headed into the church. "Hey, Jane."

Paul. She could well believe he'd given up fame, fortune, and Dartmouth for Hilltop. It was a Paul thing to do. They had grown up together, competing and sometimes cooperating on school projects, doing their homework in the rear of the conference room while his parents and Gram hashed out details for the Hilltop Festival.

"Enjoying your visit so far?" He held the heavy oak door for her.

"I am, thanks. It's more work than I expected. But Gram is so self-sufficient, they cancel each other out." She laughed. "I'd be bored without something to do."

In the foyer, Paul helped her with her coat and hung it on the rack next to his. He smiled down at her. He still had one lone dimple, deepening his smile. "I have a favor to ask you."

"Anything." She smiled up at him.

Paul chuckled, a deep and appealing sound. "I was wondering, could you watch the girls for me the first Saturday in December?"

"I'd love to."

"Great. I've got a chiefs' conference. My parents usually watch them for me, but that weekend, we're triple-booked."

"I'm not even single-booked, and Gram would love to have kids around."

"Then it's a date." Paul smiled down at her, his dark eyes alight, his voice deep and confident. "Janie, I was thinking how we've been through so much. Remember when you beat me in the spelling bee?"

"Yeah, but you edged me out in the science fair."

"Remember when we went to Bangor, Maine, for that French exam, and Tommy Marshall missed the bus? When the driver turned around to go get Tommy, she used words none of the Hilltop kids had ever heard."

"And prom," Jane said.

"Yeah, that was quite a night. I never even got to kiss you." Paul's voice turned hesitant, more like the boy he'd been. "Maybe we've got something else to catch up on."

Jane stood still as he bent toward her in the stillness of the foyer, in the mottled light from two stained-glass windows.

At the last minute, she turned her head, but his lips grazed her cheek. She still flushed. "We need to get moving. The staff meeting is about to start."

It was too soon and too late.

The festival steering committee gathered around the long table in the conference room, and Jane nodded to faces that were even more familiar now. She forced herself to smile at Hastings. Could he tell? Did she wear Paul's almost-kiss like a banner? And why should she care? He didn't think about *her*, did he?

He flashed her one of *those* smiles and took the seat across from her. She could see a tiny shaving nick on his jaw. Her gaze traveled upward to see the teasing grin swapped out for a searching look.

Jane arranged her files and folders on top of the notebook as much for protection as organization. Who she kissed, or in this case didn't kiss, was none of his business.

Greg called the meeting to order. At his request, Father Donovan prayed. Jane had to admit his simple requests to his God were appealing. Father Donovan had thrown in his lot with Hilltop years ago. He loved his hardy parishioners, including the Dumont clan and the Colarussos, and they loved him.

Jane annotated her lists during the committee report, avoiding the glances of either Noah or Paul. She gave input when asked and laughed at all the appropriate times. Her mind raced, anticipating the next obstacle. She hadn't baked cookies yet.

Maybe I could do that with Paul's girls.

She noted the progress of the cookie walk, the soup and stew café, and a tentative lineup for the coffee house and main stage entertainment. Maybe she could pull this off after all.

But Bev rose with a somber expression to give the treasurer's report. Had Mark taken a turn for the worse?

As Bev rattled off a list of figures, the group went on point. After all these years, they could read each other.

"We'll adjourn now," Greg said. "I need to see the board members. In private."

The others filed out, chatting softly as they shrugged into their coats. Monique told her husband she'd get a ride with her sister. Father Donovan clapped Wayne on the back as they laughed together.

But there was no closing prayer, and inexplicably, she missed it. Paul had stayed behind too. At a gesture from him, Greg shut the conference room door.

"What's this about?" Charlie asked. "We never have closed meetings."

Greg crossed his arms. "Bev, tell them."

Jane had never seen Bev's capable hands shake. "One of the stock certificates is missing. It's been cashed in."

Jane was the first to break the silence. "Paul, you know about this?"

"Bev and Greg have been down to the station. We're investigating."

"You should have told me. Come to me first. I'm the acting chair."

Paul looked miserable. "We're looking into it, Jane. Greg and I have talked."

She glared at Paul, but he looked away. *So much for near-misses and almost-kisses.*

"We're keeping it quiet for now," Paul told the group. "And—and I don't know how to say this—"

"Say it, Paul." Greg said, the corporate executive and business owner, no-nonsense side of him they rarely saw because he so seldom had to use it.

"It has to be one of us."

"That's impossible!" Bob said. "Why would we steal from the festival?"

Paul met Bob's gaze. "Because only five people have the code to the safe-deposit box, and only five people have access to the stamp to sign a transaction. The chairman, the three board members, and the treasurer."

"How much?" Jane finally managed to say.

"Ten thousand dollars."

"That's crazy." Genial Charlie looked like an angry Santa. "We're all Hilltop people. We all trust each other."

Exactly. Hilltop was Jane's safe place. The place where her trust was reformed.

Paul folded his arms, all policeman. "Apparently not enough."

"It's ridiculous." Bob looked close to tears. "This is *Hilltop*. We don't lock anything up. We've all been working together for years. If someone needed money ..."

Greg quieted the group with a look. "Paul, what do we do now?"

"Don't leave town. Be available. We'll need to get statements. Keep doing what you're doing. We need the festival now more than ever."

How could this be happening? Noah looked over the faces around the table. People he'd come to admire in his brief time here. Not a one of them he'd suspect of taking an extra candy cane from the Hilltop Festival.

It doesn't make sense.

People in these mountains had a hard time making it—even he knew that—and well before he'd met Fred Parker. But to steal from their own?

Didn't that defeat the purpose of Hilltop—town *and* festival?

Jane kept smoothing her hair with her left hand and browsing through her mammoth notebook with her right hand. Like lists and charts were going to help them now. If only he could comfort her. *Her*. The little girl with the big green eyes. She just found one more person she couldn't trust.

He heard his own voice, strange and raw, though he had no rights here. No roots. "Paul, you've got to find who did this."

Greg adjourned the private meeting, and no one stayed just to chat. Paul spoke quietly, gesturing often, with a grim-faced Greg. As Jane headed for the door, Noah Hastings started toward her, but she ignored him. She huddled in Gram's cold car under the stars she'd admired earlier. Stars that shone a little dimmer now.

When Jane got home, Gram was sitting in her wheelchair by the smoldering fire. Jane went on autopilot to the log holder, but Gram put out a hand to stop her.

"Honey, you look awful. What happened?"

How does she always know?

Jane dropped to the sofa, reaching her hands toward whatever warmth was left. "There's festival money missing. Someone cashed in some of the stocks."

Gram narrowed her eyes, still quick enough to grasp the implications. Quicker even than Jane. "It has to be one of the five of us."

"Unless someone swiped the code and the stamp."

"But, Janie, who? We've all worked together for so long. We're like a family."

Families could hurt, wound, destroy each other. Families could give each other away. But Jane knew what her grandmother meant.

"What do we do now?" Gram said, ever practical.

"Paul says not to leave town."

Gram looked at her wheelchair. "I've been practicing with the walker. Still, not likely in my case."

"You are getting better." She patted Gram's hand. "But we'll all be questioned."

Gram shook her head. "There must be a good explanation. But Janie ... one of us?" When the mantel clock struck ten, she yawned. "I'm going to bed. We'll let the Lord sort it out."

CHAPTER NINE

It was the Friday after the meeting, and Noah still couldn't think of anything to say for his Thanksgiving Sunday sermon for next Sunday. He wasn't a scholar. God knew it too. But God had taken the total package, and Noah would honor that. He knew from reading enough Old Testament stories God purposely called people who didn't seem worthy. *"God equips the called,"* a seminary professor had said.

Noah just needed to adapt his strengths to Hilltop. After all, he could talk about God and the Bible all day long, but perhaps if he used his passion for nature, he wouldn't be as nervous when he preached. He could even see himself sharing his testimony with the youth of the congregation. Yes, to be like the very people who saved him and save others from a self-destructive path.

Maybe one day. He sighed, stepping away from the computer to pick up the phone.

"Good morning, Noah."

He smiled at Alice Merrill's unique blend of crispness and compassion. Out of everyone, she seemed the most determined to keep up morale after the bad news.

"Morning, Alice. What can I do for you?"

He could picture her in her tidy living room at the old Victorian house, wielding her cellphone, ordering her world from a wheelchair. Was Jane there? He caught himself listening for sounds in the background and finally heard a "Gram, I'm leaving now" and Alice's "Bye, honey."

Alice was back on the line. "Pastor, I was wondering if you had plans for Thanksgiving."

Not that he knew of. He had been so consumed with thinking about the theft and praying for whoever took the money. His brothers weren't that good at keeping in touch, busy with their own friends and own lives. And Dad was Dad. There was nothing to fly back to California for.

Noah sighed. "Joe Colarusso has that dinner at the Limelighter. I was thinking of going. I'm sure he'd welcome the help."

Joe's free Thanksgiving for those in need. Or alone. *I'm certainly both.*

Paul had invited him over to watch the football game, but Noah had turned him down, feeling awkward at not knowing where the police chief and Jane stood with each other. But he had made a new friend.

There was a silence at the other end, but he knew by now that silence was Alice's way of working through a problem.

"Well ... Listen, Noah, Joe's dinner is a wonderful gift to the community, but I think you should have a family Thanksgiving for your first time so far away from home."

Noah's heart warmed at the thought. Should he tell her about those Thursdays in November when he and his brothers had reheated Graziella's turkey and watched the game without talking?

No need, Alice was in full problem-solving mode. "Joe starts the prep at nine a.m. Go on over and set tables, chop vegetables, whatever he needs done. And then come to my house at one. You can do both."

Yes, he could. "Who else will be there?"

Alice laughed her rich laugh. "Janie, of course. And the people she calls my strays. We always have a full table."

Did Jane want him there? She hadn't been near him since the news of the theft. She would cross the street when she saw him coming. Sometimes, against the traffic. Well, it was Alice's house, she could invite who she wanted. And he could think of worse holidays than one spent with Jane Archer. He couldn't figure her out. And he couldn't stay away until he had.

"Thank you, Alice. Of course, I'll come."

"Then we'll expect you." Alice paused. "One more thing. I don't want any talk about what happened. Not at Thanksgiving."

Yes, the theft of the stocks. What caused everyone on the festival committee to smile a little less, to assess each other a little more, to cut off eye contact. To keep conversation guarded, neutral, and focused on the festival.

Would the missing money divide this town and conquer its wholehearted goodness? He had seen too much division in his own family—too much in California itself—and didn't want that bitterness to corrupt this sweet town. He could feel it already, the kindness of these people healing his heart.

Is this why you brought me here, God? Noah bowed his head for a brief, desperate prayer. *Lord, help them find out who did this. Don't let it be any of "my" people.*

"Of course," he said. "Let's just have a good day." He took a deep breath. "And, Alice, would you mind praying for my dad and brothers?"

"It would be my pleasure, Noah." He loved how she was the only one to call him by his first name, the way his mother used to. "Ted and Jeff, right?"

He cracked a smile. She was now the only one who he felt he could trust with his prayers. "Yes. It's going to be our first real major holiday without each other."

"I understand." she said, and Noah felt she truly did. "It's one of my great pleasures in life to pray for others. You just let me know how else I can pray for you. I'm sorry you won't be with your family this holiday season, but we're happy to have you."

He had to blink away tears. It had been so long since he had a motherly figure in his life, and he couldn't do any better than to have Alice Merrill praying for him.

He thanked her again, hung up, smiled, and moved the cursor to a new line. "What are we thankful for?" he typed "Friends."

"That's the last of it, Joe." Noah stepped back from the loaded dessert table. "Lookin' good, pastor." Joe turned from checking a turkey. "I got other volunteers to help serve. Go and have some fun."

Noah lingered, his hand on the doorknob. "Keep an eye out for the Parker family, okay?"

Joe nodded. "We'll take good care of them. Go!"

Noah rushed home, changed from jeans and sweatshirt to khakis, a shirt, and a pullover, and arrived on the steps of Alice's house at one.

Jane threw open the door, and his "hello" died on his lips. She wore her hair swept to one side, a mass of dark curls, and a simple wine-colored dress with a frilly apron at her waist. Black high heels made her even taller and showed off her legs.

He couldn't help staring. Here she stood, all dressed up. It was his own fault. Some selfish part of him hoped her seeing him all dressed up was having a similar effect on her. He didn't want to look like a pastor, just a man.

But she smiled, at least politely. She ushered him in, hung his overcoat in a hall closet, and led him into the living room where Alice held court from her wheelchair to a roomful of guests.

The Dumont twins sat on the sofa with their husbands Bill and Bob. Noah must have looked surprised because Monique explained, "We've been coming to Alice's for years. By Thanksgiving Day, we're tired of cooking."

Ah. So, they are the "strays" Alice told me about.

"We did bring the pies," Michelle said. "But we made them yesterday."

Noah smiled at the thought of eating one of their pies, remembering how they had dropped off an apple crumb masterpiece the week he'd moved into the parsonage. And they didn't even attend his church.

When Jane disappeared into the back of the house, he followed her to a sunny and tidy kitchen and said, "Anything I can do to help?"

She turned and smiled at him. "No. Thanks. Gram trained me well, and some of the others brought things." She gestured to steaming bowls and platters on the counter. "Really, all I did was the turkey."

From the rich smell, he could tell that was more than enough.

What would it be like to have this woman in his kitchen, to come home to this? Or to cook for *her*? He didn't much care who did what, a series of housekeepers had cured him of that. What would it be like to come home to this woman and eat together?

But she seemed to be doing fine without him.

Heading back into the living room, he nodded to two of Alice's friends, Helen and Laura, both of whom he'd seen around town but never met. Alice explained they were both retired teachers. Stephanie Gregson and her daughter rounded out the group. Steph relaxed in a wing chair by the fire. Hayley glanced up with a quick smile, before going back to the game she was playing on her tablet.

Noah took the only available seat, folding himself onto an ottoman between Steph and the fireplace, and warmed his hands at the blaze. "Where are your mom and dad?"

Steph wrinkled her nose. "Beacon Hill. Mom's family. I begged off this year. I never know which fork to use. My grandparents don't quite know what to do with Hayley even though she's better behaved than Ryan or I ever were."

Noah nodded. "Is Ryan coming? Or did he go with your parents?"

"Ryan doesn't do Thanksgiving. He's probably off with some girl."

He nodded. "Well, I'm glad to see you both."

After he'd finally warmed up, Noah couldn't sit still. Was it being in Jane Archer's home? He'd been here before, visiting Alice, but that had been pre-Jane. He walked around the room, taking a fresh look at the photos arranged on a desk and piano. Alice Merrill wasn't much for knickknacks, but she loved a good family picture.

There were black-and-white images of a younger and middle-aged Alice with a handsome dark-haired man, her beloved Walter, color studio portraits, and framed vacation snapshots. There were several of a small blonde girl with a mischievous expression. *Must be her daughter Carly.* But there were no photos of Carly as a teen or young adult, which spoke for her mysterious absence.

He walked over to a picture of a pigtailed preteen Jane, sober beyond her years. By middle-school age, she had started to smile a little, and by the high-school pictures, she had a radiant grin. He looked more closely at a posed photo in a white curlicued frame of a teenage Jane and a younger, geekier Paul in a too-big white tuxedo. Jane, though, was perfection in a simple purple gown, her dark hair swept to one side and anchored with some kind of flower. If only he'd known her then.

If Hilltop had been good to her, and good for her, why does she still seem sad?

As if she could pick up on his thoughts, Jane appeared in the arched doorway between the living room and dining room. Her cheeks were flushed. "I think I've got everything out. Let's eat!"

A golden-brown turkey sat in the middle of Alice's dining-room table, ringed by steaming side dishes. White china rimmed in gold gleamed in the light of two taper candles, and each place, even little Hayley's, had a crystal goblet.

Jane circled the table, pausing to pour a bubbly amber liquid into each glass. "This is that ginger ale," she told Noah. "We don't do wine or champagne."

When everyone took their place, Alice took the hands of the people beside her, a Dumont husband and Hayley, and the others followed suit. "Our most gracious Lord, we are grateful for family and friends gathered under this roof," she said in a strong voice. "Thank you for the year we've had, and for these fruits of the harvest. Strengthen us to do your work and your will."

"Amen," they chorused, but Noah didn't hear Jane's clear voice.

She sat at the other end of the table, but he caught himself sneaking glances at her, in that wine-colored dress, and found himself isolating her voice out of the conversations.

Before his surrender to Christ, the fourth Thursday in November had been a day off from school or work. A time to eat and chill. Now, it reminded him of how far he'd come, and not on his own strength. All his righteousness like dirty rags. Now he had a passion, a purpose, and a profession. Forgiven. A forgiveness he would never forget. A forgiveness that made him who he was now.

And how thankful I still am, God.

Thanksgiving. Demoted by the world to "Turkey Day," until a crisis or disaster forced people to realize who was really in control.

He looked around the table full of glowing faces. Yes, these kind-hearted people knew about the true meaning of thankfulness. Alice for sure, especially with her prayers and presence at Hilltop, how she had gone out of her way to make him feel welcome knowing his family was far away. The Dumonts-Descrochers-Desrosiers lived out their Catholic faith, serving around town. Stephanie led the younger crowd at Hilltop Community Church and was raising Hayley in the faith. Alice's two friends had to be good seeds. Probably went to St. Dominic's.

He looked at Jane. *God, may she know how much you and these people have done for her.* She caught his gaze over the candles and stared back with boldness. *No, this is just another nice day for her.* But hers softened, especially when she looked at Alice, and he knew. Alice was the closest to a savior Jane would ever accept.

Noah stared at his plate. Their moment of exchange felt almost indecent, as though he'd peeked into her soul. *Just be grateful to be here.* He helped himself to seasoned green beans, aromatic squash casserole, savory stuffing, and two more chunks of turkey—one dark, one white. He sipped the ginger ale and found it rich with flavor.

Alice was talking with Hayley about books, Steph discussing her college classes with Bill, the other Dumont spouse, and the two bakers explaining their need for expansion to a nodding Jane.

"How are you enjoying New England?"

Noah pinpointed the question from one of Alice's friends. "So far, so good. Except I'm always cold." He waited for their sympathetic laughter to subside. "I haven't seen much of the area yet, though."

"So, you haven't been to the Old Man site? Or the Kancamagus?" Bill asked.

He shook his head. "Those are?"

"The Old Man of the Mountains was a rock formation over in Franconia," Bill said. "It depicted what people thought was the face of a man, and it was the symbol of our state. People came to see it for more than a hundred years. It's still on postcards and keychains."

"Oh that. What happened to it?"

"It fell. But people still come and visit."

"They could have put up a replica." He looked around at a table of blank faces.

Great, something else I don't understand.

Bill chewed and swallowed before answering. "Oh, we don't need a pile of rocks to remind us."

Noah nodded. Whatever was in these Hilltop people ran deep, deeper than the need to touch or see or photograph.

"And what's the, um, Kancamagus?" Had he pronounced it right?

Forks stopped in midair. Even Hayley looked up at him.

Jane held back a laugh, probably from the wrong way he'd pronounced the name.

Bob leaned forward, his eyes alert behind thick glasses. "It's a thirty-four-mile scenic road, part of Route 112, that winds through the White Mountain National Forest. It links Lincoln with Conway, and it's a major draw for leaf peepers."

"*Leaf peepers*?" He hoped he wasn't making a weird facial expression.

"Fall foliage." Alice added. "And once you've seen it, you'll know why."

Jane looked around at the sparkling table at the animated faces. The Dumonts, Desrochers, and Desrosiers ladies and Gram's friends had always been like aunts to her. She beamed at the thought to forge a real friendship with Stephanie. Hayley was delightful. And then there was the simple fact of having Gram here, Gram on the mend.

But why did Hastings keep looking at her even when he was talking to someone else? Was it the burgundy dress? It fitted like a glove. She'd brought one good dress with her, just in case. Jane was a "just in case" person.

She shied away from another warm glance he threw her way. *Wait, is he flirting with me?* She watched him laugh at something Gram said, and a selfish part of her wanted it to be true. That a man full of warmth had eyes only for her. That this was their home, these were their guests. That they were building a life together.

She thought of her own darkness and swallowed hard. No, she couldn't do it. Not even with Noah Hastings and his sunshine smile. Even if they had been different people.

He'd get the message sooner or later. If she could skim the surface with her colleagues, her housemates, and even with Gram to a point, she could hold off Reverend Noah Hastings.

The candles burned down, the bowls and platters emptied, and the sky grew dark outside with one of those early winter dusks. But the talk flowed. He looked at Jane, who looked away. *She* probably had a big old-fashioned Christmas with Alice and other people who loved her, with hand-knit scarves and homemade fudge.

Don't you realize how lucky you are?

Noah watched as Jane bent to fill his glass. When her hair brushed his shoulder, she moved away. Before the curtain of hair fell over her cheeks, he saw a flush.

Is that because of me? He hadn't exactly been flirting with her, but he did want her to feel special. Maybe it was flirting. But it wasn't like how he used to flirt with girls on the beach. No. It was special because Jane was. His heart pounded at the thought. *Oh, Noah, don't.* No good could come from this. *Just this once.*

"I don't know what I'm going to do all weekend." Did he sound casual enough? Too late now. "It's my first holiday away from California."

The older women eyed him, but Stephanie took the bait. "You should get your sightseeing done before the festival. Things kick into high gear in December. And you should go before the tourists come back in January. It's bumper-to-bumper in ski season." She pierced Jane with a glance. "Janie, you should take him. You know these mountains better than anyone."

"I think that would be a splendid idea," Alice said.

Jane bit her lip. "Gram, I can't leave you alone for that long."

"Nonsense." Gram waved the objection away, her charm bracelet tinkling. "Helen and Laura are coming over for our annual movie marathon—*It's A Wonderful Life* and *White Christmas*. I'll be busy all Saturday."

Jane met his grin head-on with a scowl. "Be here at ten sharp. It gets dark early."

"Excellent." Gram wiped her mouth on her linen napkin. "Jane, dear, could we have some pie?"

CHAPTER TEN

Noah arrived at Alice's house a little before ten on Saturday morning. Jane met him at the door again and gave him a tightlipped smile. She was tugging on her parka, and one glance at her icy stare shied him away from helping. *How could anyone look so good in jeans and an oversized green sweater?*

She tugged a cap over her flowing curls and looked *him* over from head to toe. "Good. You remembered gloves. It gets cold up there."

She turned and called to an unseen Alice, "I'll be back in time for supper."

Alice's voice floated back to them. "Don't rush."

Jane's lips thinned. "I won't. And I'll *still* be back for supper."

She brushed past him on the neatly-shoveled sidewalk. "We'll take Gram's car. I've already got it out. It's easier to manage, and I won't have to give you directions." Which, her tone implied, would be like taking medicine.

In the passenger seat, he kept his mouth shut as she navigated the way out of Hilltop. He did steal a few glances at her perfect profile as they passed the French Hens, crowded on this holiday weekend, and the Limelighter, its windows steamy from cold and the breath of patrons wedged into the booths.

How did she feel about having this field trip thrust upon her? If she really didn't want to show him around, why didn't she just say no? He had only been consumed with the chance to spend time with her and see her beloved mountains. He berated himself for not considering her feelings. Too late to turn back now. He hadn't thought. He never thought.

God, please help us to still have a nice time.

His heart pounded when their eyes met for a moment. He was in trouble now. He liked her, liked more than her stunning looks. Liked her intelligence, her fierce devotion to Alice, and the courage that had lifted her out of a mysterious and troubled past.

But it stopped at "like." He wouldn't "missionary date" as some of his classmates had called it. He had come so far in his faith he couldn't risk being tied to an unbeliever. He could never forget how God and his love had filled the void, healed his soul. He wanted that restoration for Jane, but she needed to come to her own faith for her own sake.

Jane would be nice to him for Gram's sake. Even if she had, for whatever reason, manipulated this. Had they seen the way he looked at her during Thanksgiving dinner? Could they tell? Could everyone? She bit back her embarrassment. And anger. She breathed a steadying breath. Gram *was* on her side, always had been. It was just a day trip, not a date. Plus, she could finally get away to see her beloved mountains.

She knew them inside and out. Ever since she had arrived at Hilltop and saw their majestic wonder, she had made them her passion. They were everything she wanted to be—strong, stable. She smiled at the memory of Gram teaching her mountain legends, the fact and the fiction interwoven. They'd hiked most of the trails, driven to the summits of the higher peaks. If Boston was her city, these White Mountains were her country.

She turned onto Route 93 and drove a few miles on the interstate, almost as deserted as the back roads on this chilly morning. Smoke rose from the chimneys of isolated homes and farmsteads. The gray sky promised more snow before the weekend was up.

She turned into a parking lot off the highway, cut the engine, and looked over at Hastings. "Here we are."

He exited after she did, stretching his long legs after cramming them into Gram's compact and looking around at the ring of mountains. "So?"

"It's over there." She steered him gently to look at a rocky outcrop. "That's where the Old Man was. White Americans discovered it around 1805, although people believe it's been there for centuries. It later became a tourist attraction and a symbol for the state."

"Uh-huh." Hastings stamped his feet to keep them warm and sent a longing look back toward the car.

Well, he'd asked for this.

"Nathaniel Hawthorne wrote a short story about it, 'The Great Stone Face.' And Daniel Webster in a quote attributed to him compared it to the signs tradespeople hung out along the lines of 'in New Hampshire God Almighty has hung out a sign to show that there He makes men.'"

"Okay." Hastings pulled his knitted hat over his ears. "When did it fall?"

Jane looked off, remembering every detail of that day. "I was in high school. It crashed during the night, sometime between midnight and two a.m. We were in biology class when they told us. My teacher cried. We got the rest of the day off."

Hastings shook his head. If he laughed ... But he just looked confused. "So, you mourned a pile of rocks, and now you come here to see another pile of rocks where the first pile stood?"

Jane exhaled. "Yes. That's what we do. Because the Old Man was more than a 'pile of rocks.' It's who we were. And are."

Would he understand? Suddenly she wanted him to. But in her years of teaching, she'd learned you couldn't make anyone understand anything. He was being polite. That would have to do.

She swiveled toward the car. "Come on, you'll love the Kancamagus."

Well, I guess I'd be sad if the Hollywood sign fell. At least they could make another one.

Noah stared out the window at fields reduced to stubble and coated with frost, small towns with white churches and brick libraries, and forgotten scarecrows and snow-dusted piles of leaves. Sobering sights also lined the streets with a boarded-up general store and a small brick factory with its windows shattered. It wasn't easy to make a North Country living.

He could now better make out a craggy face on postcards and T-shirts in souvenir shops. He'd never known what it meant or how much it meant to its people. California had its own treasures—the Redwoods, the Pacific Coast Highway, the early Catholic missions.

How could they be so devoted to something that wasn't there?

He still couldn't wrap his mind around the leaf peepers. *I'm all for forests, but ...* Jane swerved to the left and guided them into Lincoln, a wide main street lined with businesses, outdoor outfitters, and restaurants. Loon Mountain towered over the town with its shops, inn, and condos. She took a sharp right where a sign announced the White Mountain National Forest and no services for thirty-two miles.

"We are on the Kanc," Jane said with a smile, the first smile he'd seen that day.

As the road climbed, the houses and small farmsteads thinned out. Noah spotted a flock of birds, black against the sky, in a perfect "V" formation. Classical music played softly from the car radio. He left like he could drive on forever like this when she turned right into a paved parking lot and cut the engine.

"You've got to see this one," she said.

He looked at Jane, the joy on her face saying nature was her safe place too. He thanked God again for this insight. Something to connect them. Something for God to use to connect with her.

He gazed out at a sea of snow-capped evergreens, hardwoods in muted colors, and bare rock face stretching as far as the eye could see. "Wow."

Jane unfastened her seatbelt. "This is the Hancock Overlook. Pretty impressive, huh?"

He joined her at the rock wall. They stood decorously apart, but he picked up on every gesture as she pointed out various landmarks. Even in the too-crisp air, he didn't feel the cold, not when she stood so near. The scene spread out before them, a bleak panorama, like a black-and-white pencil drawing except for the evergreens. The unforgiving landscape reminded him of a sci-fi movie, like he and Jane could be the only two people in the world.

If we were the only people in the world, then maybe it could just be us and nature and—

"So," he said, breaking away from his thoughts. "You come here often?"

Jane laughed. Was she warming up to him? "Whenever I can. What girl wouldn't, with a mountain practically in her backyard? Gram and I used to come up here all the time for picnics and hiking. It was our go-to place."

"It's amazing."

"You should see it earlier in the fall. The color—it's everywhere. Like a giant abstract painting. People come from all over the country, the world."

"To look at leaves?" He still couldn't wrap his mind around it.

"Yes. To look at leaves. Senior citizen bus tours. Foreign tourists. The newspapers and radio stations update every day when it's going to be the most colorful. They call it the 'peak foliage.'"

Noah shook his head. "And I thought Californians were crazy."

"Well, I suppose everyone has their own brand of crazy." Jane grinned and tugged at his sleeve. "Come on, Pastor. There's a lot more to see."

Jane drove on, negotiating hairpin turns and keeping up a running commentary as she unpacked facts about her beloved mountains.

So, this is what she's like when she's in a good mood. It seemed even she couldn't resist an opportunity to show off her home.

Unexpectedly, his heart longed for his sunny California home. But being here with Jane and her joy and love for nature made him feel less lonely.

They would get through today, get through the festival. She'd be gone, and he'd go just as soon as he got some pastoring under his belt. Perhaps within a year. The majestic mountains and their remarkable people would something for the mental scrapbook.

And with today burned into his memory.

Jane looked over at him. "So ..." She paused. "Do you drive one of those wood-paneled station wagons and yell things like 'Surf's up!'?"

He cracked a wide smile. "Every chance I get." He gave her a hang-ten hand sign. "Do you say 'Ayuh,' gut deer, and give people convoluted directions?"

Jane's laugh rang out, pure and joyous. "No to one and three. Yes to the second. I did it once." A wicked grin spread across her face. "I could make an exception for the third. Where do you want to go?"

He smiled back. *Seems like she's really having fun.*

Smart, pretty, caring, funny. Even without being religious, Jane had a strong sense of morality inside her soul. Jane Archer was the total package. Whether she knew it or not. And she'd bested him, which she probably did know.

Jane turned left into another parking lot and turned off the engine. "This is the Sugar Hill overlook."

He joined her to sit at the edge of the parking lot, looking out at the patchwork of trees and slopes and rocky ledge. It made him feel small—and big enough.

"'I will lift up mine eyes unto the hills. From whence cometh my help,'" he murmured.

"Something like that." Was she thawing? "I never took you for a King James kind of guy."

"There's a lot you didn't know about me," Noah said. But he wanted her to.

Jane perched on the stone wall. "It's going to snow later."

"How can you tell?"

She lifted her face to the sky. "I can smell it."

"Really now?"

"Yep." She grinned up at him.

He lost any coherent thought. Her green eyes sparkled in the sunlight, her cheeks pink from the cold, her lips, well, kissable. Was that even a word? Snowflakes decorated her hair from a sudden gust of wind. She belonged here. Her strength came from these austere mountains, just as Alice Merrill's did. This North Country had shaped her character, whether she knew it or not.

Better get his eyes, and his mind, off those lips. "What's it like in Boston?"

Jane hugged her knees. "Well, technically, I'm not in Boston. The school is in Wellesley—a beautiful town in its own right—but we're a half hour away from, well, everything. I can take my students to the State House, the Freedom Trail, and Bunker Hill. Lexington and Concord are just down the road. There's nothing like teaching history and civics in the places where they happened."

"Night life?"

"Plays, concerts, museums."

"Social life?" None of his business, but the pastoring side of him couldn't help it.

"I have friends." The cautious way she said it told him more than she probably wanted him to know.

"You should come back," he said. "There's plenty for you to do in Hilltop, and these people love you. You could get a teaching job here."

He bit his tongue. Would she tell him just how much he didn't know her, say what right did he have to tell her what to do?

Jane only stared off at the frozen hills. "No. I can't. I can't just leave my students behind." Her voice was soft but resolute as she turned toward him. "Could you just up and leave your flock here for another church?"

Noah looked away since he had been thinking just that. "No," he said. Just because he couldn't see himself living in Hilltop didn't mean God didn't have plans for him to stay.

She stepped away. "There are so many more opportunities for me in Boston."

Opportunities. He knew about those. All those other churches on his list. All the opportunities he'd left behind forever when he turned his back on his dad's dreams and the business.

Noah closed his eyes. Jesus had died and risen again to give him that opportunity, the most important one. The chance for a new life, true life.

God, you can open her eyes anywhere, but please don't let her miss this opportunity while she's here.

He opened his eyes. "Then can you tell me why you don't want to come back?"

Noah Hastings should mind his own business. If he even knew what that was any more. He was ruining their day. True, it started off rocky, but the mountains made it better. He had to go and spoil it with all his questions. She saw concern in his eyes. Why did he seem to care so much, especially when they barely knew each other? Was it the pastor in him?

Jane looked up at him, the sculpted face furrowed with concern. His blue eyes bore into hers, his blond hair sticking out from under his cap. He looked like a Viking, like he belonged here more than she did. Ironic.

She had to say something. Maybe he'd leave her alone. Was that what she even wanted? She wasn't sure anymore.

But she couldn't lie in front of her mountains.

Heart pounding, she looked away from him, focused on the peaks and valleys before them. "It's the unconditional love. I've always had a problem with that. Always will."

He tilted his head. "They *do* love you, Jane."

She saw a kind of pain welling up inside him she never dreamed could be there. Not in Reverend Noah Hastings, the man with the sunshine smile.

She blinked the thought away. "Yes. Hilltop would take me back, whatever I did, whatever I was. Look at the way they've treated Stephanie. Cared for her, welcomed her little girl. The way they were with me when Gram took me in."

Hastings watched her with those keen eyes. "Shouldn't that be a good thing?"

She turned her face away. "I don't want anything I don't work to get."

"So, Steph deserves their kindness and not you?"

Jane bit her lip. "That's not what I meant."

Memories flooded back to her. Nights alone in her bedroom at the Victorian, memorizing French verbs and chemical formulas until even Gram told her to stop studying. Contest wins and class offices. Salutatorian. That unforgettable prom night with sweet Paul. Lonelier nights in the Cornell library, striving to make herself worthy of the scholarships and good wishes. And she'd made it. She was ... something.

Hilltop would never understand her darkness. She'd never give them or anyone else the chance.

When she looked back at Hastings, something seemed to click in his mind. He spoke in a soft voice, "I'm sorry for prying and ruining the mood. I hope we can still have a nice trip." He smiled a reassuring smile.

They both turned their faces to the cold, rocky outcropping.

After a moment of stillness, Jane turned toward the car. "Come on, Pastor Noah." She willed a smile, as if they had never argued. "There's still a lot of the North Country to see. We'll finish the Kanc. There's a place in Conway with amazing chili, and the tourists haven't discovered it yet."

Noah trailed her toward the car. He'd done it again, blundered his way through an invitation to Christ, of all things, and she had turned it down. And he had nearly blurted out his own deep pains. Would sharing his full story help her open up about her past? Help her heal? He saw the pain on her face, the tears threatening to fall.

Please forgive me for being too forceful. I know you'll be there for her when she's ready. Please show her the radical love you have waiting for her. You can be the father she never had.

Noah had to close his eyes as Jane drove away from the cliff. That's what hurt the most as a pastor, hearing people's hurts, offering them the only cure, and seeing them reject it. As if anything were too big for God.

Noah remembered that pain, had tried to drown his sorrows before they drowned him. But all that wild living, walking in his own plans, only ever added to the pain.

He couldn't bear the thought of Jane Archer without heaven—or heaven without Jane Archer.

CHAPTER ELEVEN

"Hey, Greg. Can you believe it's December already?" Jane breathed in the familiar scents of sawdust, paint, and machine oil as the tinkling bell signaled her entrance to Gregson's Hardware. An artificial tree with old-fashioned colored bulbs shed its glow from the display window. But the low interior lights made the cluttered aisles end in pools of darkness.

"Hey, Janie." Greg looked up from a laptop on the counter. "I was just about to close. Help you with something?"

Greg's voice was as pleasant as always, the crinkle-eyed smile as welcoming. Was it real or a performance? Would any of them ever be really comfortable around each other again? Not until they had some answers to questions they'd never expected to ask.

I'm the acting chair. I have a right to know. I need to know if Gram will be safe here.

"Have you heard any more about the missing money?"

Greg rubbed his eyes. He looked tired tonight, older. "No. Paul says they're still investigating. I'm not sure I *want* to know."

As it would for Gram, knowing would break his heart.

Greg brightened. "I've got something to show you."

Greg's office would have been a decent-sized space if he hadn't had so much stuff. Over the years, he'd shoehorned in books, antique and modern tools, bulging file cabinets, and his "collections" of rotary phones, vintage cameras, and a mint-green and mint condition Smith Corona manual typewriter from the 1970s. When she worked here in high school, she had fun typing the work schedules on the ancient machine.

She marveled at the old advertising signs, Mason jars full of nails, and an orphaned window shutter. "You never got rid of anything."

"Nope. Anne hates clutter. Won't even let me have a basement workshop. So, this is my Magic Kingdom."

He led the way to his worktable where a desktop computer sported a Sherlock Holmes hat. "We've found a couple of them but need to start an archive." He picked up a leatherette-covered scrapbook.

Jane peered over his shoulder at a collection of square black-and-white photos. In one of the photos, a small blonde woman in an elf's tunic and rakish hat linked arms with a handsome dark-haired man in front of the Santa Float.

"That's Alice as a parade elf, and the man is your grandfather."

"Gram," she murmured. "Oh, she had great legs."

And Gramps, in a heavy jacket and a cap with flaps, grinning for all he was worth. *I wish I could have met you.*

"He drove the Santa float for years. I took over from him. He was our chief mechanic. Walter loved Hilltop."

There were other pictures. One of a young and scrawny Reverend Clarke at the Christmas Eve service and another of the town librarian from her childhood presiding over a table at the cookie walk. Those who had gone before.

How would you have handled missing money, Grandpa?

"Someone must have thought it was important to preserve Hilltop's history. We could put out an APB, see if anyone has anything to donate."

Jane nodded and flipped through page after page of Hilltop doing what it did best. One picture depicted kids at the Regional marching band wearing jaunty elf hats. The living nativity gave the town's teens a place to belong. Children posing in vintage snow suits skating on the pond. A trio of women in cat's-eye glasses singing on the main stage in the sanctuary.

The second volume of pictures brought the festival into more recent times. There was Gram, chairing a meeting with her schoolteacher's look. Bev and Mark Smith serving soup together at the café. A young, whole Mark before his diagnosis. The Gregson's family portrait in front of the Santa float.

"Look how little they were," Jane said, pointing to a young Steph and Ryan.

"Look how young we *all* were." Greg snapped the book shut on a final page from the 1980s. "It could be our last year. Depending on how all this plays out."

Greg was either innocent, or a very good actor. Jane had never seen him act. *What would he need the money for anyway? All the board members know how tight the budget is, so they'd never risk taking any out lest the festival not succeed.*

"We'll figure this out. Or Paul will." She patted his arm. "We've all come too far not to. So, don't give up on the festival just yet."

Did she even believe it? She had no choice.

The sun had set, and the air bit at Jane as she came out into the street. She turned up her collar, headed toward home. Nice that Gram lived so close to downtown.

Main Street was settling in for the night as merchants lowered lights. The Limelighter was open for the dinner crowd while the French Hens stood closed until the twins came in before dawn to bake. The festal banners on the lampposts quivered in a slight breeze. Light streamed from the old library, turning the ancient windows into golden squares.

Jane had always loved the old library, a small building of good New Hampshire granite, with arched windows and a yard full of old-growth trees. Having outgrown the town's needs, the old library kept its doors open for smaller civic functions and the festival. The new brick library was already bursting at the stacks as Hilltoppers loved to cozy up by their fireplaces with their books. Although Hilltop had internet access, many residents clung to the ease of the old ways.

And she wanted to see Hilltop change as little as possible.

She turned the knob on the antique door. The old library still smelled of books, the good old-fashioned kind with spines and covers made of ink and paper. Although the stacks in the middle had been taken down to allow room for events, vintage wooden shelves lined the walls of the single room. She found Bev Smith there, studying the placement of a camel in an olive-wood Nativity set.

"I saw the light," Jane said.

"Hi, Janie. I was just setting up. No time during the day."

"Don't let me stop you."

"No, I'm grateful for the company."

Jane wandered the room, looking at a selection from the three hundred manger scenes in Bev's collection. She remembered some of them—wood, porcelain, and clear glass that shimmered like ice. An elongated Masai set in ebony shared a shelf with a Mexican clay set, the figures clad in bright festal garb. The smallest set was carved out of ivory and tucked inside half a walnut shell. A Cuban set was crafted from scrap metal and small appliance parts.

"They used what they had," she murmured.

"That's what fascinates me." Bev turned with a smile. "So many different expressions of the birth of Christ. He truly came for all mankind."

Jane nodded. "Any new ones?"

"Not since Mark took ill. I'm thinking of selling some, but where would I start?"

I wouldn't want to have to decide that. Is there even a market for this stuff?

"Some of them were expensive, some just novelties." Bev seemed to have been reading her mind. "They're my one indulgence."

"Like Gram with clothes." Jane looked at another olivewood set from Bethlehem. "This one was always my favorite." She picked up the miniature Mary and gazed in awe at the wonder the carver had captured in the thumbnail-sized face.

"I'll give it to you on your wedding day," Bev said.

Like I'll ever get married. What would I do with a nativity set? Jane looked from the figures to Bev. *Still, it's nice she offered.*

Jane felt the silky buffed wood, looked at the tiny, perfect features. As a child, she had been drafted to help Bev set up the collection—the only ten-year-old in Hilltop allowed to touch the sets—because she'd been so well-behaved.

She gently put the Mary figure back next to Joseph. Straightening, she caught her image in the arched window. Her reflection shimmered in the old glass and the glow from the streetlamp. Her face stared back at her, pale and unsmiling. Had she ever even *been* a child? Who was this wary woman? She didn't belong here, not with these good people.

A car drew up and the overhead light went on. She sucked in a breath when she saw Noah Hastings driving while Mark rode shotgun.

Jane watched as Hastings did the talking, gesturing expansively between blowing on his reddened hands. He'd forgotten his gloves again. Mark listened and nodded, bundled in a jacket and two scarves and the cap that covered the baldness from his final chemotherapy. Hastings talked as if his own life depended on it.

So, he really is like that to everyone.

She was about to turn back to Bev when both men bowed their heads. She couldn't look away from this minister's fierce concern for this parishioner as he prayed. Oh, he was walking through the valley of the shadow with Mark.

Her heart just about broke when she heard the news of Mark's cancer returning. For something so awful to happen to such a kind and caring man. Where was God then? But Bev and Mark's faith didn't waver, as if it really could move mountains.

And Hastings looked like he was about to go to hell and back again for Mark. Her heart warmed. Perhaps he really was a good man.

Her cheeks flushed as the memory of his concerned face, so close to hers, came to mind. She shivered and moved away from the window. Couldn't be feeling anything for him. She'd let too much of him in already, starting with that Thanksgiving weekend jaunt, ending who knew where with that look he gave her before he drove away.

"Bev, Mark is here." Did her voice shake as much as she did?

She followed Bev to Hastings's car.

Mark got out carefully, after a look passed between him and Hastings. "Hey, honey."

"Did you have a good time?" Bev fussed over him, retying his scarf.

Mark and Bev drew out of the way as Jane stood on the sidewalk with Hastings. She couldn't look at him, not after the intimate scene she'd just witnessed. Even she knew Noah Hastings was the real deal. And it only increased his appeal.

And poor Mark. Oh, how she wanted to believe there really was a heaven, a good place for good people like him to go. Bev would get to see him again, and Gram would be there one day, reunited with Walter. Would she be there?

She sucked in a breath to think of happier things.

"What are you up to tonight?" an unfazed Hastings asked.

Jane forced herself to look at him. "I saw a light in the old library, so I stopped by to see Bev. She's setting up her nativities. You've got to see them."

"I will. You working on floats this Saturday?"

They had taken a break the Saturday after Thanksgiving, but even now, on a Monday, she heard from the board members that some people had put in some work.

Hilltop business, that was safe. "I'm doing my bit for cookie decorating. Paul asked me to watch the girls, and I invited Fred Parker to drop off his boys. If I'm going to have a mess, might as well go for broke."

Hastings leaned against the car, and she could just imagine him on the beach, surfboard in hand, staring off into the waves. "Want some company?" He tucked his bare hands into his pockets. "I'm not much of a baker, but I can help out with kids. Used to give free tips to young surfers."

She tried not to imagine him surfing. "Oh, really, I can manage."

Hastings grinned that lazy grin. "Then do you mind if I invite myself? Come on, Ms. Archer—Jane. My housekeeper used to say, 'Many hands make light work.'"

It wasn't the hands she was worried about. It was her heart. But cookie baking? What harm could it do, especially with four tiny chaperones?

"Be there at two." Jane turned away before he, or she, could say more.

CHAPTER TWELVE

Been a while since a woman had rendered Noah speechless. He thought about it all Friday as he prepared his Sunday sermon. Nevertheless, his spirits were on a high ever since his positive feedback on his Thanksgiving Sunday sermon. Well, at least the people his age and younger did since they could relate to the desire to make friends. He had even dared to share a part of his story of meeting the kind people of Venice Beach Mission and about how true Christian friendship was better than anything the world had to offer.

Brad and Paul even came up to him after saying the four of them should get together to watch some football sometime. Noah had thanked God then and thanked Him now as the four of them finalized their plans for next weekend. So far, his brothers had only liked his Happy Thanksgiving message he'd sent them, but he wasn't giving up praying for them just yet. Not after he'd seen what God had done to give him some friends of his own.

He was feeling confident. Perhaps this would be the Sunday he'd use a mountain metaphor. Maybe that was the key to relate to the people of Hilltop.

Noah said another prayer for himself. *God, don't let us argue like last time.*

Jane answered on the first ring, flinging the door open to a house already redolent with spices. She wore a sweatshirt and jeans, with a white apron cinched at the waist. Her hair was in a ponytail, a few loose wisps curling around her flushed face.

And for a moment, he lost all words, shuffled his feet like a middle-schooler on a first date. But this wasn't a date. If his brothers, frat *or* biological, could see him now.

"You look like someone from a Christmas movie," he finally said.

"Well, you'd better get inside. Four hooligans are about to destroy Gram's kitchen." Her smile as she hung up his coat told him she was at least a little happy he was here.

Just don't push it like last time. Care but respect her wishes.

Noah slipped out of his snow boots and padded behind her, down the hallway to the kitchen. "Where's Alice? How is she doing, by the way? I heard from her friend on Sunday she's already starting to use a walker."

"Yes, she's nearly there. Today, she's at book group at the library." Jane shook her head. "One of her friends had room in her car for a wheelchair, so off Gram went. You know how she is."

Noah nodded, grateful for everything Alice Merrill was.

Jane had greatly exaggerated the reports of a destroyed kitchen. At the table, the two Parker boys colored in holiday coloring books with fresh crayons. They had new haircuts and new-to-them clothing, but they eyed Noah warily.

Well, it's natural for them to mistrust adults. God, please let me be a good example to them.

"Hey, guys." He made a fist bump.

Danny, the older boy, returned it with a tiny smile.

Two small blonde girls played with Barbie dolls at the other end of the table.

"You know Paul McKee's daughters," Jane said, ruffling the older girl's curly hair. "This is Emma. She's four. And Maddy is *almost* three." She held out her arms to the smaller girl, and Maddy came to her, nestling her flaxen head under Jane's chin.

How beautiful Jane looked. How beautiful she'd look with her own child. Her face held a tenderness and a wistfulness as she cuddled the police chief's daughter.

And what was her relationship with McKee? Just old friends, former prom dates?

Don't be jealous now.

Noah cleared his throat. "What do we do first?"

Jane settled the little girl back on her chair, boosted up with a vintage telephone book. Her green eyes shone merry with delight. "You've never baked Christmas cookies?"

Well, no. Three boys and a housekeeper didn't make for a Hallmark holiday. They had always had Christmas dinner at the club, until Mom and Dad split for good. After she left, they opened Dad's professionally-wrapped gifts on Christmas morning and headed for the beach. It was sunny California after all. If Dad remembered, he picked up cookies from a bakery.

He hadn't had time to think about his own Christmas, only the festival and his sermon. Perhaps now was his chance for a real Christmas.

"Teach me," he said.

His gaze held hers, and he couldn't look away. *Just this once.* A Christmas to remember before they both left. One perfect Christmas, in this place and with this woman, neither of which were like anything else on earth.

Yes, God. Please let me have a great Christmas too.

Jane gestured around the sunny kitchen and talked fast even for her. "Well, I baked most of the cookies in advance." She picked up a tray of sugar cookies shaped like stars, bells, and wreaths. "The icing is all mixed, and they can frost these. I've got about five dozen." She lifted a covered bowl from the counter. "But I wanted them to have the experience of rolling and cutting, so I kept a little of the dough out."

"Here you go, sweetheart." she said, helping Maddy into an oversized white apron as she spoke. "You don't want to get frosting on that pretty shirt."

Noah helped Emma into the apron Jane tossed him and tied one around each of the boys.

Jane set a small bowl of white icing in front of each child along with several plastic knives. "In case they lick the knife, and you know they will."

Noah stood right beside her and seemed even bigger in Gram's small kitchen. For a moment, Jane couldn't breathe. Well, the kids would provide a distraction, and he could make himself useful. She picked up a tray of baked cookies from the counter. It was still hot, and she almost dropped it, but Hastings grabbed a potholder and caught the tray.

"Whoa there." His kind blue eyes smiled down at her.

She turned away, trembling. "I'm okay." She found a cool sheet of cookies and placed it in the center of the table. "See, honey, this is how you do it." She bent over little Maddy, guiding the plastic knife.

They frosted the bell-shaped cookie until the icing reached every corner of the bell. Maddy looked up at her and laughed.

Oh, the joy of teaching something to a child. *Will I ever have a daughter of my own to do this with?* She felt Hastings's gaze on her as she helped Emma ice a snowman cookie. *Why did he want to come? He couldn't possibly like me, could he?*

He helped the Parker boys—with surprising gentleness—until all the baked cookies were iced. She didn't want to hear his low voice, murmuring encouragements and silly jokes until both boys were giggling. She had to admit he'd proven himself useful today.

Jane brought over small plastic containers. The children squealed at the sight of red and green sugar, chocolate sprinkles, little silver balls made of sugar, and cinnamon stars.

She handed each a plastic spoon. "Don't put your hands in the decorations, please."

Maddy loaded a cookie with sprinkles, both colors of sugar, silver balls, and stars. The embellishments almost weighed down the delicate star-shaped cookie.

"Are you really going to let her give that away?" Hastings murmured in Jane's ear.

Her heart pounded and cheeks flushed. He stood too close, but she couldn't move away.

"Probably not that one," Jane said. "But they don't all have to be perfect. The better ones will go to the cookie walk or the Legion supper."

She focused on the McKee girls wiping up sprinkles as they scattered them, trying not to look at the blond giant who was so good with the Parker boys.

Why did he have to be so nice?

When the children's cookies were all decorated, she drew a deep breath. "Now it's time for cut-and-roll. Brace yourself."

Well, he was seeing a different side of Jane Archer this afternoon. And he liked it. She ignored their sloppy work and kissed each child on the crown of the head, praising their efforts. Paul's girls glowed, and the Parker boys thawed under her gentle encouragement. Jane might be a perfectionist toward herself but not for children. She was something better.

While Noah hadn't grown up with parents who had a healthy marriage, he wanted that for himself more than anything. He'd like a house full of kids someday. He knew his brothers would make great uncles. Would his dad be a good grandfather to his kids? Would Nicole, his mother, be a good grandmother? Time would tell.

Jane sprinkled the table with flour and handed each child a rolling pin and a ball of honey-colored dough, explaining how to roll out the dough, cut a shape with a plastic cookie cutter, and lift the unbaked cookie to a cookie sheet with a spatula.

"These are wonderful," she said, watching the children work with the dough. "Good job!"

Noah smiled. *Don't you see, Jane? You're giving unconditional love right now.*

The cookies *weren't* so beautiful, but Noah guessed he'd better keep his mouth shut.

It happened. For reasons known only to the young boy, Danny Parker took a fistful of flour and lobbed it at his brother. Dougie rubbed his eyes and sent a handful back, a handful which floated like snow over the table and Danny. Jane started to separate them when she slipped in the same puddle of flour Noah had slid through.

Oh, why not? Noah took a small handful of the extra flour and aimed it at her. *What have I done?*

Jane shook it off like a dog shakes off water, her green eyes gleaming. She grabbed two fistfuls of flour off the table and shot them both at Noah.

Her laugh. Such a beautiful sound. Unashamed, unshackled. She started to throw another handful, but he gently caught her wrist, enough to make her writhe in his arms. She smelled of cinnamon and vanilla.

"Noah, let me go," she giggled. "Come on. We've got kids here."

But the Parkers were engaged in their own food fight while Paul's girls watched them. Maddy licked a plastic knife. Well, Jane had been right about that.

Jane, solid and real in his arms. He didn't want to release her. Her green eyes laughing up at him.

He reached down and brushed some flour from her hair. "Sorry." But he wasn't, and he knew Jane knew it.

Yes, "kissable" was a word. What would it be like to kiss her?

No, no, no. He sucked in a breath and released her, slowly.

Jane straightened her apron. "It will take forever to clean this up." She spoke like a schoolteacher.

"It would have taken forever anyway. And I'll stay." He looked her in the eyes.

There was no way he was going to leave after that.

God help me.

Is he ever going to leave?

Noah stayed till the floor was swept and the table scrubbed, till the children relaxed in front of a Disney movie in the living room, till the children's rolled cookies came out of the oven. He helped Jane cover the remaining icing, package the worst of the kids' creations for them to take home, and helped her put the best cookies in a freezer container for the American Legion potluck.

He stood there when a grateful Paul came to collect his girls and when Fred Parker drove up in his old car. Fred, still gruff, but less edgy now that Greg had hired him to manage the Christmas-tree lot, and a local mechanic had fixed his car at cost. Fred ruffled Danny's hair, sampling a cookie, trying to figure out the whole fathering thing.

Looks like he's experiencing what Hilltop's all about.

She couldn't look at Noah. She knew she was flushed. What had possessed her, to tussle with him like that?

But she couldn't stop smiling, either.

She had even started calling him by his first name when they started cleaning up the kitchen. How had she let her guard down, especially with Noah Hastings? She'd wanted the kids to have a good time, that was it. And gotten carried away. Now she had a freezer full of child-designed cookies to show for it, a spotless kitchen, and Hastings still hanging around.

He was handsome, kind, and obviously flirting with her.

She shook her head. They shouldn't be alone, not after what had happened in the kitchen, not after what had almost happened. She looked at the white-and-gold anniversary clock on Gram's mantel. When would Gram be home?

She trembled a little just thinking about it.

Why did it have to feel so nice for him to hold me? He had touched her so gently, so respectfully. The way intimacy was supposed to be. The way she'd always wanted it to be but never let herself have. Larry was the reason Jane's dates ended at the front door or at coffee with one of her roommates at home.

Would the ghost of those nightmares ever stop haunting her?

As the light faded from outside, Jane switched on the lamps. Noah showed no sign of leaving. He had poured himself a cup of coffee from Gram's ever-ready pot, sat in a corner of the sofa, and crossed one long leg over the other. Settled in for the rest of the afternoon. Oh, this was too intimate, the two of them here in the lamplight in this cozy house.

How do I ask him to leave?

Jane perched on the edge of the flowered wing chair. "Thank you for helping, Noah."

"You're welcome. It was fun, Jane." Noah grinned that heart-stopping grin.

Oh, he was charming, and he had said her name. *Well, we are something like friends now.*

"I didn't think you'd let it get so messy. That doesn't seem like you." he said.

Jane closed her hand around her own cup of coffee until she feared it would break. "I wanted to give the kids a good time. They need to be kids. Paul's girls don't have a mother. Maddy doesn't notice it as much, but Emma remembers her, and it shows. The Parker boys, who knows what they've been through?"

Noah smiled into his cup. "You must be a good teacher."

Jane shrugged, though the praise warmed her. "This isn't my age group, but kids are kids. Even in fancy Boston prep schools."

Noah settled in even more, if that were possible. "I could start a fire." He looked at her. "Or you could. You'd probably be better at it, having done it more often. I think the last time I made a fire was when I went camping as a kid."

A fire. No. That would be far too intimate. Too homey. Too much like *their* home. Too romantic. Too much like a date.

"I talked to Alice," Noah said. "She really wants to start going back to church. She's getting around so much better. Do you think you could bring her tomorrow?"

No wonder he'd been so nice to her. He wanted Gram back in church. Well, what pastor wouldn't? If anything, it truly seemed as if Gram and Noah had become good friends.

Of course, he didn't like her. She should be glad. Hang out a flag or something.

That's right. She bit her lip. *Snap out of it already. It would never work.*

"I don't know." Jane could hedge it with the best of them. She was a schoolteacher, after all. "I'd be worried about the ice."

"Jane, she's in a wheelchair. She won't fall out. Plus, the greeters could always help."

She set her cup down. "I know, but ..."

"I know how much you love her, but do you know how much she loves you?" Noah bit his lip. "You said you don't deserve love, but God's love is unconditional." For a moment, she could have sworn he was preaching to himself. "He knows we can't ever earn it. That's the whole reason why he sent Jesus. So, Jesus could be enough on our behalf. Jesus paid it all, remember from the hymn? It's a free gift. No strings attached."

She could tell some part of him seemed on the verge of tears with the gravity of his own words.

He looked at her, setting his cup down to stand up. "Are you afraid of that too?"

Jane took a deep breath. It wasn't about what God had done for her. She recalled memories of being in church hearing the gospel, the good news. To her, it was old good news. It was about what God hadn't done for her. Oh, there was so much Noah Hastings didn't understand, even with his Bible college degree.

"There's nothing to be afraid of," she said crisply. "It doesn't exist for me. I just don't care."

Noah took her hands in his, and for a moment, she rested in their strength. "Jane, God does love you. He has a plan—"

"For my life?" She pulled away, her anger rising. "Do you think I haven't heard the pitch? You're not telling me anything I haven't heard."

A hurt bloomed in his eyes. She knew the question there. Why couldn't she believe? Would it be so hard to acknowledge his faith, his God? He was a good man. He believed. Gram believed. Could at least just try?

The depth of the care in his eyes for her made her want to cry even more. *No, don't. Don't you dare care for a lowly thing like me.*

She'd gone through the motions for Gram's sake, Sunday School, youth group. She was done faking the day she left Hilltop.

"If this is about suffering, Jane, I've had my share. We'll all have trials in this life. Even Jesus suffered and died for us. He's the only one who didn't deserve it."

She stopped him before he could say more, for then she really might cry. "I just want my own plan." It came out in a small voice, but she forced herself to smile.

Noah's heart broke for her. He had meant it to be a natural turn of the conversation but could see now just how much he'd overstepped. "Jane, I told you my lowest moment. But you grew up in this household, with one of the finest Christian women I've ever known—"

Jane held up a hand. "That's a story for another day, Reverend Hastings."

He had been "Noah" all afternoon.

"Okay, well, we have Bible studies, support groups. We have a couple of women's Bible studies. I think Stephanie is in one. You could go together and catch up. And I'm always available." He cleared his throat. "You have my cell number." He attempted a smile. "It's in that notebook you haul around."

"Thanks, but I won't be here that long."

Jane got up, with the grace that characterized all her movements, and crossed to the hall closet. She took out his coat and scarf and hung them on the newel post and moved his snow boots closer.

She crossed her arms. "Whenever you're ready."

He was obstinate enough to finish his coffee but watched her from under his lowered lashes. In his brief career as a pastor, he'd learned there was always more. Wasn't it his job to help her unpack it?

What did it take for her to hold it together, to give the appearance of someone she maybe wasn't?

He knew about appearances. Every time he counseled someone, every time he led a pastoral prayer. And don't get him started on preaching. That old doubt that began from his father's hurtful words crept in—who was he to explain the Word of God to anyone?

Better to have been an engineer where people's souls aren't at stake.

No. In a powerful prayer, he shoved away the doubt and fear. He would stick with this. He had a calling. Even if some days it was all he had. He would stumble, get up and try again. Jesus was his perfection, after all.

But Jane Archer. However did she do it?

How did she do it? Some days were better than others. She could hold her head high, teach her students with efficiency and insight, keep the townhouse pristine, manage her private life. Sometimes, she had to brace herself just to go into a coffee shop and stand in line. Sometimes, she had to sit outside the school in her car and nerve herself up to go in, even though she'd been teaching for six years.

Sometimes, it took all she had.

But she did make it work, preparing her lesson plans down to the semicolon, keeping house on a rigorous schedule, planning her wardrobe and weekends for maximum efficiency, and now running the Hilltop Festival.

If I let my guard down, it will all descend into chaos.

God? She thought of what Noah—Hastings, rather—said. But what had God done for her she couldn't do for herself?

She would run Hilltop, though not with Gram's grace and grit, and get out of here. Go back to St. Hildegarde's, teach privileged children about civics and history, draw from the richness of Boston to supplement her lessons and her life.

Go back to where she had some control. Far away from Reverend Noah Hastings.

Jane smiled a knowing smile at Noah. "I can take her tomorrow, if she's up to it." She watched his face light up and added in a casual tone, "I can always drop her off and come back."

She had the satisfaction of seeing the light drain from his eyes.

It's not you, Pastor. It's your boss.

CHAPTER THIRTEEN

"Gram, I'm going now." Jane coiled her scarf tighter and peeked through the oblong window next to the front door—at a frosty Winter Wonderland.

What a night for a sleigh ride—maybe the best ever—crisp and dry and spangled with stars. Jane looked back at her grandmother, nestled on the sofa with the remote and her beloved books. "I wish you were coming. You've made so much progress with your walker now."

"I know, but I just don't want to rush it. The chairman always gets the first ride of the season. But there's no way they could get me up in the sleigh. I'll go next year." Gram sipped at her green tea. "Are you sure you don't want to take the car?"

"Not tonight. The barn isn't that far, and it's a perfect night for walking."

Jane checked the fires in both the fireplace and wood stove, fed in smaller sticks until they caught the blaze, and put in larger logs. She recalled what Noah had said about her being good at making a fire but brushed it away. She had to be back before they burned down too far.

"Janie?"

"Yes, Gram?"

"Be careful." Jane knew she wasn't talking about the fire.

As Jane struck out on foot, Hilltop sparkled under four inches of new snow, snow that the moonlight turned to diamonds. Most people had their Christmas lights up by now, everything from austere white electric candles to strings of colored bulbs wrapped around anything that didn't move. There was the sense of promise only December could bring.

Most of Hilltop was home tonight, light glowing in the windows like one of those porcelain Christmas villages. She passed the old Victorian building where Stephanie had her apartment and saw lights in the first-floor window. Steph and a pajama-clad Hayley cuddled on the sofa. Watching a Christmas special? She passed Bev and Mark's tidy cape and saw the couple at their kitchen table, Bev leaning forward as if she were trying to convince Mark of something. More chemo? Greg and Anne's brick Colonial stood down a side street. Were they home, doing whatever pillars of the community did in their down time?

Who else was thinking about the theft? If only she could put Hilltop under a glass globe, protect them forever.

Charlie Wenholm's barn was a fifteen-minute walk from Gram's house. Smoke poured from the chimney of Charlie's white farmhouse, the last home in the village proper. His classic red barn was a favorite photo op for tourists. His property stretched beyond it, twenty acres of open meadow, farmland, woods, a narrow rushing brook. He'd made a life and a living off this land, one of the few full-time farmers left in the county, in the state.

A red-cheeked Charlie beamed at her from under a knitted hat and layers of scarves. He stood by the sleigh hitched up and ready to go, two of his Percherons stomping their feet, and a teenage boy in the driver's seat. "This here's Mikey, my grandson. He'll be your chauffeur."

Jane extended a gloved hand. "Hi, Mikey. I'm Jane."

"And you've got company." Charlie gestured to a figure coming around the side of the barn.

Jane knew him by his height, his gait—and those shoulders. *Wonderful.*

"Pastor here wanted to give it a try. Can you believe he's never been on a sleigh ride?"

She could. Did it have to be tonight? She tried not to think of the cookie baking and their argument. The way he had held her and looked into her eyes.

But didn't he look handsome even swaddled in a parka and scarf, that wide grin beaming out from under a snug hat?

Jane shoved her hands in her pockets and looked away. "Maybe I should try it out some other time."

"But the snow's perfect," Charlie said. "Come on, Janie. The chairman *always* gets the first ride. How else you gonna brag about it?"

Noah's grin challenged her resolve. "Okay. You can dig me out of the snow if I fall out. Remember, you did it before."

She really shouldn't. But if he was willing to be professional for the sake of the festival then she could too. One ride wouldn't hurt.

Besides, she'd tasted cookies at the twins' bakery and sampled soup at Joe's. She'd be vetting acts for the main stage entertainment and the coffee house.

This was research, and who better to get an opinion from than an outsider like Noah Hastings?

Jane ignored Noah's proffered hand and climbed into the sleigh on her own.

As soon as Mike clicked to the horses, they were off, the thump of the hooves the only sound as they flew across the meadow behind Charlie's house, leaving the town behind. The moon made a path over the unbroken whiteness of the snow. Jane could see her breath as she sat erect on the seat across from Noah.

She had always loved sleigh rides, proudly accompanying Alice on the test run early in December. She'd always sneaked in a ride during the festival. She loved skimming over the fields, the jingle of the sleigh bells, ducking into the woods and coming out into open meadow, the smell of the fresh pine and the stillness of the night.

Did Noah like it too? She made herself look at him.

He was grinning, even laughed a little. "This is great!" he said. But the laughter died when he looked at her, and she couldn't look away.

Her heart pounded and cheeks flushed. It was too late.

Noah stared at Jane. Exquisite as always. He remembered the way she had looked when he was at her house to bake cookies and found her in his arms, her green eyes looking up at him, her lips very kissable. Her curls and a green knit hat that matched her eyes framed her face tonight. Her cheeks were pink from the chill, her slender shoulders erect. If only she'd sat on his side. He could have put an arm around her, shared the wonder of his first sleigh ride ever with a woman who was becoming way too important.

The jingling of bells and the thump of horses' hooves provided a backdrop for his thoughts. The air stung his cheeks, but he wouldn't turn back for anything.

He had followed her here tonight, engineered this outing after Charlie had told him he was planning a test run. He had nobody to blame but himself.

Story of my life.

He sat helpless before this woman, cut off from rational thought, isolated as he'd been when surfing inside the tube, nothing around him but shimmering green and gold water.

Yeah. Like that.

Noah hadn't even dated since he got saved.

Could he ask Mikey to turn back? No. That would embarrass all three of them.

The festival chairman and the Hilltop pastor. Purely professional.

He glanced at her. "How's the festival coming?"

"Really well. You know Gram, she did a lot of the prep work ahead of time." She tossed him a grin.

His heart nearly stopped. *Don't do that, woman.*

"Still scared about preaching to five hundred people?" she said.

"I was never scared." But he knew she knew better, and he was afraid of something else now. "Yeah, guess I am. It will be the biggest challenge of my ministry so far." Except for her.

He had to ask and dreaded the answer. "So, when are you going back?"

Jane lifted her face, bathing it in moonlight. "January at the latest. Gram's already using a walker in the house. She'll probably be driving by then."

The stars shone overhead, bigger and brighter than he'd ever seen them.

How he wanted her to stay, needed her to stay.

Maybe her true friends were here. But she couldn't stay.

Mikey had his back to them with wireless earphones playing music only he could hear. Three feet separated her from Noah, and he looked at her with none of the teasing, flirtatious looks she'd come to expect from him. His blue eyes were dark with emotion.

I don't know what to think any more. She knotted her gloved hands in her lap until they hurt. *If he loves to talk so much, let him talk.*

"Tell me more about your family."

Noah took a deep breath. "Even though my brothers and I don't talk often, we get along well. I even recruited Alice to pray for them." He exhaled, hesitating. "My mom took off years ago with another man. We don't hear from her."

She saw the depth of the pain in his eyes. *Looks like we're not so different, after all.*

"Oh. I'm so sorry." She met his gaze.

Noah shrugged halfheartedly. "I was a kid. You get over it."

No, no he hadn't. She knew that pain.

He really was a good man. She'd seen that in his dealings with Hilltop. Sometimes children's trauma made for compassionate adults, and who knew that more than she?

He was handsome and kind. If only—If only what? He gave up his faith? She wouldn't ask that of any man. She wasn't worth it. If he gave up the ministry? No. Not after all the good things Gram had said about Noah, raving about his caring heart as a pastor, his Biblical insight, especially as she gabbed with her friends who shared the sermon notes with her. Even a strayed lamb like Jane recognized a calling.

She met his watchful gaze and couldn't look away. Oh, he saw into her, on a level neither of them wanted to admit.

The lost boy and the lost girl.

Mikey crossed a wooden bridge over a frozen stream, passed Charlie's hunting camp and sugar shack. He picked up speed in an open meadow and ice crystals peppered their faces. Jane didn't take her gaze from Noah, nor he from her.

They plunged into the woods, through a narrow path carved from between the majestic evergreens. The smell of pine and spruce rose all around them. They couldn't see the stars in here, but the horses knew the way, their steps confident against the packed snow. A gentle wind ruffled the treetops. She didn't feel the cold anymore. Did he?

"'The woods are lovely, dark and deep,'" she whispered, looking at the trees.

"'And miles to go before I sleep,'" Noah completed the couplet. "Robert Frost. I *do* read, you know."

Jane blinked. "Oh, I didn't know you read anything but the Bible."

Noah smiled. "I may not surf anymore, but I do still like to read."

Jane looked at the scenery. "Yeah. Reading can be relaxing. That's what I tell my students."

He reached out, over the three feet separating them, and covered her hands with his big ones, gloved for once. She almost wished she could hear him speak more poetry. Her heart pounded when he crossed the three feet, sitting beside her at last, one arm slung around her shoulder.

Mikey did the loop at the end of Charlie's property and turned around, urging the horses on, back to the barn and warmth and safety. Safety for Jane, anyway. As she curled into Noah, Jane knew she would carry the memory of this night with her as she went back to the world of grades and papers and field trips, of tenure, college recommendations, and the mannered dance that was St. Hildegarde's.

A good enough place, but it could never be Hilltop.

With a "whoa" from Mike, they pulled into Charlie's yard. Only the upstairs window shone with light. Mike unhitched the Percherons and led them to the barn.

Weak in the knees, Jane let Noah help her down from the sleigh. *What's wrong with me?*

"Too bad it's so late." She knew she was babbling. "Charlie's wife, Edith, used to invite Gram and me in for hot chocolate. Maybe next time—"

Noah took her by both shoulders. His eyes shone dark in the faint light from the barn, even as the moon's light cast a milky glow around them. He said her name as though he tasted peppermint candy. He pulled her to him, their faces separated by a distance that shrank as he bent to kiss her. His lips felt rough and cold on hers.

Surprised at her own boldness, Jane kissed him back.

CHAPTER FOURTEEN

They belonged to each other. She forgot the cold, losing herself in his kisses. She plunged her hands into his thick hair. Wanting more. Needing more. He looked down at her, stroked her cheek with his thumb before he claimed her lips again. His arms tightened around her, and she melted into him.

Noah.

How good it felt to be held, and to be held by Noah. Something gentle and loving. A romance with someone who wanted her kisses as much as he wanted to give them. In this moment, she wasn't alone. Didn't have to pretend. Could just be.

When they finally broke apart, Noah's voice shook. "I've wanted to do that all night. For weeks, really. Ever since we took that trip together. I'm not sorry. I mean—"

"I'm not either."

Jane steadied herself against the side of the sleigh. *Oh, Noah.*

Hadn't *she* wanted this for weeks, had a taste of it at the cookie baking? His arms. Not Paul's, not any of the up-and-coming young businessmen she spent time with in Boston. Noah.

Reality hit her like the news of the theft. They couldn't, for more reasons than she could enumerate with him still so close and Mikey in the barn.

"We should talk." Noah held her by both forearms, looking down at her.

She saw his heart in that gaze as her own heart became distant once again, even though it was tearing her apart inside. "There's nothing to talk about." And everything.

Her cell phone buzzed, and she took it out of her pocket. A text from Gram. Jane read the text and read it again—*Please come home.*

Jane's breaths came in gasps. "I have to go. It's Gram. Maybe she fell."

"Did you bring a car?"

"No, I walked."

"I'll drive you." Noah raced toward his SUV, opened the passenger door for Jane, swung himself into the driver's seat, and flashed her a reassuring look. "Come on, Jane. Whatever it is, we can handle it."

There was no "we."

As soon as they arrived at Gram's, Jane jumped from the car even before Noah had cut the engine. No ambulances or police cars sat in front of the house. But Gram wouldn't call her back home for nothing.

With Noah following close behind her, Jane pushed the front door open. "Gram?"

"In here, honey." Gram sounded calm enough, but her voice held an odd tinge, a tinge of excitement. Good news? On a weeknight?

Jane stopped on the threshold of the living room and smelled Noah's piney aftershave and heard him breathing behind her. She only saw her grandmother sitting erect in the wheelchair looking paler than normal.

"Are you okay?" Jane took a small step forward.

"I am." Gram nodded in her most regal way. "But we've got company."

Jane's gaze traveled to the woman in the wing chair by the fireplace. She wavered, and Noah gripped one of her arms, but she wriggled out of his hold.

"Mom?"

The woman's smile trembled with uncertainty. "Janie. You're even more beautiful than I expected."

Which was more than Jane could say for Charlotte Merrill Archer, the woman who'd abandoned her. Carly, as Gram had always called her, had been petite but curvy, with a mane of naturally blonde hair and the blue eyes Gram had passed down to her. She'd had no trouble attracting men, almost like a fly strip, in any one-stoplight town where they washed up. Now, Carly, as Jane herself began to call her the day her mother left her at Gram's, looked whipcord thin. Her now gray hair curled around her lean face. Calloused hands gripped a steaming mug of tea.

Did Gram make her tea? Isn't she just as hurt by her own daughter leaving?

Jane took a step closer, arms crossed. "What are you doing here?"

Rude, but she'd been holding it in for eighteen years.

Carly's face held no emotion. Her eyes held a spark of what? Hope? "I got tired of moving around so much. Thought I'd see how you and Mom were." She gestured to the photos around the room. "I'm proud of you, Janie. You done real well."

Seems like the only thing she could ever hang onto was that accent, the sound of bars and smoke and hopelessness.

If only Noah didn't have to hear this. For his sake, she'd keep it polite. "So where have you been?"

"Here an' there." Carly punctuated that with a shrug, but Jane knew what "here and there" meant in Carly's world. "I broke up with Brian after I sent you here. Been married twice. Neither of 'em took, but it bought me some stability for a while so I could go to school. I got my LNA, and I've been working in nursing homes."

There was more, there had to be, but Jane didn't want Noah to hear. She had already been through enough with him tonight.

"Your mother thought she'd visit with us for a while." Gram spoke carefully, afraid to shatter whatever this was. "We've got the room."

Jane steadied herself on the wall. *No, she can't stay here.*

Noah touched her shoulder, reassuring her of his presence.

She put on her brightest smile—the one that had gotten her through everything—and opened the front door to an icebox of an evening. "Pastor, I can take it from here. I'm glad Gram's all right. Thanks for bringing me home."

Noah lingered on the front porch with her, the light highlighting the planes on his face. "You're sure you'll be okay?"

How was he asking? As a friend? As a potential pastor? As the man who had kissed her in the snow and turned her world upside down?

"I'll be fine," Jane said. Her cheeks burned with the memory of his cold lips warming hers. His warmth warming her. She had never been kissed like that before.

She would never be again.

Noah Hastings was a dedicated pastor, and she a dedicated agnostic-apostate-whatever schoolteacher. Miles apart, physically and spiritually.

When he didn't budge, she said, "Noah, please go!"

Noah gave her hand a reassuring squeeze before backing down the steps. "Call me if you want to talk."

"Sure." But she knew she wouldn't.

When he was finally in his car, Jane took a minute to compose herself before going back into the living room. She steeled her nerves, thankful for Noah's encouraging touch.

Gram stood with her walker by the piano, holding the prom photo. "That's her with Paul McKee at the prom," she told Carly. "Wasn't she gorgeous? Janie was Prom Court. Anne called in a favor to one of her designers and got her that dress at cost. And here she is at graduation. Salutatorian."

Jane interrupted the graduation story. "So, what will you do?"

Carly's hands tightened around the mug. "I thought I'd stay with you folks a while."

Jane took a deep breath, but bit back her words after the look Gram gave her.

Gram set the photo on the piano and turned to Carley. "You can sleep upstairs in *my* old room. Jane can help get it ready. Jane, would you see what else the room needs?"

A retort died in her dry throat. Jane turned away, hung her jacket in the closet, and slipped off her boots. She climbed the stairs like a wind-up toy.

Mom. How could this be happening?

Jane found the sheets and made short work of the bed in Gram's old room. She could dust and vacuum in here tomorrow. Her mother probably wanted to go to bed soon. Did she even have any luggage?

She practiced smiling as she made her way downstairs and entered the living room. "The bed's ready."

"Thank you, Janie." Carley heaved herself from the chair. "I got a bag. Came by bus, so I couldn't bring much." She pulled a battered wheeled suitcase from behind her chair. She paused at the staircase, almost as though she were asking permission.

"Go ahead up," Gram said with a sort of choking sound.

Perhaps she was more affected than Jane gave her credit for, but Jane had nothing left to say.

Noah parked his car in the side driveway of the white New Englander-style parsonage. He fumbled for his key. Wouldn't it be nice to have Jane waiting for him, to see her silhouetted in the light from inside? They'd have a cup of coffee or tea while they caught up on their day, say grace over dinner, share what was going on with the congregation.

In another lifetime.

He stumbled on a patch of ice and found himself kneeling in the snow. He put his hands over his eyes.

What had he just done?

He had gone on a romantic sleigh ride with a nonbelieving woman, kissed said woman under the cold December sky. Held her in his arms for a few glorious moments. Felt her heartbeat under coats and layers. Felt her full, soft lips on his. Beautiful, giving Jane.

Trusting him to do the right thing.

A million stars. Two people. Two kisses too many.

Had she felt what he felt? Like she was coming home? Like they belonged in each other's arms? He had kissed plenty of women during his wild phase but never like this. Never like they were two halves of a whole. Never with this sense of belonging, completion.

Had all that free time reading poetry made him into a hopeless romantic?

But this was *Jane,* the most remarkable woman he'd ever met. No, more than remarkable. She was beautiful and bright and caring. But without Jesus, they wouldn't have anything.

He was finally winning over the congregation and getting the hang of their ways. How would they feel about their new young pastor marrying an unbeliever? Did they even know she wasn't one?

Noah bowed his head. *Please, God, don't let me mess this up.*

He was the man, man of God. It was up to him to see this didn't happen again.

Jesus, do You understand how I feel?

Yes.

"In Hebrews, you say you were in all points tempted as we were," he said, still kneeling in the snow. "You know what this is like. You're the only one."

He would keep to business from here on out. Help where he could to pull off her beloved festival. Treat her with respect as the chair. And never, ever engineer another private meeting. Continue to pray for her, nudge her toward Christ.

For her sake. It was his calling.

Some day, she would be just a memory, a star-spangled night on the top of the world, as he went about his business and she went about hers.

Father, help me to be strong. Because I can't do it on my own.

CHAPTER FIFTEEN

Jane usually slept well on the sofa. But the "usual" didn't cover the reappearance of mom-on-the-lam, following the kiss of a lifetime. The images swirled in her mind, Carly hesitating at the staircase, Noah's cold-whipped red cheeks and cold, full lips on hers. His kind blue eyes boring into hers with a passion deeper than kindness. His strong arms at her waist, a hand cupping her cheek. The total lack of barriers between them for once. And for once, she didn't miss the barriers.

If she hadn't gotten the text ...

Could she give herself to this man?

But she couldn't linger over it, not while Charlotte Merrill Archer was under their roof. What was her game? Jane had been Carly's daughter long enough to know that there was a game—somehow, somewhere.

They were already up. She heard murmured voices from the kitchen. She darted into the bathroom, splashed water on her face, and rinsed out her mouth.

She'd need every tool in her arsenal to face this day. Scrambled eggs would be a good choice. The whisking, cracking, pouring would give her hands something to do.

There they were, Carly in one of the kitchen chairs, her arms crossed on the table. Her hair lay in wild wisps on her head, and she wore a mismatched pair of sweats. Her eyes looked bloodshot. Well, she'd probably slept as much as Jane.

"I can fix some eggs," Jane said, her voice coming out too loud.

A cold, pale sunlight streamed in from the large windows, and a chill seeped in around the edges.

I'll have to get a fire going soon. I doubt Carly remembers how.

Gram had wheeled her chair closer to Carly. They were conferring in hushed voices. Jane's smile disappeared. When Jane walked over, they lifted sober faces to her.

"Jane, dear." Gram's voice quivered. "Your mother has something to tell you."

What now? Little her mother did would surprise Jane. She'd been Carly-proofed for a while.

"Janie, honey, I've been sick for a while. Lung cancer. I had two rounds of it, twice with the chemo. That's when I lost my hair, and it come in gray. And curly." Carly sucked in a breath. "This time it's spread to my lymph nodes, and there's no point trying anything else. That's why I came back to Hilltop. I'm dyin', Jane."

Jane sank into an armchair. Well. If there was a way to make the situation worse, Carly would find it. Did she want the woman to die? Of course not. She'd be happier if her mother lived—somewhere else.

"What about chemo? Radiation?" Was she really saying these words? To her mother?

"Tried 'em. Two times for each. They beat it back, but not enough. My second husband couldn't deal with it. When it come back, he left." Carly grinned, and in that grin, Jane saw the ghost of her old carefree mother. "Maybe he didn't like me flirting with the doctors."

Mom. *Carly.* "How long?" Jane bit out and hoped her sharp tone showed some concern.

"Three to six. Up to a year, one doctor said, but I got no faith in 'up to.'"

Lost for words, Jane looked at the skeleton of a woman in front of her. It all made sense now. Shivering in her baggy clothes, clothes she would never have worn for one of her boyfriends.

Mom. Here for less than a year left on this earth. How much work would *that* take? And how bereaved would Jane have to pretend to be?

Gram had always taken in strays, for the holidays and for longer periods. Could Jane treat her mother like one of Gram's projects? Could she summon up at least as much compassion as she'd have for a stranger?

It was the right thing to do, and Jane Archer always did the right thing.

"Of course, you'll stay," she said. To the woman who had robbed her of a childhood and cast her aside. To the woman who had set the whole horrible chain of events in motion. "I'll get dressed and then work on those eggs." Jane went toward the stairs.

Gram reached out a hand, but Jane ignored it. She was breathing heavily by the time she crested the stairs, stairs she'd been climbing all her life.

She leaned against the door to Gram's old room. *Can I even do this?* Mom, Carly, here in this house. Reminding her every day of what she'd lost. Of why she was here in the first place.

She should have grown up here, with two parents who loved her fiercely, like Greg and Anne. Did Stephanie and Ryan even know what they had in their parents? And

Gramps, gone too soon. Should have had Hilltop, the town that came as close to healing her as she'd let them.

Should have been safe.

Where was Gram's God? Where was Noah's God?

Not in Hilltop. Not this morning.

CHAPTER SIXTEEN

Her mother's cancer diagnosis was all Jane could think about during their festival meeting. At least, it made it easy not to look at Noah and his perfect lips. Instead, she told the board members her mother was back in town, only detailing she was sick.

She determined not to let her mother's presence interfere with her festival duties.

The next evening, Jane sat through the mainstage rehearsal, laughing and clapping, enjoying both the earnestness and the imperfections as children from Hilltop Elementary danced around the stage. She made notes on her clipboard and in the notebook for the needed props and areas that needed propping up.

"They're adorable," Jane whispered to Wayne, as the antler-bedecked second graders finished their medley of "Up on the Housetop" and "Rudolph."

As the children filed out, one tiny, freckled boy ran back for a second bow, and the small audience laughed and clapped as he preened.

Wayne marked something on a clipboard. "Good thing it's a school night, or we'd never get that one off the stage."

Jane nodded with a smile.

Wayne couldn't sing, dance, or act, but he could put together an entertainment lineup that would fill this sanctuary. Despite the cloud over the festival, he had enough talent booked for the first two nights.

Jane stood, stepping out of the aisle. A tall, live tree in one corner of the room glittered with tiny white lights. The tree's scent perfumed the sanctuary. Frost gathered in the corners of the darkened windows.

Where was Noah? What would she say to him? *You kissed me, and I liked it. You're a pastor, and I haven't believed for a while. So what?*"Ms. Jane!" Maddy McKee hurtled toward her, almost tripping over the hem of a white robe, a circle of tinsel drooping from her blond hair. "Me angel! In a play!"

Jane scooped her up and smiled. "Of course, you are."

Emma followed more sedately, beaming under her own tinsel halo. A uniformed Paul brought up the rear.

"They just got their costumes," he said. "Guess what I'm going to hear about on the way home."

"You will be the most beautiful angels ever," she told the girls.

Paul grinned down at her. "It's going to be a busy time, but it's worth it."

Yes. Even a skeptic like Jane knew the worth of Hilltop.

"And I'll be in the front row for at least one performance," she said.

If she attended the mainstage pageant, she wouldn't have to go to an actual church service. There was a question that hung between them, and she knew they'd never regain their old easy footing till it was answered. When Gram had told Carly of the theft, Carly had closed her eyes briefly in a "what next" gesture and fixed her gaze on her mother with a power Jane hadn't expected.

"They'll figure it out, Ma." Carley had said. "That Paul's a smart guy. It'll be okay."

"Paul," Jane added, "have you come any closer to finding out who did it?"

Paul rubbed his eyes. Oh, he must be tired. Hilltop was a small department, and he was probably assisting its only detective.

"I couldn't tell you if I knew. It's scary, Janie. To know that one of us—" He followed Maddy and Emma as they dragged him toward the Christmas tree. He turned back in mid-tug, his dark eyes haunted. "Only I don't think I want to know. Do you?"

She bit her lip. *Maybe not, after all.*

She watched until all the children drifted off with their parents, and only she and Wayne were left in the sanctuary.

"Go home," he said. "The festival will still be there tomorrow."

But for how many other tomorrows? It was almost mid-December.

Jane went out through the office wing, passing by Noah's office. Would he step out, either by accident or design? Why hadn't he come out to watch the kids rehearse? It would be nice to see him. They could be friends, couldn't they?

Was she still here? Noah cocked an ear to the sounds of a rapidly-emptying building. He'd passed by the sanctuary earlier, heard her clear laugh from the hallway, and caught a glimpse of her holding Maddy McKee, Jane's shining head nestled against the little golden one. Would she cast her lot with Paul? Had she already? They had a lot in common, like practically their whole lives. Maybe they would be better together in the long run.

But he wanted Jane. He knew from the kisses he'd found himself reliving until he asked God, once again, to help him forget. *It can't be. At least not now.*

He opened the door to his office and was rewarded with the sight of her, the red wool coat and tumble of dark brown hair, a splash of color in the diminished light.

She paused in the hallway, almost as if it were planned. "Oh."

"Are you heading out now?" *Brilliant, Noah.*

"We're done for the day." Jane fiddled with her purse strap. "We have some wonderful talent this year."

"I know. I looked in earlier." He'd looked only at her, but she didn't have to know that. "I'm leaving now. I'll walk out with you."

She matched her stride to his as they headed out into the blast of cold night air. A moon glowed under a kind of yellow filter, and even he knew now it was a sign of snow to come. He stood beside her as she fumbled with the door handle to Alice's car.

He couldn't stand it. "Jane."

She looked up, her green eyes wide but shielded in the hazy light. She knew. "It was just a kiss. It didn't mean anything."

His gut twisted. "It did. But we can't let it happen again."

She crossed her arms. "I didn't ask you to come to the sleigh ride. Or Thanksgiving. Or cookie baking. Or to follow me around town."

She was too sharp for him. "No. You didn't. And I didn't ask to—to be—" What exactly did he feel? He loved her. Yes, that was it. "I didn't ask to be *intrigued* by you."

Jane seemed to mull that over. "Good. *Intrigue* is something that can go away, with time. I have enough on my plate right now with Hilltop and—" she swallowed hard and said in a thin voice, "and my mother."

"How is that going?" Anything to get them back on a normal footing.

"It isn't. Good night, Pastor." She slid behind the driver's seat, and he stepped away.

Intrigued. She should be glad it wasn't more. She had enough to deal with. But even Jane, with her carefully curated social life, knew that a kiss like that wasn't just from someone you *intrigued.*

If only ...

Could she believe now?

No. Not just to "get" Noah. Even Jane knew a conversion for a man wouldn't take.

She spoke into the darkness. "You did this to me. None of this was my fault. Even Noah isn't worth you. Nothing is."

Had God heard? She hadn't spoken directly to him in a dozen years. Did he care?

What *did* she feel for Noah? Well, a little more than intrigue. But she'd beat this, with the self-discipline that had carried her through her life, before Hilltop, during her life here and now.

Jane drove past Gram's house. The lights shone downstairs, in the living room, dining room, and kitchen. Gram had started cooking again, and she'd probably held supper for Jane. Gram and the mother who had appeared out of nowhere, too little too late. "Home" was a minefield now, with Gram fussing over her prodigal daughter and Jane staying out of the way, flying under whatever radar she had left.

Gram in her element, arranging Carly's medical care, wielding her cellphone like a weapon, researching treatments. Only Jane heard her crying at night, through the door of the downstairs bedroom. Jane hadn't cried yet. She wasn't sure she ever would.

Jane drove around, as she did most nights after whatever Hilltop business kept her out. Tonight, she landed at the edge of town, where the only chain restaurant in Hilltop, a national doughnut franchise, sat in bland solitude. She ordered a hot sandwich, booted up her laptop, and tried to think of anything besides Carly, Noah Hastings, or God.

But she couldn't hide at the doughnut shop forever.

"So, you're home for once?" Gram said as soon as Jane walked through the front door. Her voice held a buoyancy and hope as she called from the living room.

"Yes." Jane plugged in her laptop on the dining room table. "Stephanie and I talked about a movie, but it's a school night, and she decided not to keep Hayley out. Maybe we'll have a movie night over the weekend."

Gram probably thought they'd spend the evening together as a family. Were they a family? What did that even look like?

Jane tried to drown out the sounds of Gram and Mom watching a gameshow in the living room, their shouting out of answers, the laughter, and high-fives when they got one right. Gram never watched game shows, or much TV beyond the news and PBS costume dramas. Who was this new Gram?

Jane had to admit Carly was good at the gameshows, filling in the blank letters on "Super Crossword" and shouting out answers on "Pop Quiz America." Carly was smart enough, the daughter of a teacher and an engineer. What could she have become if she'd used her mind?

Well, she had gone into nursing, and had her sights set on more. She could have been more.

Carly. What right did she have to even be here? Why couldn't she die with her friends? The ones she'd given Jane up for?

Jane should feel something, she knew she should. But she didn't.

Carly took a lot of naps, got tired easily, and coughed a lot, coughs that shook her small frame. Today, even as cold as it was, she was having a good day. Carly brewed a pot of decaf Earl Grey to share with Gram as they matched wits with the manic gameshow candidates.

As Carly passed through the dining room to the kitchen, she put a hand on Jane's shoulder. "You're working hard, Janie."

Jane looked up into the blue eyes, so like Gram's, so unlike. "Hilltop Festival takes a lot of time. It'll be Christmas break soon, so I'll have a break from work emails."

Jane smiled politely, the way she would to any house guest of Gram's. But Carly wanted more. Jane could see it in the way the light faded from those eyes, flickered and died, the way the hand dropped from Jane's shoulder. Well, what had she expected?

Gram was big enough to take Carly back, without reservations. Jane wasn't.

Gram was working on insurance tonight, the dozens of different liabilities and waiver documents Greg had forwarded for her review. As Carly and Gram returned to their gameshows, Jane tried to shut out the noise from the living room. She'd almost succeeded when the doorbell rang.

Paul, in uniform, stood on the porch. She stammered a surprised greeting, knowing Paul wasn't a drop-in kind of guy, but noticed the middle-aged man wearing a suit at his side.

"Jane, this is Lieutenant Patterson, our detective. Patterson, this is Ms. Archer."

She managed a nod. "What can I do for you?"

"We'd like to see Mrs. Merrill." Detective Patterson said.

Wordlessly, she led them into the living room.

Gram shut off the TV while Carly stared open-mouthed. Had Gram known they were coming? But her voice was pleasant, steady. "Good evening, Paul. Eddie. What can I do for you? You look cold. Coffee? Tea? Carly, please get us some more tea."

"No thanks, Mrs. Merrill." Paul crouched on an ottoman next to Gram's walker. The detective remained standing.

"Mrs. Merrill, we'd like to ask you a few follow-up questions about the theft." He swallowed hard. "You're aware only five people have the code to the safe-deposit box?"

Gram nodded. "Yes, Chief McKee. I am aware of it."

Jane noted the subtle shift in tone, the shift to his official title. She moved to the fire, stirred it up with a poker, and clung to the corner of the mantel. *Not Gram. It can't be.* The rock of her childhood, her only rock. *Don't take her away.* Was she addressing Paul or the God long absent from her life?

She'd hedge her bets on Paul. But Paul would do his duty. He always had.

She locked eyes with Carly and saw no fear there. Carly already had one foot in another world. Whatever that world was.

Paul pushed his glasses up his nose, a gesture she remembered from childhood. "Mrs. Merrill, I have to ask again. Did you open the safe-deposit box and cash in the stock certificate?"

"From a wheelchair? Really, chief."

Paul blushed but plowed on. "It was cashed in early October. You were still walking then, still driving. Mrs. Smith didn't realize it was missing till November. It could have happened."

"Was I *seen* opening the box?" Gram's pleasant tone held an edge, an edge only Jane could recognize.

"No. You weren't seen. But none of the other board members were, either. The bank manager said it was especially busy that day. And the bank doesn't have security cameras. Never had a need to."

Oh, that was so Hilltop.

Gram eyed him. "Then why question me again?"

Behind his glasses, Paul's eyes held a dark misery. But Jane couldn't afford to care about anyone but Gram.

Paul nodded to the detective, who stepped forward, holding out a small glassine envelope. "Ma'am, do you recognize this?"

Jane let her death grip on the fireplace go, peered over Gram's shoulder, and drew a single sharp breath.

No.

A silver sleigh the size of a thumbnail glowed like metallic fire in the light from the Christmas tree and the burning logs.

"It's from my bracelet." Gram's voice was calm. "Walter gave me that one in 1985."

"Do you know how it got in the safe-deposit box?" Paul said.

"If I knew, we wouldn't be here, would we?"

Why didn't Gram tell me one of the charms was missing?

Paul looked from Carly to Jane to Gram. "Yes, well, as soon as we found the charm, we ran for fingerprints to make sure. Whoever did it used gloves. As soon as we found the sleigh, I said we should check around, since the charm is

153

not as rare as we thought. But I could only hold this off for so long since you're our only lead."

Paul drew a ragged breath and motioned to the detective, who began to read Gram her rights. Paul went over to one of the windows where he leaned his forehead against the cold glass.

Jane tried to stop shaking. "Wait, wait. I remember Gram had all her charms on her bracelet the day I came back in town on November third, so how could it have been in the safe-deposit box since October?"

Paul seemed to be taking a mental note of that fact. "That's something, but do you have any proof that it was still there?"

Jane bit her lip and shook her head in defeat. Paul nodded to Patterson. She went over and stood near Paul so she couldn't see her grandmother being arrested. But she heard Patterson's businesslike tone, heard Gram's calm responses.

"Paul, you've got to get her out of this." Jane said.

Paul turned to her. "Janie, I'm sorry. I don't know how that charm got in the safe-deposit box. I'm doing my best here."

"You're not going to—"

"I have to book her. It's strange there weren't any fingerprints. Makes it feel like someone was being sneaky about it. The charm alone isn't enough to convict. My gut says it was planted, especially after what you said. We'll get her right back home after her bail." He attempted a small smile. "The Hilltop jail isn't handicapped accessible."

It wasn't funny. Nothing would ever be funny again.

Jane moved to her grandmother's side and put an arm around the slender shoulders. "You don't have to cuff her."

"We're not going to, Ms. Archer. We'll make this as easy as possible." Patterson knelt before Gram. "Here's what we're going to do, Mrs. Merrill. We've got to take you down to the station and book you. But we'll get to the bottom of this."

"I promise we will." Paul joined them. "Do you trust me?"

"I trust my Lord, Paul McKee. Then you. But I can't walk." Gram winced, probably from standing for too long.

Jane bit her lip while Carly sat in stunned silence.

"Then I'll carry you."

Gram looked so small as she held up her arms. She was already dressed for bed, this night in pale blue sweats. Jane helped her into a coat, and Paul lifted her as though she were one of his girls.

"Get the door, Patterson."

Jane bit back a cry and grabbed her own coat and purse. "I'm going with them," she told Carly who now stood in the entrance to the dining room, her face pale. "Call Greg Gregson and ask him to get down to the station and post her bail. And—and—call the Reverend Hastings."

CHAPTER SEVENTEEN

Greg and Hastings arrived at the police department minutes after Jane. Greg's plaid wool jacket hung open, and Noah hadn't even bothered with a coat. She felt her gaze straying to Noah even as Greg gave her a comforting hug.

"I'm so sorry, Janie." Greg said. "We'll get this straightened out."

Jane clutched the back of Gram's wheelchair she had brought for her. "You don't think—"

"Of course not. It couldn't have been Alice. I've known her since I was a kid. She's the most honest person in Hilltop."

If only there were cameras inside the bank. Her life seemed full of "if only" lately.

The sentence he didn't dare voice hung between them— if not Gram, then who? Who of the group of insiders who had worked together for decades? People whose children had grown up playing in the back of the conference room while their parents conducted Hilltop business. People who had rejoiced with each other's successes and shared their sorrows. There were newcomers like Brad King, sure. But he had been so willing and ready to see the festival succeed, in his own way, and the core group went back generations.

And who'd want to disrupt the festival? Who would go so far as to plant Gran's charm?

Greg went over to the counter to begin the bail process, leaving Jane standing alone with Noah.

She looked down and choked out a laugh at his disheveled state of an unshaven face and untucked shirt. "You have two different socks on."

Noah looked at his feet without interest. "Yeah. I'll find the other ones." He locked eyes with her. "Hey, Jane. I'm so sorry."

"You know she didn't do it."

He put a comforting hand on her shoulder, but it burned through her coat. She couldn't look away from him, the eyes deep with concern and the "something else" neither of them wanted to acknowledge.

Intrigue.

"Alice is the heart and soul of this community. Why would she jeopardize the festival? Plus, she's one of the finest, truest Christians I've ever known."

She dared to lean closer to him. "And Paul thinks the evidence was planted."

Noah furrowed his brow. "Well, if anyone can figure this out, it's Paul."

Poor Jane. Dear Lord, please comfort her and Alice. Let the truth be revealed.

Jane was shivering. Did Noah dare wrap his arms around her, even as a friend? She looked so small, so lost. Like a little girl with long pigtails who never spoke or smiled.

He wanted to be the one to comfort her, but he didn't dare.

Greg was posting bail now, Noah reassured himself. Alice would come home, be home until they worked this out.

Paul McKee would unravel it. He'd clear Alice's name, even if he had to implicate someone else from the inner circle. Paul knew how this town worked. Paul belonged here, in a way Noah never could.

When they finished the bail, a strong young officer lifted Alice as if she were a piece of china and placed her in her wheelchair. Paul came over to them. His face looked gray with the responsibility for his people, but he put out his big arms, and Jane moved into his hug. A friendly hug, a comforting hug. *I can't even give her that.*

Her gaze met his over Paul's shoulder. Tears shimmered in the green depths. For her grandmother, sure. For whoever had done this to Alice? Probably. Her heart was that big.

And his work was done, at least for tonight. If it had ever even started.

He leaned over to Alice and gave her hand a reassuring squeeze. The moment he heard the news of her arrest, it was like losing his mother all over again. But then he saw Alice's smile.

"It'll be okay, Noah." She squeezed his hand in return. "God is on our side."

Noah held back tears and nodded. "Yes, ma'am."

And to think I came here to comfort her.

When Paul and Jane fixed their attention on Noah and Alice, Paul let Jane go.

"I'll be going now." Noah took a step back. "I'll be praying for you all. I'll call you tomorrow."

When they arrived home, Carly looked even more pale, if that could be possible. To Jane's surprise, she embraced them both before heading to bed. In coming home, poor Carly had gotten way more than she bargained for.

The next morning, Jane sat at the kitchen table across from Gram. She could tell neither of them got much sleep, but Carly was still asleep upstairs.

"Gram, do you have any idea who it could have been?" Jane said as she refreshed Gram's coffee.

The sweet smell of a French toast bake filled the kitchen. Jane had assembled it last night, with her final ounce of strength. This morning would be hard enough.

Gram warmed her hands around the thick white mug. "I've been going over and over it in my head, ever since you told me it was a setup. I've known all these people for thirty years, trusted them. I've worshiped with Greg, Bev, and Charlie. And Bob Desrochers used to shovel my sidewalk."

Jane looked out at the unbroken expanse of the back yard, where the evergreen branches made lacy shadows against the snow. "So, who needs the money?"

Gram sipped her coffee. "Jane, really."

"Come on, Gram. You and I are both teachers. We're used to analyzing problems."

Gram sighed again. "Surely not Charlie. Farming is a tough life, but he's got so many things going–the hayrides and corn maze in the fall, the sleigh rides, the maple sugaring, the farm stand. Charlie's resourceful."

They all were. People in the North Country turned their hands to many things to make ends meet. Growing up, Jane's favorite was a woman who ran a hair salon in her home, built picnic tables, and sold live bait from a cooler.

"Bev? Mark's treatments must cost a bundle."

Gram shook her head. "Then why would Bev make the announcement?"

"Because she knew it would come out sooner or later."

Gram made a dismissive gesture. "Bev's not that good an actor. She couldn't lie to save her life. What about Greg? Has he gotten in over his head with all those branch stores?"

"I suppose he could have." Jane looked out the window again where a squirrel left feathery prints as it ran lightly over the snow. "But Greg's a shrewd businessman. I find it hard to believe he'd overextend himself."

Gram snorted. "I find all this hard to believe. What about Bob? The twins really want to open a second shop, but startups are expensive."

"I—don't know." Jane straightened a fold in the tablecloth. "Gram, what about us? Besides the charm, is there *anything* that could cause people to suspect you?"

"No. I own this house, have for years. My teacher's pension isn't—well, it's a teacher's pension. But I made some good investments over time."

"Mom's treatments?"

"I *allegedly* stole the money before we even knew your mother was sick. Plus, she said the treatments weren't working for her anymore." Gram drained her cup. "And if you still have doubts, I guess this is as good a time as any to tell you. Walter left me fairly well-fixed. We owned a business block and a small apartment building in Littleton, and I've been collecting the rents for years."

No wonder they'd been able to live so well, and Gram was able to raise someone else's child on the down slope of midlife. Modest vacation trips, clothes as good as any child in Hilltop, except for Ryan and Steph. Clarinet lessons, a year of piano. Not extravagant but always enough.

This beautiful house, like something from a story book. This *home*.

Jane looked at gram. "Why didn't you tell me?"

"I was planning to when I went over my affairs with you. When I became infirm. Which I am not."

No, she wasn't. Gram could still step into a fifth-grade classroom and teach any subject.

"But all that property ..."

Gram shrugged. "I didn't think it was time. You were doing well. I was doing well."

"It was on account of me." Carly's voice spoke like rusty iron.

Their heads swiveled toward the doorway.

Carly wore a faded plaid men's bathrobe cinched twice around her slender frame, her gray curls flattened from a night of sleep. "You didn't want me swooping in. Because I'd probably waste it. Or gamble it. Or drink it."

"Carly, don't be absurd."

"She didn't tell me either," Jane said. "It's got nothing to do with you." At least they could agree on that.

Gram pinned them both with her schoolteacher's look. "Jane, you're getting this house and the stocks and bonds. And Carly, you're getting the rental property in Littleton. I figured you might need a regular income at some point. But I intend to be around for a while, so don't spend it yet."

"I won't live long enough to do that." Bold words, but there was no getting around them. "And I'm not going to cost either of you a dime. I've got my own insurance. I learned in nursing you got to have it." Carly turned to go, holding the doorpost briefly for support. "I have to get ready for a doctor's appointment," she said around a cough.

"Do you need a ride?" Jane busied herself rinsing the plates and setting them in the dishwasher.

Say no.

"Anne said she'd take me. We used to be close, way back in the day, so it's nice to see an old friend."

"Great." Jane nodded. Well, Anne was always willing to help out.

Was this Jane's voice, falsely brisk, insanely chipper? She had to get out of here.

Jane slammed the dishwasher shut. "Well, I'm off to do Hilltop stuff. Be back in the late afternoon. Gram, Meals on Wheels is pot roast today. And you—" She stumbled as always on what to call this woman. Carly? Mom? Judas? "I mixed up some tuna salad. You could have that as a sandwich, and there's some of the pulled pork from Sunday."

"I'm sure she'll find something. She was raised in this kitchen." Gram's voice held a pleasantness as always but with an undertone of exasperation.

Well, let her be. Jane hadn't asked for any of this. What had she asked for? Before Carly gave her up, she couldn't have voiced what was "normal" or "not normal." But she'd known what she didn't have.

"And I'll pick up your meds," Jane said. "I have to stop and see Bev anyway."

She brushed past a mother she no longer knew. Carly started to say something, but Jane gave her a swift, false smile.

"Gotta go."

On the porch, she leaned her forehead against one of the pillars. The cold wood soothed her burning brow. She couldn't do this. Couldn't play daughter when she'd never been one. Couldn't see Gram stand trial in January. Couldn't walk downtown and smile at people, talk festival, and wonder who had betrayed Gram.

A pristine white SUV glided to a stop at the curb, and Anne Gregson came up the walk. She wore a camel's hair coat belted over her slim waist with shining high boots encasing her legs. The sun glinted off her pale-gold hair, and her eyes lay hidden behind huge sunglasses.

"Good morning, Janie." Anne smiled. "Is your mom ready?"

"I guess." Jane collected what was left of her composure. "She's ... inside." She waved vaguely at the tall old house.

But Anne could read her after all these years, almost as well as Gram, and put a gloved hand on Jane's arm. "Honey, nobody is sorrier about Alice's arrest than Greg or I." She gave a little shudder. "It doesn't bear thinking about, does it? Couldn't it have been someone from the outside?"

No. There was no "outside."

"If you ever want to talk, I'm here."

"Thank you." Jane forced a smile. "The truth will come out sooner or later."

Jane ran into Stephanie, hurrying along the sidewalk at double time, her booted feet sure on the ice.

"Janie!"

"Hi, Steph. On your way to work?"

Steph didn't break her stride as they walked together. "No, I'm off today. Comp day from the day after Thanksgiving, and not a minute too soon. I've got to shop for Hayley while she isn't around. How's Mrs. Merrill? How's your mom?"

They were both conversational minefields, but Steph meant well.

Jane shrugged. "Gram's okay. You know she's not going to let this get to her. And my mother is—She's holding her own."

"Oh good." Steph smiled. "Hey, I'm sorry if I pushed you to go out with Hastings."

Jane blushed. "Oh, it's fine. We ended up having a nice time."

Steph paused at a display in the Five and Dime window. "Oh, look, Janie, they've put up the dollhouse again."

"Every Christmas." Jane nodded, pretending to focus on the miniature Victorian figures going about their porcelain and plastic business. "So, Steph … Do you remember Gram coming in, sometime in October, and going into the safe-deposit box?"

Steph frowned. "Nope. And I'm glad I don't. Janie, I can't even think it was her."

Neither could anyone else. Except the person who had seized the tiny silver sleigh.

Jane nodded. "Okay. I have to pick up meds. Talk to you later."

Hilltop's Rexall Pharmacy had changed little over Jane's lifetime. The Christmas window display was always the same, the 1960s aluminum tree, which caught the sun by day and gleamed under colored revolving lights at night. The wooden floors from the 1940s slanted under her feet. She and Paul had once rolled marbles from one end of the store to the other for a physics class experiment.

Bev stood at the pharmacy counter, her head bent as she listened to Mrs. Barnes who had seemed old even when Jane was little. What was she now, ninety? She still puttered around town in her ancient Oldsmobile, "Victoria." The locals knew enough to give Mrs. Barnes and Victoria a wide berth. And the tourists learned it fast enough.

Bev's head was tilted, in that way she had, making you feel like the only person in her world. Jane thought she knew the woman whose heart beat under the crisp white coat and crisp manner. Bev would not cut Mrs. Barnes off, no matter how many people stood in line.

Mrs. Barnes finished her story, which had something to do with a cat, her late husband, and her property taxes.

When she meandered off, Bev gave Jane a smile more professional than usual. "Picking up, Janie?"

"There's something for—for—" *Spit it out, Jane. She has a name.* "My mother."

Bev pulled the plastic bag from a spinning rack and dumped out the small bottle. She placed it in a paper bag and tapped out something on the register. "That'll be six dollars, please. Isn't insurance wonderful?"

The impersonal banter Bev would use with any customer, but an opening for Jane. "Sure is."

"How's Carly? I heard she'll be in town from now on. We were so sorry to hear of her cancer. The whole church team is praying for her."

Jane nodded. "She's all right. You know." She didn't really know how her mother was. She'd made purpose and passion out of not knowing.

"And Alice?"

Jane looked for guilt, for some kind of tell, but Bev's face was as open and honest as ever. "She's all right." It would have to do. "How is Mark?"

Bev sorted a stack of receipts. "About the same. It's palliative care now, same as for your mother. Mark finds little things to do around the house. He reads all the time. I'm at the library twice a week."

"Is it—is it costing a lot?"

"His job's picking up most of it. They've been wonderful to him."

Jane tried to remember what exactly Mark did. Or had done. "That's good. I wasn't sure. I remember you were talking about selling some of the nativities ..."

Bev's eyes glinted behind her glasses. "Because I'm running out of room at home, and I'll probably downsize once Mark goes. That's all. Jane, dear, I do not need more money."

"Oh." She was terrible at this. She should leave the detecting to Paul. If it were anyone but Gram, she'd do so gladly.

Bev and Gram had worshiped together at Hilltop Church, worked their way up in the festival hierarchy, from blowing up red and green balloons to board positions. Gram had seen Bev through her struggles with, and acceptance of, childlessness and through Mark's cancer. Bev had seen Gram through, well, everything with Carly.

How could I have even thought it?

"I'm so sorry, Bev."

"It's all right, Janie." Bev sighed. "I'd like to see Alice out of this nonsense as much as anybody. I don't think it was her. But it wasn't me either." She looked over Jane's shoulder, and her voice ironed out to a professional smoothness. "Picking up?"

Noah saw Jane leave the pharmacy. Well, really, he'd been waiting since he saw her go in. She looked unguarded for once—her slender shoulders bent, a look of bleak sorrow on her face. A sorrow that was suddenly his to bear too.

"Jane, wait!" His boots thumped against the snow-packed sidewalk.

She turned, and he skidded to a stop.

"I thought we could walk together. I'm—going to the bank," he improvised.

"Sure."

He looked down at her as he matched his stride to hers. Her cheeks shone pale despite the crispness of the morning.

"Listen, I'm—I'm sorry."

She plowed on, and he touched her shoulders, but she wrenched herself away.

"I'm sorry." He held up his hands, praying for the right words. "I just wanted to see how you're holding up."

Her big green eyes looked tearless but as full of misery as any he'd ever seen. "How am I supposed to 'hold up'?" But she asked it genuinely, without the irritation she'd shown in the past. "My grandmother, the one person who's always stood by *me*, is accused of theft from an organization she's been part of for thirty years."

Yes, it was crazy. He couldn't make sense of it himself, so how could he expect her to? Only God could.

"Are you getting any flack around town?"

Jane shrugged. "People are just hurt, wondering how this happened. I'm wondering myself. I think my mom's sudden appearance and the news about her cancer has softened the blow, if anything."

Noah swallowed hard. He heard the church board chat about Carly's reappearance and the rumor she looked unwell, but he never could have guessed it would be this bad.

To go through so much, without God ...

He hoped his words didn't come out as pity. "Oh, Jane. I'm sorry to hear about that. How about the committee?"

Jane sighed. "You were there. Everyone was barely speaking to each other last week. I can't imagine what this week's meeting will look like. Paul told me they ran her bank account information and didn't find the missing funds, didn't find it in anyone's account. None of the members even went to the bank in October. But people still think Gram did it."

They lived in a world of offshore accounts and shell companies. Anyone could do anything.

He remembered that last meeting—the camaraderie absent, the members sticking to the facts of their reports, afraid to look too long at each other. And now one of their own targeted, undone by a tiny silver charm.

Yeah, he was already dreading the next committee meeting.

Jane swiped at her eyes with a mittened hand. "Nobody's mean to me. I think they feel sorry for me. They're just guarded, especially the people who don't even know Gram. But it still isn't the same. It isn't Hilltop."

It wouldn't be. Even a newcomer like him could notice the difference. A pillar of their community had crumbled. If they couldn't trust Alice Merrill, who could they trust?

God. We're all supposed to trust you.

He couldn't even imagine any of the others doing this. Avuncular Charlie Wenholm had given free produce to the poor in summer and fall. Bev Smith, school board and church choir member. Bob Desrochers, part of Phil Donovan's Parish Council. And Greg Gregson and his family had supplied the town's hardware needs for four generations, sponsored teams and floats and fund-raisers for burned-out families.

Any one of them would have been a nightmare come true.

But only Alice awaited trial.

Only Alice's life could change forever.

The worst for him was seeing Jane hurt. If only he could hold her, let her pour her grief and confusion into him.

No. There was only one route left for him. The only one that mattered.

"I would like to pray for you." He looked her in the eyes. "Please, Jane."

She never agreed before, but then, she nodded wordlessly and pulled him into an alley where he took her hands and poured out her need to the Father. Jane didn't speak. Was she praying herself? Didn't matter. Noah prayed hard enough for them both.

He released her hands at last. It had been good to touch her, even that little bit. "I'll let you go now. I've got to get to the bank."

A smile tugged at the corners of Jane's mouth. "Yeah. The bank."

She had seen through his ruse, but he didn't care. As he watched her walk off, he accepted a powerful truth. Love was when you took the loved one's pain as your own.

God, now I know I love her.

CHAPTER EIGHTEEN

She had let him pray for her. Never in a million years ...
Did it make her feel any better? She didn't know yet.

But Noah believed. Gram believed. What would it be
like to have that confidence, to know that someone besides
yourself was in control?

What would it be like for her to *give up* control?

She couldn't control any of this, that was for sure.
Couldn't configure it into her notebook where she wrote
everything down. She'd structured her life for the least
possible disruption, built a fortress, and shame and despair
had entered through an unguarded crack.

How could Gram do it? A close friend had failed her.
Implicated her. Let her take the fall. How could Gram sit
there, day after day, and trust that her Lord would work
this out? How could she have this inner peace despite
everything?

Wouldn't it be nice to have that kind of peace, something
more stable than any mountain? If only Jane could be like
Gram. Or Noah. But she didn't dare let go, even now. If her
house was a house of cards, she'd hang on until someone
else removed the crucial piece.

But Noah had prayed for her. If *his* God cared enough to
get her out of this, so be it. Had she sensed something else

in the prayer, something more personal than a plea for one of his flock?

I'm not even that.

Yes. Something in the way they connected. Something more than intrigue. He cared for her, and she cared for him, far more than she'd expected, far more than she should. Something straight out of the sappy romcoms she and her roommates laughed over.

Jane squared her shoulders. She would get this done, helm the best Hilltop Festival ever, help Gram get well, help her clear her name, help her decide what to do about Mom. Then Jane was out of here. Back to the condo and lesson plans, field trips and finding a doctorate program. Where she belonged.

Noah could hurt her, but she could hurt him more. Best to get out while there was time.

Jane's boots thumped on the sidewalk as she hurried through Hilltop to her final meeting with the police. She kept her head down, watching for ice. If she looked up, she'd run the risk of knowing someone was avoiding her. Better to avoid them first.

The red brick town office building was a Hilltop treasure with its tall windows, gables, and turret, with the transoms over the doors and opaque glass windows. Paul stood there in the conference room.

Paul was going over some documents and lifted a tired face to her. "Hi, Jane."

She stepped inside the room. "Hey. How are the girls?"

Paul's face lit up, as it always did over Maddy and Emma. "They're fine. Looking forward to the festival—and the next day."

Oh, yeah, Christmas was in there somewhere. How would she celebrate? A quiet day with Gram and her mother, probably. She should pick something up for Carly.

"How's your mom?" Paul scrabbled through some papers. "Must be nice—" He couldn't finish the sentence. Even Paul didn't know what it meant to have Carly back. Even he had heard the stories about Alice Merrill's wild child.

"She's all right." If one more person asked her … "Paul. How is the investigation going? I mean, at least you can tell me you think she didn't do it."

Paul took off his glasses. "That's a given. Someone planted that charm because there was no other DNA in or around the safe-deposit box. Someone made sure to clean up their mess to only leave the evidence." He rubbed his eyes. "And we can't even find the missing money. It's just gone. We've got the means and opportunity but no motives."

Gram had an attorney now, a nice man from Littleton. They'd agreed she couldn't use Paul's father or Sutton Davis, the man who had handled hers and Gramps's affairs for years. Too close for comfort. But how good was he against a little silver charm?

Paul's voice changed. "How is she?"

"You know Gram. She's toughing it out."

Paul took her hands, kneaded them between his big ones. "You know I'd do anything to make this go away. But I can't. We'll just have to pray the truth will come out."

Yeah. Pray.

But it worked for Paul, made him who he was. Got him through his sweet wife's horrible death.

That first Sunday in Hilltop, she'd clung to Gram's side until the after-service coffee hour. She had a new outfit—a pleated plaid skirt and a sweater of a softness she could only have imagined. She didn't want to get even a cookie crumb on the clothes, so she'd taken one of her new books and gone to sit on a bench against the wall.

Until a tall, thin boy with floppy brown hair sat next to her. *"I like Harry Potter too,"* he'd said, pushing his glasses up his nose. *"Which House do you think you'd be in?"*

Paul McKee, her first friend in Hilltop. First friend ever. However, she'd never told him. Others had come after that, Samantha Wexford, now Sammi Morton, Jean-Paul "J.P." Beaulieu, others forming a solid nucleus of Hilltop pals she took with her to Regional. She'd made more friends at Regional. But Paul had paved the way.

He wanted more. She could feel it. Or he wanted to find out if there could be. He was a good man. He would take care of her, shoulder her burden as if it were his.

But there was a huge conflict of interest, and not just because he was investigating charges against Gram.

He still wasn't Noah.

Determined to get both men out of her mind, Jane visited Charlie at the farm to fine-tune details for the sleigh rides. She found him in the barn, rubbing down one of the draft horses.

At the sound of her footsteps, he turned toward her. "Hi, Janie."

Charlie's farm, a labor of love for four generations. There was always something going on—the sleigh rides, the bustling farm stand, the giant bale of hay he kept in front of the main barn for tourists who wanted their picture taken. He'd even been known to pose with them.

She breathed deeply of the smell of horse, hay and, yes, manure. She'd taken a few riding lessons here during her horse period, loving both the ambience and the animals.

She held out her hand to one of the horses. "Hey, Charlie. Which one is this?"

"Ozzie. He's the life of the party, this one." Charlie stroked the giant horse's mane, and Ozzie neighed and nuzzled him.

"I just wanted to check on the sleigh rides. The weather forecast says we'll have enough snow to do them from the Common, so what do you estimate as the time? Will people have to wait?"

"Prob'ly." Charlie chewed on a straw. "The Common's more convenient, but it's another ten minutes to my place. Full ride's an hour. That's what I gave you and the pastor."

She blushed at the memory of Noah kissing her. No, she wouldn't trade that trip for anything. She hurried past the images of that night. "So, we don't want people to wait too long ... Should you trim it back a little?"

"Prob'ly. We'll use the sleigh for small groups or courtin' couples." He looked away. Was he also remembering that night? But then, he went into the details.

"How's Carly? I remember when she was a little girl and came on the sleigh rides with Alice and Walter. Oh, she was a lively one."

Jane smiled, trying to picture the scene of them together. "She's not as lively, but she's doing all right. You know."

He knew. He told her with a nod. In his long life, Charlie must have seen enough cancer.

Charlie looked older, not that he'd ever looked young, but she sensed a tiredness under the red cheeks and hearty laugh. And a chance for Jane. "Have you ever thought about selling out, maybe moving South? Winters would be easier."

"Winter ain't supposed to be easy." Charlie worked the straw, his blue eyes thoughtful above the white beard. "I may have to do it down the line, maybe for Edith. She's got emphysema, and I'll need to take her someplace dry."

"Emphysema? But she never—"

"Yeah, my Edith was a smoker. Before we gave our lives to Christ."

Jane had never wondered about a before. The Wenholms had been stalwart Christian soldiers for all her life, at Hilltop Church every time the doors were open, sometimes opening the doors themselves.

"I can't imagine Edith with a cigarette."

"Neither can we, now."

Good for them and an opening for her. "So, you may have to take Edith somewhere warm. That would be expensive, wouldn't it?"

"Maybe. But I get offers on this place five, six times a year. Big offers. City folk want to live here, fancy themselves farmers. I could buy two, three houses in Arizona for what they offer me."

"Oh."

Charlie looked at Jane until she felt her cheeks redden. "It wasn't me, Janie-girl. I wouldn't do that to Alice even if I needed the money."

Of course, he wouldn't. Jane heaved a sigh. "I'm sorry, Charlie."

"So am I. Sorry you didn't know me better and sorry I didn't know *you* better." He slapped Ozzie on the rump and folded Jane into a clumsy hug. "Give it up, Janie. Let the police take care of this."

If this were anyone but Gram ...

He didn't invite her into the house for tea and cookies with Edith, and she wasn't sure she wanted to anyway. Maybe she'd eat a quick dinner, take her laptop to the library, do some work in peace. Research some topics for the sabbatical St. Hildegarde's was almost certain to grant her. Email her substitute, see how things were going before the Christmas break.

It was a perfect December night, cold with stars twinkling overhead, dark before supper, but the Christmas lights strung up on the homes more than lit up her way back to Gram's.

What was Noah doing now? Did he cook for himself? Was he thinking of her? Was he praying for her? She hoped so, even though her heart wouldn't let her believe.

She stopped at the mailbox and withdrew a sheaf of papers. Sale flyers. A fistful of Christmas cards addressed to Gram. What was this plain, white envelope addressed to her? No stamp, no return address, just "Jane Archer" in block letters. She tucked the other mail under her arm and tore it open. And read the words three times before they sank in.

Stop asking questions. Or you'll wish you hadn't.

CHAPTER NINETEEN

Jane peeled off a glove and dialed Paul's cell.

"McKee," came the voice, crisp, professional, and unaware.

"Paul. I—I got a note."

His voice shifted into what she could only expect was his cop mode. "What kind of note?"

"A threat. To stop asking questions."

Paul sucked in a breath. "Come to the station," he said at last. "My mom's here. I'll have her watch the girls. And don't handle the note. Okay?"

"Okay."

She went in the house by the back door. Good, Gram and Carly were watching their gameshow. She pulled tweezers from her purse and slipped the note into a sandwich bag.

Paul and Lt. Patterson, both in street clothes, met her in the station.

Paul took the plastic bag from her shaking hands. "We'll run this by forensics. It'd be better if it were handwritten, but we'll find something. And, Janie, I know there's a lot of loose ends, but I promise you we will find who did this. So, please, stop asking questions."

But they both knew she wouldn't.

She made her way back home through the cold, quiet streets. Most families were indoors by now, relaxing by their Christmas trees, doing whatever normal intact families did in December. She parked in the garage and braced herself for the short walk up the steps to the mudroom, then the kitchen. Should she tell Gram?

Not yet. Not quite yet.

Jane shrank into a corner, her nightclothes clammy as she pulled the sheet from her bed. Could she throw it out a window, use it as a ladder? The footsteps came closer. She ran to the one window, rattled the latch. It wouldn't budge. And the sheet began to evaporate in her hands as the footsteps came closer.

Jane screamed. Was it real, or was it in the dream? She pulled herself upright on the couch. No, it must have been in the dream.

She shuffled to the kitchen, poured herself a half-glass of orange juice and hit the "on" switch on the coffee maker. Five a.m. She'd never get back to sleep now.

Okay, she *had* screamed. The thump of Gram's walker told her that. Gram looked like she hadn't had a good night either. But then why would she?

Gram tapped her way over to the table, and Jane pulled out a chair for her. "You shouldn't be up."

"Neither should you. Another bad dream?"

"Yeah. Doesn't matter now."

Gram reached out and lifted Jane's chin with one small hand. "It does. Are you worried about me?"

If only that were all.

"Of course, I am. You don't deserve this."

"No. I don't." Gram nodded as Jane handed her a cup of coffee. "But I'll be all right, Janie. You don't serve the Lord for as many years as I have without knowing, well, that all things work together for good."

"Gram, they don't."

"To those that love him, they do."

Gram pulled herself back into the walker and thumped her way into the living room. A few seconds later, Jane heard the sound of the television.

Gram never watched TV in the morning, and as Jane rubbed sleep from her eyes, she cocked her head at the older woman. "What's up?"

"Laura was going to take me Christmas shopping, so I wanted to check the weather. If it's dry, I may use the walker."

"Do you think you should—"

Gram leveled a glance at her. "Jane, dear, I am not going to hide in this house forever. I did nothing wrong. We're going to have to depend on the Lord to prove that up. In the meantime, well, I'm not going to let it stop me from anything I want to do."

"It's hard, Gram."

Gram took her hand. "It is, honey. And you're out in public getting the brunt of it. But has anyone who matters turned their backs on us?"

No. Their dearest friends, the Hilltop Church members and the festival committee, hadn't deserted them. Church members came over regularly. Steph had brought Hayley, who enthralled Gram with her new book series. "It's a mystery *and* it has horses!"

Gram knew about the cattiness, knew about the people who had turned against them. She knew Hilltop inside and out. Did she know about the note? Did she suspect?

Gram knew enough. She had seen too much of what people could do to each other.

Even in Hilltop.

Jane turned her attention to the television, where a well-turned-out redhead presided over the anchor desk of the crack-of-dawn Boston newscast. "Oh, there's Jillian. Our local celebrity. I went to school with her. You remember, Gram."

"Yes." Gram's expression motioned for silence.

"The small town of Hilltop, New Hampshire, home of the popular Hilltop Christmas Festival, is on its guard this month after a longtime community member was arrested for allegedly taking money from the festival funds." A headshot of Gram popped up in the corner of the screen. "Alice Merrill, sixty-seven, has chaired the event for more than twenty years. Evidence was found linking her to the cashing-in of ten thousand dollars' worth of stocks. Merrill's trial is scheduled for January."

Jane took the remote and shut off the TV. "How dare she! I was in Student Council with that girl and French Club. And ..."

"That poor girl. As I remember, her family didn't give her much support. She's done well despite it all." Gram took the remote. "Let's see if anyone talked to her." She turned the TV back on, but the show had gone to a snow tire commercial.

Jillian Despres, a classmate from the Regional. Did Jill still have contacts in Hilltop? Who had tipped her off?

"I'll kill her." Jane's fingers tightened against the cord of her bathrobe.

"No, dear." With an effort, Gram pulled herself up from the wing chair and into her walker. "The truth will come out, or it won't. Let's see what we can do about breakfast."

It was Monday again, after an awkward float-building session and a too-quiet Sunday, when Jane made her rounds downtown, opening the door to the sugary steaminess of the bakery.

She focused on the task at hand, trying to get her mind off the threatening note and Gram's arrest in the news. Paul had advised her not to tell anyone about it, at least not until they had a suspect. He had also assured her this meant for sure the charm was planted, which was at least some good news. With Christmas break in full swing, there were finally no more work emails to go over. Her sub did let her know the students missed her, which brought her some comfort.

She stared into the plateglass window of the Five and Dime, where retro toys beckoned the eye under a Christmas tree decorated with old-fashioned bubble lights. A simpler time—or so everyone said. She'd thought any time in Hilltop simpler than that in the wider world. She'd been wrong.

"Hey."

Noah had materialized at her elbow.

"Hey." Could she infuse her voice with enough indifference? She'd done well with other prospective boyfriends over the years, kept them at arms' length, but they hadn't been Noah.

Nobody was Noah.

He looked down at her with that familiar glint in his blue eyes, the glint she knew now was only for her, and something else. Far beyond intrigue. Compassion.

She wouldn't let him of all people feel sorry for her. Nobody felt sorry for Jane Archer. Not since the mill towns and the mining towns, when the girl in hand-me-downs had bested the other kids on every test, every spelling or other kind of bee, every assignment. She hadn't had many friends, but she'd earned their respect.

Noah would be harder to ignore. It would be harder to conquer the flutter in her stomach every time he grinned his easy grin. And she couldn't stop thinking about how he had prayed for her. Better than thinking about their kiss.

And it seemed he knew it.

He gently took her by the arm and steered her toward the Limelighter's battered wooden door. "You look like you could use a cup of coffee, and I'm between appointments. Would you like to talk?"

Cause a scene on Main Street? Yeah, that was all either of them needed.

This couldn't look like a date. No, it was simply the acting festival chairman and the pastor of the sponsoring church hashing out details.

Jane shrugged off her own coat, and when the teenage waitress came to their booth, she asked for separate checks. That ought to do it.

They were quiet until the girl brought their steaming cups. Joe served only one kind of "Caw-fee," but it was good enough. Although Jane usually took hers black, she made a show of doctoring this cup with cream and sugar. Anything to keep her hands busy. Anything to keep her mind—and eyes—off Noah.

Where were the Colarussos? Could they break this up with their banter? She cocked her head, heard the usual sound of pots banging from the kitchen, strained toward the noise, and finally heard the names of two New England Patriots players over the metallic din. The Joes were arguing about football. No help there.

Noah shredded a paper napkin in those big hands.

"You didn't invite me here to talk about the festival. Did you?"

She was almost hoping he would, as long as it wasn't about Gram's arrest being in the papers and the news.

That grin. "Nope. It's running fine, as far as I can tell. Everybody knows their job."

She used to know hers or thought she did. Work hard, study hard, make the right kind of friends. Get a good job, make Gram proud. And never, ever depend on anybody.

Why isn't it enough anymore?

Noah looked her in the eyes. "We need to talk about what happened."

She looked away. "Nothing happened."

"That's why we need to talk."

Jane was so beautiful, casually elegant in a forest-green sweater and dark jeans, a lighter green scarf bringing out those eyes. Did the woman ever hit a wrong note?

But he could see the ragged child underneath it all.

Did *she* see it?

"I think—what I mean is—" He gazed into the coolness of those green eyes. She wouldn't make this easy. "We can't be together because you don't serve the Lord." There, he'd said it. "And I need to know why."

If Jane could have absorbed herself into the cracked vinyl of the booth, he bet she would have.

She sat up straight. "I'm grateful you prayed for me, but that's none of your concern."

He pressed on, desperate now. "Yes, I think it is. If that's the reason I can't have you, then I deserve to know it."

Jane clasped and unclasped her slender fingers. "If I do, will you leave me alone?"

"Probably not." He gave her what he hoped was a charming grin.

Please, God. Let her open up about this, for her own sake.

Was that a small smile blooming on her lips? "Okay. You've met my mother."

The husk of a woman who seemed to be fading when he last visited Alice. "Barely."

"She wasn't always like that." Jane stared out the window to Hilltop's Main Street, postcard pretty in the snow. "Carly ... Mom was a blonde, a natural blonde, and gorgeous. I never knew my father since he left us when I was still a baby. When Mom took off from Hilltop with me, we lived all over the East Coast. Mom would hear about jobs and move us to another town, then another. Wherever the grass seemed greener. But sometimes there wasn't any grass.

"Mom met guys in every town. Sometimes, the man was the reason we moved there. Sometimes, he was the reason we left it. She was always going to strike it rich in some new town, and every new guy was, well, the love of her life."

He could see it. Californians made poor choices too. He had heard as much from the people he had preached to on the streets that one semester. His heart went out to that girl. He reached toward Jane. He couldn't help it.

"Must have been hard on you." He gently touched her cheek.

Jane removed his hand and shrugged. "I was an afterthought. Clothes from Goodwill, toys from yard sales or her boyfriends. Dirty until I learned how to clean myself. No friends, because who invites friends back to a motel room?"

It had to get better. He couldn't stand the idea of this woman, this girl suffering. "Then—Alice? Alice took you in?"

"Mom gave me up." An oh-so-subtle distinction. "Gram decorated a room for me, bought me clothes that fit, got my teeth fixed, sent me to a proper school. Gave me a life."

Noah closed his eyes. *God, please let her know you'd never leave her.*

He opened and said, "We would say God's grace saved you. God's grace brought you home to Hilltop."

"*You* would."

Jane would always feel the shame, deep inside, of being the child nobody wanted.

Until first grade, she'd stayed with neighbors while Carly worked or went out with men. That all changed in the mining town, when Carly took her to a big stone building and enrolled her. Jane didn't know what "enrolled" meant. She just knew Carly walked her to that building, handed her two pieces of white bread and a piece of processed cheese, and kissed her on the forehead.

"*Bye, hon,*" she had said, "*you come home with Rita's kids, and I'll see you after work.*"

Jane couldn't even remember now what Rita, her babysitter, looked like. She'd been just one of the fast, super-glue alliances Carly made in each new town.

Jane had worn too-short jeans and a too-big shirt on her first day of public education. She sat when she was told to sit, rose when told to rise. Like being part of a machine. She colored with crayons longer than the broken ones she used at home. She couldn't take her gaze from Miss Barrister, her new teacher, as the woman read from a book with bright pictures, moving the book from side to side so everyone could see the drawings of a little brown monkey having adventures. Jane couldn't understand how Miss Barrister could read the words and still move the book around.

Jane liked the little tables and the unbroken crayons and the whiteboard where Miss Barrister wrote stuff and wiped it off. She liked circle time, sitting on the carpet around Miss Barrister's rocking chair.

On Friday, Miss Barrister invited Jane to sit next to the rocking chair in circle time. In science, she let Jane stick on the correct weather symbol. And on Friday afternoon, when the class was watching a video, Miss Barrister had Jane sit in front of her, combed out the knots in Jane's long hair, and put a ribbon around it, the red ribbon from the teddy bear Miss Barrister's boyfriend gave her for a first-day-of-school present.

Was it any wonder Jane became a teacher? There was Gram's influence, yes, but the first seed had been planted by a young woman in her first job in a tiny mining town.

But Jane had to do her part, borrowing books from the class library, picking words and sentences apart on the old Formica table in the trailer after Mom picked her up at Rita's. She'd count cans on the shelves, count Carly's nail polish, or count anything else in the trailer.

Even at six, she'd known somehow education was her ticket out. But the shame of their poverty was nothing next to the shame that came later.

When Jane was silent for a while, Noah said, "I wish I'd been there."

Oh, how he wished it. He'd do anything for her now.

God, please let her know she can open up about her past.

Jane shrugged. "It's done. Mom sent me to Gram, and that the first year was better than the other ten combined."

She sipped her coffee and looked out at Main Street, where a light breeze ruffled the banners hanging from lampposts and the sun turned the tinsel to fire.

Poverty was bad enough, neglect bad enough. He knew neglect and abandonment. But he grew up in a mansion of a home with a maid. But she'd had Hilltop to make up for it. She'd had *Alice*.

"So, that's what turned you away from God?" Noah bit his lip.

She avoided his stare, her slender fingers gripping the thick white cup. "It doesn't matter."

Yes, it does. Because she mattered. She mattered to Alice, to Hilltop, to him. There had to be more but—conviction settled in. He was pushing too much again. He did care too much.

Jane watched Noah from the corner of her eye. Why the pained look? Could she tell him? Surely, he'd heard troublesome testimonies. From what he had told her about his own upbringing, she knew he wasn't perfect. But at least, he had come to the light. But she was stuck on the edge of darkness. And if she confessed her past, the darkness would surely swallow her whole.

No. Jane gathered her things and shoved her arms in her coat sleeves. She'd already risked too much by coming back here. Risked too much by loving him.

The room spun. *Oh, no. I love him.* She loved his kind heart, his gentle spirit, his concern for her even though he could see a "they" could never happen.

She saw her future like the calendar pages in those old movies—decade upon decade of striving, trying. Reaching for the next rung while working desperately to cover what she'd been.

But she'd never be good enough. A second master's degree, a doctorate, tenure. The townhouse, the nice clothes. She would always be the child in rags, the child Gram—and Hilltop—had taken in. Always be the dirty girl.

And in the shadows, she would stay.

She sucked in a breath, forcing the topic of conversation to change. "Was there something else?"

"Sort of." Noah shrugged his big shoulders. "I was wondering—that is, I thought—you've never been to a service. Or heard me preach, so, I wanted to invite you."

Hadn't she known this would come around again? He never gave up. *That's what I love about you.*

"I wish you would come to church at least once before you go back to Boston.

"Make it my Christmas present." He smiled, that dazzling smile.

The smile that was always a little broader, and deeper, for her.

A Christmas present? Gram would appreciate me going with her. She sighed, *even if Carly goes too.*

She faced him. "I'll be there on Christmas Eve." She smiled to herself. It would be fun to hear the choirs, to see Maddy and Emma in their angelic glory.

They locked eyes and exchanged smiles.

Her head pounded as her whole body shook. "I have to go." She pushed past his restraining hand and ran from the booth.

But where could she go?

Anywhere but here.

CHAPTER TWENTY

Jane woke gasping for air, weak from her scream. She clutched both pillows to her chest. Her body shook, drenched in sweat. He wouldn't get her. Not anymore.

No, here she was in Gram's parlor. In the faint light from the street, she made out desk, wing chair, Gramps's old recliner. Gray ghostly shapes, but familiar ones.

And no Larry.

"Janie, honey." Here came Gram, managing her walker with one hand, holding a plastic tumbler of something in her other. "Drink this."

Jane gulped the cold, clear water. No town had water like Hilltop. It ran through her like a mountain stream. She could breathe again, but her hands shook, and the water sloshed as she set the tumbler on the coffee table.

"Thanks, Gram. It was nothing."

"Doesn't look like 'nothing.'" Gram settled herself on the flowered wing chair. Her old eyes were clear, wise—and relentless. "And it didn't sound like nothing. That's the third time this week, and the worst. What's going on, Janie? Is it about your mother?"

Oh, Gram was sharp. Mom and so much more.

"Hope I didn't wake—her."

"Your mother took two pain pills before bed. She'll be all right for a while."

"It was just a dream." Jane pulled her covers up to her chin. "A man was hurting a little girl. That's all."

Gram's expression said she wasn't buying it. Jane had never tried to fool her. Never lied to her. Only when it came to the nightmares.

She should blame Noah for prying again, then maybe she wouldn't have dreamt of that. Why couldn't she have dreamed of her prom night or her first Hilltop Christmas? Why did memories from nearly twenty years ago still have to haunt her? She could really use Gram's peace. At least Gram was there with her.

Gram thumped across the room and bent down to plug in the Christmas tree, a burst of color that sent its light into the dark corners of the living room. "If we're going to be up, we might as well have something pretty to look at." She sat in the wing chair. "Remember when you were little, and I let you sleep on the couch so you could look at the tree?"

Jane remembered. Friday and Saturday nights, going to sleep in the glow and sparkle of the most beautiful Christmas tree ever. Waking up to it, with Gram bringing her a cup of hot chocolate or tea, the smell of waffles drifting in from the kitchen.

"You were so good to me." Jane smiled.

"I ... I was lonely too, Jane. But I don't want you to be alone. I'm not always going to be here. And your mother ..." Gram's eyes teared up.

That's right. Jane wasn't only losing a mother. Gram was losing a daughter. A daughter who had a whole life with her own mother before Jane was born. She tried to picture it. Tried to have compassion at least for her grandmother.

Jane patted Gram's hand. "Sure, you will." The words rang hollow, but she had to say something. "And I've done well without a mother this long, I'm sure I'll be fine when it's Carly's time to go. You're in perfect health now you've had the hip replacement. You'll probably outlive me!"

Gram was outliving her own daughter, wasn't she?

Gram cupped Jane's face. "You need a family of your own."

"You're my family. And—and Mom." She made herself say it. It would make Gram happy.

"You're a good girl, Janie."

For the sake of the depth of the love in Gram's eyes, Jane, for once, let her kind words linger.

Jane hadn't realized the extent of what had happened to her until college. Abnormal psychology, regular psychology, a special seminar for education majors dealing with troubled children.

A robbed childhood, not that she'd had much to rob. A diminished self.

She'd read deeper on the subject, beyond class requirements, until she couldn't read any more. She hated knowing she wasn't the only one out there this happened to, but a small part of her was glad she wasn't alone.

The psych books advised victims to tell someone, but Jane never did. She was managing on her own, wasn't she? Jane didn't need therapy. She'd made a life for herself. Top of her class, then top of her profession. Gram had opened the door for her, and she'd run through it and never stopped. Despite it all, she had done something with her life. Her students needed her. And she needed them. That was something not even the memory of Larry could take away. She couldn't let it.

So, what if she had nightmares once or twice a year? Okay, since she'd been back to Hilltop, once or twice a week. Dreams didn't mean anything. Getting up the next morning and working hard, that meant something.

Running so fast nobody had a chance to know the real you because they probably wouldn't like you. *That* meant something.

She recalled Noah's touch, so gentle, so caring. And the respect in those blue eyes. He was pushy but only when he came to showing her how much he cared. For the first time in her life, she wondered what intimacy would be like. With Noah. But how could she ever tell him about what Larry had done?

Telling someone, dealing with this through counseling would only slow her down.

"Honey, I'm going back to bed." Gram's voice brough her back to reality. "But you think about what I said." With one tender backward glance, Gram shuffled off toward the downstairs bedroom.

Jane thought about what Gram had said all the time. She just wasn't prepared to deal with it.

Noah couldn't stop thinking about Jane and her story about being on the road with her mother. The hurt in her eyes. A hurt that went deep and wide.

He rubbed his eyes as Wayne MacDonald set the first of two crates on one of his office chairs. "You've got to be kidding. What happened? I packed that one myself."

"Miz Hopkins don't want it." Wayne said. "Said she can manage."

"But it's a Christmas basket! A gift! She's behind on the taxes, and her son—" Noah rubbed his eyes again, calming his tone, trying not to think about how young Jane could have used a Christmas basket. "If Bernice Hopkins doesn't need a Christmas basket, I don't know who does."

Noah thought of the marathon basket-stuffing session this past week, with half his congregation coming together to make sure nobody went without this Christmas. Parents brought children, teaching them how to give. Children learned to give, with even little Maddy McKee holding up a box of stuffing she "bought with my 'lowance," as she put it. It wasn't charity. It was Christianity.

Wayne shrugged. "Bernice is a hard case."

"Fred and Melissa accepted our help, for them and the boys."

"They ain't from here."

Four words that defined his congregation, this town. Defined these stubborn, prideful Yankees. Would he ever get to know these people, to understand them, to know them the way Wayne and Charlie and Alice did?

Well, no one is perfect. Not even in Hilltop. God, help us understand each other.

Would he ever stop making mistakes? He shook his head, reassuring himself of his own humanity.

Ever since his chat at the Limelighter with Jane, he felt closer to her. But there was still a distance. A wall she wouldn't let come down.

"I'm going to Bernice's. I'm gonna go." He sounded childish, petulant even to himself.

"Fine." Wayne slapped his glove on the desk. "Iffen you want the door slammed in your face."

"I don't." Noah could feel himself wilting. "I just wanted to share Christ's love with her."

That's it, God, right? I'm not being stubborn, am I?

Wayne rubbed his tired face. "I know, Pastor. Me and Bernice, we went to school together. She's always been poor, and she's always been proud. You got to get to know her first."

Which had been the point of the Christmas baskets in the first place. "Okay, then please tell me how."

Wayne left and poked his head back in the door like an aging flannel-clad turtle. "Bernice is a beekeeper. She might bring you a couple jars of honey, and she makes decent jam. Could be she'd take a turkey if you 'cepted a couple of jars."

So that was how it worked. Noah thanked him. When Wayne left for good. Noah cleared off another chair and made room for Bernice's second rejected basket.

Well, I do like jam. If all else fails, maybe Father Donovan knows a needy family.

Nobody in Hilltop would go hungry.

Oh, God, help me break through. You put me here for a reason. There are so many people who need you. Help me know what to do.

Jane would have known.

Noah shrugged off the bright image of her, scoured his Bible commentaries, and took notes by hand for his next sermon, the Sunday before Christmas. But Jane's perfect face superimposed itself on his Bible and materials. Her pinched expression, the way she went deep inside herself when he asked her about her past. The little girl who had nothing.

If I had been there ... He'd have been a child himself. *But God, you were there.*

Exasperated, Noah flailed around the church, rearranging Sunday School materials and straightening the hymn books even though the lyrics now came on the overhead.

Jane, Jane, Jane. Was God trying to tell him something? If he was, it was a waste of celestial time because Noah was listening. He just couldn't do anything about it.

Only God could.

CHAPTER TWENTY-ONE

"Whatcha doing?"

Jane couldn't help cringing at the tone and the speaker, but she schooled her face to politeness as she swiveled to face her mother. "Just going over some things for the Hilltop meeting tonight. It's our second to last meeting before the festival. So many details."

I just hope they don't bring up Gram's arrest being on the news.

"Anything I can do to help?"

Nothing that would let her into Jane's world. "I don't think so," Jane said, choosing her words with care. "It's all, you know, detail work."

"Okay." But Carly lingered, her hand on Jane's shoulder. "Seems funny to see you like that. Reminds me of when you were little and doing your homework."

Jane hadn't done her homework in a clean warm dining room, and she hadn't had a laptop. And Carly hadn't been able to help her, well, ever.

It was as if Carly had read her mind. "Sure wish I could have helped you more with your homework. I just wasn't smart enough. I was lost after you got into fourth grade."

She hadn't helped much before that, but Jane didn't want to start an argument. She just wanted to get out of here.

"I got my GED and my LNA," Carly was saying. "I was going for RN, but I got sick. Not much beside all your degrees, but I did try to better myself."

After you gave me away.

"You did fine," Jane said with a sigh. She just hadn't done fine by Jane.

Carly ruffled a stack of papers, and Jane resisted the urge to straighten them.

"Do you think Ma will beat this?" Carly's gaze remained on the shiny tabletop.

"I don't know. She's beaten everything else in her life." *Including dealing with you.* "She had to have been framed. Set up. Whatever they call it."

"She doesn't even need the money."

"Well, somebody did."

"I don't—I can't—"

Jane had always been able to read her mother, even when she couldn't do anything about it. She got the subtext right way. *I don't want to die without her.*

I'm not sure I want to live without her.

Carly cleared her throat. "I did think about you. Missed you."

Jane met her gaze, searching her mother. Tears threatened to fall, but she pushed them away.

Carly paused then said, "I'm going upstairs to take a shower." She turned at the door, her smile a ghost of the old Carly. "Good luck with your meeting."

Carly believed in luck. Gram believed in God. Jane believed in work.

The festival would go on, at least for this year, and maybe a few more. There would be enough money. There was always enough money somehow. But trust couldn't be bought, especially in Hilltop.

The Bonhomie was jammed with commuters in business attire lined up to get their forgotten milk or bread. Jane tapped her foot as she fumed in line, and finally returned her sandwich to the cooler. She'd go to the doughnut shop after her meeting.

She stopped by the elementary school, where Anne Gregson's sewing crew worked on costumes for the children's Christmas pageant, the living nativity, and the parade. Women and a few men bent over portable sewing machines or knelt on the parquet floor of the school gym. Sammi Morton walked by and waved to Jane, who waved back.

Stephanie saw her and rushed over, giving her a hug. "Oh, Janie, it's so good to see you again. How's Mrs. Merrill and your mom? How are you?"

"She's all right. Dealing with it. You know Gram." Jane sighed and faced Steph again. "And my mother is ... well, we're trying to move forward. And I'm hanging in there."

"Hayley and I are coming over Saturday to visit. She has a new book series she's excited about."

Dear Steph. She and other Hilltop stalwarts stood by Gram—visiting, calling, sending cards. Did it make up for the people who looked at Jane, then looked away? Maybe.

Steph turned to Jane. "That reminds me, what are you up to this week?"

"More Hilltop. Details, details. Good thing I like details."

"You're like Mom. She never met a detail she didn't like."

Jane smiled. "Well, I've got to run over to Littleton Friday evening. The hotel has a check for the festival. With the news of the theft, they don't trust mailing it in. Oh, but you could come with me. We could get some dinner. Hang out like old times."

Jane couldn't bring herself to tell her friend she'd be staying after all, to care for Gram and mostly for Carly. Perhaps she could tell her over dinner.

Steph shook her head. "Can't. The bank's open late on Fridays. But would you mind bringing Hayley along? There's a book for her at the Littleton Library, and she just can't wait for them to send it over. I told her we could just download the e-book, but she loves to hold the real thing, you know?"

Jane smiled, reminiscing over memories of Gram taking her to the library. "Yeah. Well, that'll work out perfectly, then we can get to know each other."

"Great. You'll have to pick her up from school if that's all right. I'll send the school a note giving you permission."

Jane made a note of her own in the notebook. "That works. Is Hayley here?"

"I sure hope so." Ryan's voice, coming in behind them, with the swagger that seemed to grow stronger with the years. "I'm taking her out for pizza."

Ryan smiled, dressed in a denim shirt that must have cost a hundred dollars, judging by the logo on the pocket, and tucked into professionally-ripped jeans. With his hair curled around his collar, his face shone in that carefully not-quite-shaven mode. His eyes beamed bright with the wonder of being Ryan Gregson.

But he seemed like a good uncle, evident as Hayley ran to his side and said, "Are we going now?"

"Sure are. Get your coat, Munchkin." He tossed a smile over his shoulder as Hayley struggled into her jacket. "Great practice for being a parent."

"Your girlfriends are great practice for being a parent," his sister said. Before he could answer, Stephanie tugged Jane's arm. "Come on, Janie, you've got to see this."

Jane put down her purse, laptop, and the bulging notebook. They threaded their way through the humming machines and people cutting out patterns on the floor. Anne bent over a machine, examining a seam with a volunteer, and she sent Jane a quick smile.

Jane gazed in wonder at a flowing white gown with pearl insets and layers of lace on the dressing dummy. "Wow."

"Old Mrs. Carmody gave us her wedding gown. It was a Paris original. She doesn't have any granddaughters, so she said we could have it. I'm remaking it for the head angel's robe."

"Wow," Jane said again. People gave their best to Hilltop.

When they walked back to where Jane had left her things, Stephanie veered off, distracted by a question from a seamstress.

Anne joined Jane for a minute, looking out over the gym, the buzzing machines, and the buzzing conversation. "Quite an operation, isn't it?"

"It's amazing." Jane nodded. "Do you still do the costumes for everybody?"

"We do. The parade, the living nativity, Hilltop Church's Christmas pageant, and St. Dominic's Christmas pageant. They each have their own garment racks." Anne swept a manicured hand over the scene before them. "At the end of the season, we rack the clothes and pin a note on anything that needs repairing. Then we're ready to go in November. We get started on the mending, and when the pageants are cast, we work on alterations."

"However do you keep track?"

Anne shrugged. "One of my crew members does it on the computer. Something called Excel. I don't bother with that. I keep most of it in my head."

The woman could organize anything. Even Jane's head swam with the thought of keeping track of two hundred holiday costumes, from a preschool angel to Santa himself. She'd need a lot more than the notebook.

"Of course, there's a lot of back-and-forth," Anne added in a brisk tone. "St. Dominic's will have a year with a high number of shepherds, and they'll borrow from Hilltop Church. Or Hilltop will have a surplus of angels. It all evens out in the end."

It could only work in Hilltop, where the two churches complemented each other rather than competed.

But even Hilltop wasn't Hilltop anymore.

Anne excused herself, and Steph reappeared at Jane's side.

"I'll walk you out," Steph said. "That way I can make sure Ryan didn't bring the motorcycle."

"Ryan is good with Hayley," Jane said.

"He is." Stephanie grinned. "He takes his uncle-ing very seriously. Of course, she's not that much younger than his band mates—or the girls he's getting now." She rolled her eyes. "Hey, can you come over and sew with us some time?"

"I'd love to." Love to spend time with other Hilltop people with a shared goal, here in this gym where she'd spent so many happy hours. Gram had taught her some basic skills, like Greg had taught her woodworking.

"I'll try," Jane said. "Maybe next week. And I'll see you Saturday."

"With what Alice stole, you could probably *buy* all new costumes." said a voice.

Jane turned but not fast enough. The group of women behind her all bent their heads to their hand-stitching. They were women she didn't know well, not enough to recognize a voice. Did it matter at this point?

Stephanie's lips thinned, and she took Jane's arm. "I can't wait to see Mrs. Merrill cleared and back with us again, especially now that your mother is back," she said in a distinct, carrying voice. "Nobody does angel wings like Alice Merrill."

Maybe Jane should measure Stephanie for a pair.

Jane drove up the hill to the church, a little faster than she needed to. Being on time mattered, now more than ever. But Wayne MacDonald had gotten there ahead of her.

"Glad you're here, Janie." he said, looking up from an Excel spreadsheet. "Couple of the mainstage acts want to change their slots."

"Not again." Jane thumped her purse and the notebook down on the conference table but had the presence of mind to be more careful with the laptop.

"Yup. Mountain School of Ballet wants their *Nutcracker* excerpt on the first night, on account of they're a 'real' ballet school and Miss Rita's isn't. On account of Miss Rita also teaches tap and jazz. *And* acrobatics."

Jane rubbed her temples again. "Is Miss Rita okay with switching nights?"

"She don't care, long as she can get the Rit-ettes out there doin' something."

Miss Rita and the Mountain School of Ballet had sniped at each other since Jane came to Hilltop. Gram chuckled about it. Jane didn't think there was anything funny about the rivalry, at least not tonight.

"Is that all?" *Please let it be all.*

"Nope. The madrigal group and the guitar player from Concord want to go on earlier, so they can get home before it's too late."

"They knew it was an hour-and-a-half drive when they signed up."

Wayne spread his big hands, scarred from the years he'd spent as a logger. "Just tellin' ya."

Quick tears formed, the tears that were so near the surface these days. "Why can't people leave things alone? The schedule was set. December is almost over. We can't accommodate everyone."

"Hey. Hey, Jane, don't cry." Wayne laid a clumsy hand on her shoulder. If Greg Gregson had been a father figure, Wayne had been right behind him as an uncle. "I'll call everybody, get it all sorted out. That's my job. I was just keepin' you in the loop."

But she couldn't stop. "Why don't they make the best of it? This is a community festival. It's not about them."

"No. It ain't. But it's how people are." Wayne handed her a tissue from the box on the table. "Jane, maybe you oughta step back. You got a lot on your plate now—Alice and your Ma and all. Maybe you should let someone else take over. Maybe Greg, he's got a finger in just about everything anyway."

"No. The chairman can't be a board member. It's a safeguard they built in when they incorporated." When Gram inflicted the job on her, Jane had spent one Saturday afternoon reading the bylaws. It was what Jane Archer did.

Although the balance of power hadn't done Gram any favors. Oh, *there* was one for the fat-lot-of-good department.

She mustered a smile for Wayne. "Sorry. I'm a little on edge these days. But I can handle Hilltop if everyone else does their job. We'll find a place for the Rit-ettes."

The others came in, talking quietly or not talking at all, the way they'd been since they learned of the theft. Did they grieve over Gram's downfall, the last person in the world anyone would suspect of embezzlement? Or did they believe in her innocence?

But they'd have to suspect each other. There was no right answer.

She schooled her face to professionalism. She would do this, she could do this, and then go home. Or whatever home was these days.

Noah was there, breezing in next to Bob Desrochers, saying something that brought a reluctant smile to Bob's round face. Oh, Noah was a charmer. If only she could leave him at her first impression, the shallow party boy. If only they'd never kissed. No, if only they'd never talked, that had been the start of their plunge.

But he'd showed himself to be much more, in the way he cared for his flock. For the dying Mark Smith. For lost lambs like the Parkers and troubled lambs like Gram. He visited Gram twice a week, praying with and for her, mostly when Jane wasn't home.

And in the way he cared about *her.* He was a decent man and deeper than anyone realized.

He threw her a quick smile, and she froze. No. Not again. But didn't he look good tonight, in dark jeans, crisp shirt, and a pullover a shade darker than his eyes?

She gave him a curt nod and bent to her paperwork.

Noah had timed his visits to Alice to days and hours when he thought she'd be out. He'd tried to minister to Carly, who usually left the room. But he couldn't avoid Jane at Hilltop meetings. He took a seat at the far end of the table, but he was intensely aware of her. If only he could wipe the sorrow from her eyes.

But there was only one person who could help Jane, and she wasn't having any.

Dear Lord, give her strength.

The group looked tense this evening, had been since Alice's arrest. None of the usual joking, the good-humored insults honed over the years. Father Donovan looked at Noah over the bent head of a Dumont twin. Father Donovan didn't know what to do either, and this had been his town a lot longer.

Greg called the meeting to order and, with a brief nod at Noah, said, "Pastor, you can pray."

He shot a glance at Jane, but she looked at her clasped hands. Her curtain of hair hid her face. Well, she didn't care about that anymore. He supposed he should be glad. He prayed aloud for the festival and silently, with all he had, for her.

The committee members delivered their reports with little embellishment, and Jane marked things down in that notebook of hers. She was more businesslike than he'd ever seen her—and more grieved.

Under the table, Noah clenched his fists. *If only I could fix this for her. Fix the thing she never spoke of.*

He roused himself when Greg spoke. "Thank you, Janie. Looks like we're in pretty good shape. Only one more meeting before Hilltop, so we'd better be." He consulted a piece of paper. "I need a head count for the ski lodge dinner. It's next Saturday, and it's at Waterville this year."

"Ski lodge dinner?"

Had he not been paying attention? *Maybe I could learn a thing or two from Jane and be more organized and get my own notebook.*

Bev Smith grinned at him, her first smile of the evening. "It's when the local ski areas honor the festival committee. See, Hilltop brings *them* business. They go in together on a nice dinner, and then, they give us a check for last-minute expenses."

"We all pile into the church van and go together," Greg said.

"It's so much fun!" Michelle said, with her first smile of the evening.

Jane's voice fell like a rock into the sudden joy. "I don't think I can make it."

Of course, she wouldn't. It was too much to ask with the real festival chair under suspicion.

"Of course, you can." Greg's tone was brisk, the spirit of the community's problem-solver, though worry darkened his eyes. "The chairman always goes to the dinner. You deserve it after all the work you've done."

"Really, I can't." Jane looked away. "I can't leave two people alone who both need help."

Did they realize what they were asking? But then Noah saw some heads nod, acknowledging the fact her mother needed help just as much as Gram did. As nosy as he had come to know the people of Hilltop to be, he hadn't heard a single mean word spoken about Jane's mother, Carly, despite her wild past. Perhaps because now she had a short future ahead of her.

The look on Jane's face had little to do with her mother, but rather with her grandmother.

People were still people. And Noah would pray God would take away their fears. Especially that they should have forgiveness toward Alice who was the most forgiving person he had ever met.

And dear Jane Archer. She felt ashamed. Noah knew it with heart-stabbing certainty. Even though she hadn't done anything wrong or Alice either.

He knew about shame. Had been schooled in it at his father's knee. Only when he disappointed Dad.

Here was something Noah could ease, if not fix. *I couldn't help Jane when she was a girl, but I can now.*

"Of course. We understand. You wouldn't want to leave your mother or Alice for that long." His voice sounded too loud, but he focused on reading the room. "Tell you what, Ms. Archer." Her head shot up at the "Ms." Well, he was trying to be professional. "I could drive you to the dinner, and we can leave whenever you want. I'm new to all of this, so it won't hurt me to miss a little."

Jane shot him a look. If anything could mix fear, gratitude and, yes, shame, that look did it. "Thank you, Reverend."

Noah sighed in relief. *Thank You, God. I said the right thing.*

The other members nodded in agreement. Some thanked Jane for coming while others told her they'd catch her up on anything she'd miss.

He lingered after the meeting, but so did Paul. Both vying for her attention.

"Can I walk you to your car?" Noah grinned at her.

Jane shot him a quick, impersonal smile. "No thanks. I've got to talk to Paul about a few things. I'll see you at the dinner."

But as he headed to the door, he heard light footsteps as Jane came up at his side. "It is not a date," she said in a low voice.

"Not a date," he repeated dully. "Good night, Ms. Archer."

Noah had put her on the spot again. But his motives were pure enough this time. It wasn't his fault that—that what? That she *wanted* to go with him?

Jane stacked and restacked her materials. Avoided looking at Paul. If only he hadn't worn his uniform tonight, the thing that separated them the most. The unsettled issue of the theft. But Paul, of all people, would honor his office and be professional.

Once Noah left, Jane said, "Have you found anything to clear Gram's name?"

Paul leaned against the door jamb. "Well, the good news is, from the fact there was an obvious cover up, the money's nowhere to be found, and now the threatening note, we agree she's being framed. But she's all we have for now."

"Anything on the note?"

"Forensics is still looking at it. If it were handwritten, we could test board members' handwriting, but it's set in this strange, typed font."

Jane nodded.

"How—how is she?" Paul asked.

Jane opened her eyes and sighed. "Braver than I would be."

She hoisted her shoulder bag and tucked the laptop under her arm. When she reached for the notebook, a piece of paper fluttered to the ground. She reached for it, smoothed it out on the table, and began to shake.

Paul read it over her shoulder. "'Mind your own business.' Oh, Janie."

Her teeth chattered. "It's another one. Paul, it's another note."

"I know. Shh, it's all right." He pulled out a pair of tweezers, lifted the note, and settled it between two tissues. "I'll take care of this. Now we know whoever is doing this had the chance to be close to you. Did you have the notebook with you the whole night?"

Jane shook her head. "I sat it down when Hayley wanted to show me some of the costumes. Someone there could have put it in my notebook."

Paul nodded. "Ok, I'll try to get a head count of who was helping."

Tears formed in the corners of her eyes. "You've got to find out who's doing this."

He gave her a reassuring smile. "We will."

He pulled her into a hug and made little murmuring sounds as she leaned into his strength. But he wasn't the one she wanted hugging her.

CHAPTER TWENTY-TWO

Noah turned off his computer and stretched back in his office chair. That was that. A decent Christmas sermon and not that hard after all. Not when he thought of how Jane would be there, sitting in the front row smiling up at him next to her mother and Alice. And now they'd be going to the ski lodge dinner together. It might not be a date to her, but it would be for him. Perhaps someone was praying for him or maybe even *he* couldn't mess up the journey to Bethlehem and what it meant today. Brad, Doug, and Paul had even given him some pointers during their football watch party. Plus, a few mountain metaphors related to Scriptures couldn't hurt.

Now all that's left is to preach it to five hundred people.

Noah struck out along Main Street. The tinsel in the shop windows glittered in the sunlight, sunlight that bounced off the piles of snow. Hilltop was pretty enough, but if he wanted to look at snow, he could have bought a New England calendar. He put on his best "pastor face," waving to parishioners and friends. Surprising how many people he knew after a little less than three months. But did he really know them? Did they really know him?

No. Some had given him a chance, like his few guy friends, Alice, and even Jane, at least a little. He didn't know what made these people tick. He thought it was the mountains. He even learned to properly pronounce all the names of the streets. But, despite all his efforts, the person he wanted to get to know the most, Jane, wouldn't let him inside. What was the point in it all?

He could just hear his father's last words to him, the words that still plagued his mind and nightmares. The words that chipped away at his confidence. Not in himself. He had let that go a long time ago. His confidence in God's calling. He had never before related so much to Moses. *Are you sure you've got the right guy, Lord? The right place?*

Should he get out now? Run in the opposite direction like Jonah? He had some money. He could go back to California, get out of this nightmare of a climate. California, scene of his greatest follies and greatest victory.

He would finish out the Christmas season and work on his exit strategy. Apply for California churches, maybe. Throw himself on the mercy of Dad? Dad would take him back but not without a lecture. His brothers would. He could be an engineer. He'd be an okay one and serve the Lord at night and on weekends.

He'd finally be able to surf again. *Perhaps I could teach surfing lessons for a youth group. That'd be less pressure than being a full-time pastor.*

He couldn't even imagine January in this desolate place—without the glitter of the Christmas lights and the excitement of the festival.

He could only imagine it with Jane at his side.

What would happen to Jane? What would happen if her beloved Gram was convicted? What would happen to her mother, the party girl come home to die?

And what was Jane hiding?

Would anyone here even miss me? He thought of his chats with Alice, the wonderful and spiritually strong woman who had become like a mother to him. Dare he say a spiritual mentor? Alice would, but Alice had the strength to survive without him or without any pastor. A few of the Hilltoppers would miss him, he'd made some friends, especially Paul who he had gotten coffee with on occasion. His football buddies. Greg Gregson, patriarch to the town.

Have I left an impact on this sweet little town yet, Lord?

Would Jane Archer miss him?

He would certainly miss her.

Jane had time for a quick scroll through her personal e-mail. Some of her students at St. Hildegarde's had written her. She shut her eyes and pictured it, the stone buildings warmed by the sun and mellow with age, the heated discussions around the oval tables, the almost reverent silence in the library full of girls who knew how to use a library. The interchange of ideas with her colleagues, the best in their fields, far better than Jane.

She had thrived at St. Hildegarde's. She could thrive still. If only—

She heard the faint thump of Gram's walker, which had mostly replaced the creak of the wheelchair. Gram came into the dining room, lowered herself into a chair.

Jane snapped the laptop shut and reached for the notebook. "Would you like me to put more logs on the fire?"

"I'm not worried about that." Gram's voice had an unfamiliar edge to it. "I'm worried about how you're treating your mother."

Jane's heart began to pound. But she'd known the lecture was coming. "I'm civil to her."

"'Civil' isn't enough, and you know it."

Jane slumped in her chair. "Gram, you know what she did to us. She abandoned me and left you to raise me. She wasn't a mother at all. And you got stuck with everything."

"I know what she did and didn't do, but ..." Gram laughed softly. "'Stuck'? Is that how you see it?" She covered Jane's hand with her own. "Janie, I thoroughly enjoyed raising you. I had the energy, money, this big house—and I was lonely after Walter died. You and I had some wonderful times. But she is your mother."

Five words Jane couldn't run away from, no matter how hard she tried. "She wasn't much of one," she murmured.

"No." Gram sighed and ran a hand through her cropped silver hair. "The verdict is in on that one. But she is my daughter, and I'm thrilled to have her home."

Gram's soft voice went on, but Jane could feel the steel underneath. "And I need you to reconcile with her. Because I may not be here."

Jane hadn't let herself think. "They'll probably let you off with a fine. Paul told me they're sure you were framed."

"A fine for money I didn't take." Gram nodded. "But, Jane, this time, I need your help. I need to know you'll take care of your mother."

Anything but that. "I'm no nurse," Jane managed.

"Hospice will take care of that. But she'll need someone to be with her. Janie, I don't know how this is going to play out. I need you."

If Gram only knew what she was asking. No, she knew perfectly well.

They had made a good team, and Jane had never wished for a younger "mother." She'd been proud to introduce the chic, smiling woman with the silver hair to her friends and her friends' parents, to college roommates and casual boyfriends. It had been enough for Jane then. It was enough now. Why did Carly have to come along and spoil it?

She was dying, was why. And Jane could do this for Gram, if for no other reason.

She'd survived worse.

Jane rose and dropped a kiss on her grandmother's forehead. "I'll try. That's all we can do, right?"

She shrugged into her coat and opened the kitchen door.

Gram's voice followed her. "What about supper?"

"I'll grab something while I'm out. But thanks."

That was what mothers did.

Jane let herself into the dark, chilly garage, into the even chillier car, and rested her head on the steering wheel. There it was. The truth she'd run from since Carly brought her ruined body back to Hilltop. Gram's arrest had accelerated it, but the truth was already there.

I can't go back.

Too much to do here, too much only she could do. She would not turn her back on her mother, for Gram's sake if not her own.

She'd have to talk to the headmistress. The sub would be glad for more work, and they'd left it open-ended. Jane had the comp time coming. St. Hildegard's was generous that way. She'd have to make a trip to the townhouse, pick up more clothes. After the festival ... the festival ... the festival.

She massaged her temples against a rising headache. She hadn't planned on any of this. Well, Gram hadn't planned on raising a granddaughter. Bev Smith hadn't planned on losing the love of her life when he hadn't even reached retirement age.

How do they do it?

No, Jane knew how. And it wasn't an option. God had left her alone all those years. She'd built her own life. And

God presented himself on earth as a father, something she'd never had and was no longer sure she wanted.

Stuck in Hilltop, at least for now. With Noah so near and so far away, with the memory of his kisses and every other interaction still blazing in her mind. The Kanc outing, the cookie baking, and oh, the glory of that sleigh ride. The joy of belonging, even if only for a few minutes.

Hayley Gregson was good company, Jane had to admit. Although she wasn't a chatterbox like her mother had been, she made pleasant, relaxed conversation on the way to Littleton. The little girl talked about her classes, her favorite books, and the riding lessons Greg had promised. At ten, Stephanie had already been talking about boys, but Hayley was still a little girl, albeit a growing girl.

She was the child Jane should have been, if she'd started and stayed in Hilltop. Loved, protected, cherished. Free to explore her passions, growing from strength to strength.

If only.

"Thanks for bringing me," Hayley said as they cruised the snowy back roads. "I really wanted that library book. Mom told me you love to read too."

"You're welcome, and I do." And Jane knew what it was like to be a kid longing for a book.

They split up in the larger town, with Hayley headed for the library and Jane accepting the check from Thayer's Inn, an antique and boutique hotel on Main Street. She had the traditional photo taken with the manager. It should have been Gram. Would it ever be Gram again?

I'm just glad they didn't bring up Gram's arrest.

Jane sneaked in a walk, admiring the decorated shop windows and dodging the red-cheeked shoppers. She and

Hayley reconnected at the Chutters candy store, billed as "the longest candy counter in the world," and giggled their way through filling several paper sacks with candy.

The skies had threatened snow when they headed out, and flakes were falling before they left Littleton. Jane turned on both the heater and the radio as she headed out the back roads toward Hilltop. She and Hayley sang along with Christmas music sung by the smooth baritones of the likes of Perry Como and Bing Crosby and others.

The snow came down harder, swirling around them. Jane fought to see the road ahead of her. She stepped up the speed on the windshield wipers and slowed Gram's car. She'd been driving these roads all her life, hadn't she?

She strained to see through the heavy snow. Was that the old Texaco station, long abandoned? She couldn't see the yellow line in the road, but it didn't matter. No one else was out.

Beside her, an unconcerned Hayley tucked away the candy sack.

Jane masked her growing fear, though her hands tightened on the steering wheel. Nothing must happen to Stephanie's child. Or Anne and Greg's grandchild.

She combed the landscape for landmarks. Was that the small engine repair place, run out of a barn? She could barely see the curved roof of a barn. Lots of places had barns. Had she made a wrong turn?

The road grew slippery under her, like driving on a pancake griddle. She slipped once and looked over at Hayley who was staring straight ahead.

Gram's car had front-wheel drive with new tires. She'd gotten them before the operation. That was Gram, always planning, looking for ways to make this stay easier on Jane. Well, they'd missed the mark on this one. They should have left Littleton earlier. Jane knew what a mountain storm could do. They should at least have come back on Route 93, where the plows would probably be out by now.

Jane saw the fear in Hayley's eyes when she shut off the overhead light, put her book away, and braced herself on the narrow seat.

"We'll be fine," Jane said. "I know this road like the back of my hand."

Yeah, the back of her hand covered by a fierce Nor'easter.

"How about you get my phone from my purse? Pull up the GPS to see how far away we still are and if it wants us to take a different route."

Hayley nodded, and a moment later, said, "We're only about thirty minutes away, but since you're supposed to drive slower, it's going to take about an hour now. All the routes are about the same estimated time."

Jane thanked her but slipped again and righted the car the way Greg had taught her when he'd taken it on himself to supplement her driver's ed program. He'd made her practice on his trucks, first with the small fleet of pickups and then with the flatbed. She'd learned to change her own oil and to drive a standard. Greg had been a strict taskmaster, at least where cars were concerned.

In the dimming light, she could barely make out an abandoned one-room schoolhouse. *Good.* There was a curve coming up and then a dip. Jane didn't dare look at Hayley. What if it all ended tonight?

If only she'd told Noah how she really felt. Well, he knew how she really felt.

Think, Janie.

They were almost there. Coming up on Old Lancaster Road—she could take a right there, and—she looked in her rearview mirror and saw lights, two white orbs surrounded by a haze of snow. Another car. Who would be crazy enough to be out in this?

The other vehicle came closer. Jane worked the steering wheel, desperately trying to stay upright. The other car's lights reflected off her front grille. She swerved to avoid an impact, and the slickness forced her off the road with one wheel in a snowbank.

Her head hit the steering wheel, but she jerked it up and looked over at Hayley. "You okay, honey?"

Hayley's lip was bleeding, but she nodded and said in a shaky voice, "Yeah. I'm used to it. My mom's a terrible driver."

Hayley handed Jane back her phone as Jane punched in the numbers for roadside service. It wouldn't take long, the chipper voice at the other end assured her and added, "Don't worry. We've got lots of trucks out tonight. Everyone saw it coming."

Everyone but Jane.

Jane left the heater running. Hayley was bundled up. She'd be okay, and they had blankets and water in the back. Gram knew how to stock a car for winter.

Jane took bleak stock of her situation. It hadn't been a mere accident. The other vehicle had been headed directly for her. Someone wasn't happy with Jane Archer, and someone knew she'd be on this back road this snowy night.

Could it be the same person who sent the notes?

Hayley was reading her book again, with the little flashlight on Jane's phone. *Tough kid.* Jane would have to tell Steph. Word might get out, even to Noah. First, she'd have to figure it out, as best she could. The lack of visibility left no hope for a license plate. But perhaps Hayley had noticed something.

"Did you get a good look at the other car?" Jane asked.

Hayley glanced up from her book. "Sort of. It was moving fast, and it was covered with snow, but it looked like one of the trucks from my grampa's store."

It wasn't that cold with the heater on, but Jane couldn't stop shivering.

The auto service arrived within a half hour. The service was professional and friendly, no surprises there, because Joe Colarusso's second son drove the tow truck. Johnnie Colarusso hugged Jane, kissed her cheek, and asked about Gram before hooking up his machinery and coaxing Gram's car back on the road.

"It's drivable," Johnnie said as he handed her the keys. "No problems, it was just too slick. Tell Mrs. M. I said hi. If you got any questions, call me at the station."

Oh, I got questions all right.

Since Johnnie knew Steph from attending school together, he insisted on taking Hayley home. What a story to tell her friends tomorrow. The little girl climbed high in the cab with her book and waved to Jane like a parade princess.

But Jane stayed in Gram's car, rubbing her eyes and rubbing her hands to warm them.

A Gregson's Hardware pickup. It might have been. Jane didn't know the other men who worked there, but she knew Ryan. He was staff, no matter how seldom he engaged with the job. He could have appropriated a truck, but would he stoop to run someone off the road? He'd never been cruel, even as a child or a teen. He'd just been, well, Ryan.

Jane thought about what Paul had said about the second note, that whoever it was had to have been there at the school to slip it in her notebook. Ryan had been there. But he had also been so nice to Hayley. He must have only known Jane was going to Littleton.

Was it a disgruntled employee? But what would they have against Jane—or a child?

Well, Hayley was a *Gregson* child, born to as much privilege Hilltop could offer.

But Greg treated his employees like family. Many had been with him since before Jane came to Hilltop. They were loyal and rightfully so. Greg believed in raises, bonuses, and promotion from within. He'd even offered to let Fred Parker stay on after the tree lot closed. Greg gave his staff more than he got.

She should tell Gram. She wanted Gram walking through this with her.

CHAPTER TWENTY-THREE

Saturday morning. As she pulled warmed muffins from Gram's microwave, Jane tried to remember what Saturdays were like back at the townhouse. Cleaning in the morning, plays or concerts or museums in the afternoon with her work friends, roommates, or an occasional date. Weekends were a time of fun after the necessary chores and errands, and she'd made the most of them.

But they hadn't included coffee with Gram.

Since her nightmares came back, Jane had formed the habit of waking early. It wasn't much of a habit—high school teachers got up at dawn anyway, and so, apparently, did retired elementary teachers. She and Gram met in the kitchen, with one doing coffee, the other pastry. In the hush before the cold sunrise, they worked through their day.

Here came Gram, thumping along in the walker, more confident every day. What good would it do her if she went to prison? Jane couldn't think that far ahead. There was too much to dread right in front of her.

Gram poured the coffee into her thick white "morning" mugs. "Morning, honey." She dropped into a chair. "What's your plan for today? Hilltop stuff?"

"Not till evening." Jane stirred in sugar and real cream from Charlie's farm. "I've got the ski lodge dinner. Don't want to go, but ... Hey, Gram, couldn't you do it? Or at least come with me? You're pretty good with the walker."

Gram broke off a piece of the French Hens' pumpkin muffin. "Someone needs to stay with Carly. And I love the dinner, but Janie, this is your festival. You did all the work."

Was Gram afraid to be seen in public? No, she was in town every time she could get a willing driver. Shopping, book club, coffee with friends. Gram kept her head high, and Jane could do the same. But it was hard with the media involved now, and the ripples from the Littleton trip. Who knew what, and when?

News of Gram's arrest had already spread in the state newspaper, garnering more distrust from casual passersby. Jane could feel the stares when she went out in town.

As soon as Jane had made it back to her home safely and knew that Hayley was home, she called in the incident to Paul, and Steph had called Jane. Jane told her about the truck but warned them not to say anything to anyone but Paul. A little later that night, Paul had come to each of their houses to take their statements. He told Jane he would have gone to the scene of the crime if the snow hadn't covered up the tire tracks. He had offered to station an officer outside the house, but Jane settled on having one drive by on the hour to watch out for any suspicious activity and that truck.

When he had left, Gram had hugged Jane, saying how glad she was Jane and Hayley were all right. God's protective hand. Maybe. They both agreed to keep this news from Carly. Less for her to worry about.

But it seemed Jane had an infinite number of things to worry about.

It was all becoming too much and not enough. Paul and the police department were looking into the notes, conducting interviews with everyone who was there at the school sewing costumes, and looking into who in this town drove the type of truck that tried to drive her off the road.

She couldn't do much, but she could lend a shoulder to Gram. "Why don't you get out today? Call Laura or Helen and finish your Christmas shopping. I'll stay with Carly."

Carly would sleep all day, or most of it, Jane knew. And Jane could do paperwork at the dining room table—and psych herself up for the ski lodge dinner.

After Gram came back from shopping, Jane had a quick bowl of canned soup, just enough to hold her until the ski lodge dinner and went upstairs to page through the closet in her old room. She wouldn't wear the burgundy sheath again, not with the way Noah had looked at her. There, a cobalt blue cashmere sweater and a mid-calf-length tweed skirt, both left over from college. That would do for a not-a-date she hadn't wanted to go on in the first place.

She did her makeup in the downstairs bathroom while Carly leaned against the door jamb. She was looking better today, after a day of resting. She'd even mentioned going to the Christmas Eve service.

"I've got a necklace that would look really nice with that sweater," she said.

"I'm good. Thanks." Jane's hands shook as she applied her mascara.

"You need a little something with that neckline ..."

Jane's hand shook more, and the mascara swooped onto her eyelid. "I'm fine."

But Carly wasn't one for taking hints and only looked Jane up and down. "This is kind of fun. Wish I'd been around when you were getting ready for proms and such."

The tension bubbled up inside Jane, the tension that had been her companion ever since her mother had arrived. *Play nice. You told Gram you'd play nice.*

"Wasn't my fault you weren't." She repaired the mascara glitch, avoiding Carly's eyes in the mirror.

Carly looked down. "Are you ever going to let me forget that?"

Jane stroked on lip gloss and snapped the tube shut. "I forgot it for eighteen years."

She heard footsteps on the steps and went to switch the porch light on. Peering through the side panels, she saw him. Noah Hastings, unguarded for once, with hope and worry on his face, in those incredible crystal-blue eyes. He looked nervous about their not-a-date. Well, so was she.

He looked so handsome in a dark suit, only helping his eyes stand out against the night. But there was a troubled look in those blue eyes.

She could plead a headache, run upstairs, be done with this, at least for tonight.

No, this was her job. Gram wasn't afraid of the newspapers, the TV, the gossip. Jane had her blood and would hold her head high tonight.

As soon as she opened the door, she knew Noah could tell right away something troubled her.

He took her arm, his touch warming her through the thickness of her sweater. "What's the matter, Jane?"

"Nothing, of course. I'm good." She gave him her most brilliant smile.

Noah smiled back but looked far from convinced. "You sure? Hey, can I say hello to Alice? And your mom?"

Anything but that. Jane couldn't be in a room with the three of them. Gram would read her, know how she felt about this man. And what would her mother say?

She plunged out the door, her coat unbuttoned, only one hand gloved. "We'll be late."

Noah knew something wasn't right and hadn't been since Jane's mother came back to Hilltop. Jane crackled with tension. Should he face the issue, find out what was bothering her? No. He wasn't her boyfriend, and he surely wasn't her pastor. He had no right. Plus, he had been pushy before and didn't want this beautiful night to be spoiled by his big mouth. Again. If he were leaving Hilltop soon, he wanted to enjoy every moment of this night with Jane Archer.

Noah smiled. "Of course. Don't want to be late."

Jane smiled back, though without warmth or humor. "Thank you."

But as soon as they were at his car by the curb, and Jane was opening her own door in the best not-a-date fashion, the front door of Alice's house swung open.

Alice stood as a tiny figure braced inside a walker, silhouetted in a rectangle of yellow light. "Jane Archer. Please come back in this house this instant."

Jane turned, one still ungloved hand on the door handle. "Gram, the dinner's at six-thirty."

"You never talked to me in that tone, and you won't talk to your mother that way. We are going to settle this tonight."

Noah stared at them. *Alice must have a good reason if she's willing to embarrass Jane like this.*

Jane was a grown woman, and he'd already seen her will in action. She didn't have to obey. But she did. Alice's will trumped whatever this was.

Jane looked up at him, her eyes guarded, her cheeks pale despite the cold. "You'd better go on ahead. You don't want to miss the banquet."

"I can wait in the car. Or go over to the parsonage and come back."

Whatever this was, he'd see it through with her.

But Alice decided for them. "No, Pastor, you come back inside too. This may be more than I can handle."

Did she think *he* could handle it? Whatever had happened between Jane and her mother went wide and deep and bitter. They needed a psychiatrist. Or a miracle. But tonight, they had him. A green-as-grass, reformed party boy from California, only a pastor by the grace of God.

He took Jane's arm and guided her back up the sidewalk, their boots crunching on the packed snow. At the top step, she pulled away and went on alone. She looked back once, her green eyes dark and despairing.

Noah bowed his head. *Father, I don't know what I'm doing. I never have. I am nothing without your guidance, especially where Jane's concerned. Help me tonight.*

He drew a deep breath, squared his shoulders, and stepped inside, clicking the door shut behind him.

Carly huddled under a quilt in the wing chair by the fire. Her earlier energy appeared to be spent. She always seemed to be cold, and she coughed more than usual. Her oxygen tank stood at the ready, the two slim tubes at her nose, so familiar now she barely noticed.

But Jane's gaze went automatically to Gram, sitting upright in Gramps' old leather recliner and looking at Jane with a mixture of compassion and sternness.

Gram nodded toward the sofa. "Sit down, Jane."

Noah leaned against a door jamb, his overcoat open, one of his long legs looped over the other at the ankle. He looked relaxed, but when his gaze connected with hers, she saw alertness in those blue eyes.

Jane loved him.

And she didn't want him to hear this.

"I don't see why—" Gram began.

Carly chimed in. "Mom, is this really necessary?"

At least we agree on that.

"It is. I want to know what went wrong between the two of you. What's still wrong."

The fire crackled, and Jane saw her mother strain toward its warmth.

"Janie, I care about you. I want to have a relationship, at least in the time I got left." Carly's voice sounded hushed and hesitant, all the brass gone forever.

"It's too late. There's nothing to have a relationship with."

"I had to send you away." Carly stared into the leaping flames. "It was best for everyone. I knew you'd have a better life with my mother."

"It *was* better. Gram and I did just fine." Oh, *why* did Noah have to hear this? "You did the right thing. Is that what you wanted to hear, *Mom*?"

"I know you did fine." Bitterness tinged Carly's voice. "I kept up with the paper online at the library, whatever town I was stuck in. Every award, every honor. All the honor rolls, all the Girl Scout badges, all the awards you won before you were even out of fifth grade. You think I could've given you that?"

"You could have tried."

"Janie, I was a high-school dropout. With a kid." Carly spread her arms in a gesture of appeal. "I was a kid myself."

Jane was on her feet, the white-hot anger now surging through her. "Don't use that as an excuse. I could have lived with eating mac and cheese. I could have lived with the motel rooms and the moving around. As long as we were together. But even a kid knows better than to put me through what you put me through."

From the corner of her eye, Jane saw Gram sit up even straighter.

Carly grew even paler. "I don't know—I'm not sure what you mean—"

Carly had told her last lie. And for Jane, there was no turning back.

"I'm talking about Larry, *Mom*."

Who was Larry? Noah's gaze bounced from one woman to another. His hands clasped in prayer, the tension reminding him too much of how his father and mother used to argue. His glance rested on Jane's mother, the gaunt woman who coughed a lot and made herself scarce whenever he visited Alice. The woman who had gone deep inside herself at the name of "Larry."

Alice looked between her daughter and granddaughter. "Who's Larry?"

"I broke up with him before I even sent you here. Larry is nothing to me."

Don't, Jane. He couldn't bear it. Whatever this Larry was—

"Larry was nothing to me either, just another one of your boyfriends. But he liked *me*, Mom. A little too much, if you know what I mean."

Noah's heart sank. He wanted to scoop her up, take her away from here. No child should have to bear that. No one. He looked at Alice. Her face was frozen in a mask, but she nodded to him that she was all right, would be all right.

Jane's voice peaked in derision. "What did you think was happening all those nights you worked graveyard? Didn't you know him at all? Didn't you care?"

Alice's hands trembled. "What are you both talking about?"

Carly pushed herself up out of her chair and faced her daughter. "I thought I did. He seemed nice. And Janie, I was so lonely."

Alice's face went pale as she sank deeper into the old leather recliner.

Noah had had enough. "Did he—he didn't—"

He would kill this Larry if he ever saw him. For a moment, he imagined choking the pervert or bashing his head against a stone floor. He clasped his hands tighter. No, he wouldn't. But he'd make sure the man was locked up for life. Even a life sentence wouldn't make up for the childhood this Larry had robbed from Jane.

"He didn't penetrate." Although Jane answered Noah's question, her gaze remained locked on her mother. "But he made me touch him, and he touched me. What could I do? I was nine years old." Jane was on her feet now, her arms crossed in a protective stance.

How had she tried to protect herself before? Had she screamed in the night, though no one could hear her? How did she face what she did every day?

Carly spoke in a quiet tone. "You could have told me."

"Would you have believed me?"

Carly shook her head, her short gray curls flying. "That's *why* I broke up with him, Janie. Soon's I figured it out. I wasn't gonna leave you anywhere near him." She warmed her hands at the fire and turned back to Jane. "The night

I came home early from the Quick Stop. I had the stomach flu. Came upstairs and saw Larry leaving your room—and zipping his jeans. I'm not stupid, Janie. We moved out the next day. Spent two nights in the homeless shelter, but it was worth it."

"I remember." Jane's voice felt like it came from far away. "I thought we left quickly, even for us."

Carly nodded. "The thing with Larry scared me to the bone. I wanted to make things better for you, fix it so nobody messed with you again. That's why I sent you to my mother. To Hilltop, the safest place in the world. I figured as soon as I got on my feet, made something of myself, I'd send for you."

"Well, you didn't." Jane's eyes filled with tears.

Eighteen years of bitterness, rejection, loneliness, and confusion all released at once. Why didn't Jane feel better?

"No, I didn't." Carly looked down at the polished oak floor.

"And this whole time you knew, and you didn't tell me it wasn't my fault. Why didn't you get me the help I needed to heal? Why didn't you report him?"

"I got you the best help. You thrived in Hilltop. How could I compete with that?"

"It's not about stuff! I just wanted my mom." Jane wiped away tears. "I guess we'll never know. You could at least have visited. Gram had no idea how to find you."

"I didn't try." Gram's voice spoke, as strong as ever.

All three swiveled toward her.

"I didn't try," Gram repeated. "I knew how to use the internet, even back then. If I'd wanted to find Carly, I imagine I could have."

Jane went numb. What was Gram saying? It didn't make any sense. Gram wouldn't do such a thing. Right?

Carly's head snapped to face Gram. "Then why didn't you?"

Gram looked down at her knotted hands. "Because I was selfish. I didn't want to give Jane up. You were my second chance, Janie. A girl who was more like me, who loved studying and learning, working hard, making a difference."

"No." Jane and Carly, blurting their objections at the same time.

"Yes. With Jane, I felt like I could make up for the ways I failed you, Carly. And the ways you failed me. I blame myself for keeping you away. But I thought God was giving me a second chance, Janie."

Tears welled up in Jane's eyes. *How could you?*

Gram only nodded. "It's no excuse for depriving you of a mother. *Your* mother."

Gram looked her daughter in the eyes. "I'm sorry if Walter and I ever made you feel unworthy, Carly. We know how much you struggled in school, and when you and Jimmy split up, we just wanted to be there for you, not judge you. I love you, Carly." Tears streamed down her face, and she turned to Jane. "I'm sorry if I ever took out my frustrations about Carly on you, Jane. I just wanted to do better this time."

Jane cried, remembering all the moments Gram had been there for her, supported her. "I didn't mind that it was you." She crossed the room swiftly and knelt, leaning against Gram's knee. "I loved living here. I had *everything.*"

Gram stroked her hair. "And so did I. But it wasn't right. And I'm sorry for not telling you the truth, Janie." She turned to Carly. "I know how well rumors can spread here, so I'm glad you didn't tell me about Larry for Jane's sake. It doesn't matter what anyone thinks, but I'm glad you didn't grow up with everyone thinking ill of you, Janie."

Carly took Jane's hand. "I'm sorry for making it seem as if I didn't care, Janie. All that time, I missed you like crazy. But what we did wasn't right." No. It hadn't been. Except that it had been so right. "But you did do well," she added, desperation threading her thin voice. "Didn't you? You did so well. Still are."

Jane looked away. "I did because I was determined never to lose control again."

CHAPTER TWENTY-FOUR

Noah had always been good at putting puzzles together, a skill which had helped him in his engineering studies. The puzzle of Jane Archer became clearer as his gaze bounced between the three desperate women.

"That's why you were so upset about the Parker kids." he said.

Jane didn't meet his gaze. "Any kind of child abuse upsets me."

"That's why you won't come back to Hilltop." He licked his lips, staring at the defiant Jane with her walls down at last. "That's why you can't accept unconditional love."

Jane shrugged. "Even without everyone knowing, I still felt dirty all those years."

"Oh, Janie, you were just a child. You did nothing wrong." The words burst from Alice as she grasped Jane's face in her hands. "And this Larry was a monster."

Jane pulled Gram's hands off her face and held them in her own. "Still."

Noah reached back to the memory of his too-short class on pastoral counseling in difficult situations. "Larry was a pervert. It had nothing to do with you. It wasn't your fault, Jane."

She turned a ravaged face to him. "*Reverend* Hastings, do you know what it's like to not be good enough? To go through life knowing there's something wrong with you? To never measure up?"

His heart pounded. He did.

"That's why I had to be the best at everything." Jane said. "Not to please Gram, not to get scholarships. To protect myself. So people wouldn't know what was inside. That's why I can never move back to Hilltop."

What walls had Noah built around himself? Used his charm, his easy ways, especially with women, to get what he wanted. But Jane at least had substance, under the safeguards she'd built for herself.

Was there any substance to Noah Hastings?

He crossed the room, took Jane by the shoulders, looked down into those tear-filled green eyes as his hands trembled. "I know what it's like to be not good enough, Jane. My father told me I was stupid whenever I did something to disappoint him. In elementary school, that was about once a day. By high school, I'd given up trying to please him, and he'd almost given up asking. And my mother, she didn't think our family was good enough for her, or that I was enough for her to stay."

Alice and Carly stared at him, open-mouthed. He didn't care. Nothing mattered but Jane. His sweet Jane. Someone who he could and would lay down his life for.

That's the kind of love God had for him and Jane.

"Jane, who you see now is the changed Noah, the redeemed Noah. Because I accepted God's offer for a new life. Do you honestly think I deserve anything? I told you I dropped out for a whole year. I built surfboards and drank. It's a wonder I didn't saw my arm off. It was dark, Jane—the darkest year of my life. And I couldn't make myself better.

I couldn't make myself good enough. None of us can. But God was waiting at the end of that year."

Jane looked away. "I'm not good enough for your God."

"Neither am I. Neither is Alice." He shot a glance at the older woman and received a sober nod of confirmation. "And neither are the people of Hilltop. We all need God." He fought back tears. "Jesus was broken, bloodied, and bruised on the cross. That is what we all deserve—to be punished and die for our sins. But Jesus took on that punishment and shame for us. Because of His amazing love. Jesus alone can wash you clean, Jane."

Three women, all needing whatever he could give. One broken in body, one broken in spirit, one strong in the Lord but flawed.

One whom he loved more than life itself, second only to his Lord.

He'd led frat brothers, homeless people, Venice Beach strippers to Jesus. But nobody had ever mattered as much as this. Jane, trembling like a candle flame, and just as vulnerable. What if—

Noah stopped the negative thought. Time to take his own advice. He was a minister of the gospel. A pastor sent here by God to minister to Jane and her family for such a time as this.

"Jane, did you know that ever since I got here, I've felt unworthy?" He watched her shake her head. "Well, I have. I was so new to all of this, and let's just say, not everyone here has made me feel welcome. Every time I turned around, I was terrified of making another mistake. Afraid they'd make me leave, and I have nowhere else to go. I wondered if anyone would miss me. I was actually planning on leaving after the winter season, to go back to my dad and beg for a job."

Alice caught his gaze, a look in her eyes asking for him not to leave.

Jane grabbed his hand. "You can't go. Whether most of them know it or not, your people need you. Gram needs you. Mom will need you, and I ... need you, so you can't leave."

Was this the gauntlet she had to run to enter the Kingdom? Abuse by a monster, in a childhood already bleak. If only he could take her shame upon him. He could handle it, if it were for Jane.

But somebody else had already done it.

Noah knelt beside the shaking woman, his hands still on her shoulders. "Jane. Jane, look at me."

She twisted her head. "You can't fix it, Noah."

That's right, God. It was never about me. It's always been about you.

"I know." Oh, how he knew. "I'm just the messenger. Jane, do you know how much Jesus loves you?" Before she could answer, he said, "Jesus's heart broke for you when Larry was abusing you. His heart breaks for any child in that situation. His heart broke when your mother put you on that bus." He cut a glance at Carly, who gave him a grim, tired nod.

"God could have stopped Larry, but he didn't. We all have free will, Jane. Larry made the wrong choices, big time. So did your mom. So did Alice. But God didn't. Although this was meant for evil, God meant it for good. He was betting you'd take all the broken pieces and become a strong, smart, giving person."

"I'm not strong." Jane hiccupped on a sob.

"You did well." Noah's heart hammered. "But there are cracks in the foundation. It's gonna fail you, Jane. I was never good enough for my earthly father, but my heavenly

Father loves all of me. He sees what I *can* be. He sees what you can be—in him."

Noah sneaked a glance at the two older women. Alice's head was bent, her lips moving, but Carly stared at him, her eyes wide in her thin face.

Jane, at the end of her endurance. "I can't," she rasped. "I can't lose control."

"Janie, honey." Alice's voice, laced with tenderness. "You've already lost it. You can't control what happened to your mother. You can't control what's happening to me. The wolf is at the door, Jane. And you need the shepherd."

The room was too small and too warm. Jane broke from them all, darting out to the front porch where she stood shivering in her sweater. She locked her arms across her chest, but the cold went right through her. It was only what she deserved.

Forgive Mom and Gram? It would be easier than forgiving herself.

"Dirty girl," one of Larry's pet epithets for her, the only one she could bear to repeat. The "endearment" he had murmured as he abused her. Well, wasn't she? The little girl her mother hadn't wanted, the little girl nobody really wanted except for a grandmother in a place called Hilltop, which became more of a dream with every passing year.

How could she ever be good enough for God? Could he really make her clean?

Paul was. Paul was perfect. No, he wasn't. How did she know what kind of a heart beat under his crisp blue uniform? How did she know what he felt as he faced each day without his beloved Sarah, with Emma and Maddy to mold and guide?

Gram was. No, she wasn't, Gram had kept Carly from Jane, for Jane's sake—and for her own.

Stephanie hadn't been. But God had reached down and touched this troubled, promiscuous young woman and changed her into someone as beautiful on the inside as the outside.

Noah wasn't. But his God had made something out of him anyway. Used him with the Parkers at a dark time of their lives and Mark near the end of his. Used Noah to stand by Jane and Gram. Made him what he couldn't have made himself.

"Janie. Come inside." Gram's voice came compelling yet gentle.

Jane looked out over the snowy lawn, the snowy lawns of their neighbors. She was crumbling, her white porcelain shell breaking apart, revealing a coiled mass of rotting garbage.

But was it really the same for everyone else? Sure, most of them didn't have a Larry in their past, but they had enough. Stephanie, struggling with the reality of being second-best to Ryan. Noah, never able to meet the demands of his earthly father and a mother who left him and his family.

If she had a son like Noah, she'd love him. Never let him feel inferior.

But somebody already did. Somebody who loved his big blundering body, his even bigger heart. For who he was and what he could be.

That's what fathers did.

Jane hugged her arms around herself. A light breeze stirred the bare branches of the woods around Gram's house while the pines and bushes cast blue shadows across the snow.

Am I really worth something to you, God?

Carly's voice, slightly exasperated, came through the sliver of the door she'd left ajar. "Janie. Would you get in here, please? You'll catch your death of cold."

That was what mothers did. Jane went back to the house and knelt again beside her grandmother. But her gaze fixed on the broken woman on the couch. "Mom, I'm sorry. If I'd known—"

"No." Carly's voice was strong despite the rasp. "I'm sorry, Janie. Sorry for everything. I thought I was doing the right thing."

"We all did." Although Gram looked played-out, her voice was still strong. "I should have tried harder to find your mother. It was selfish of me. I should have taken you both in, cared for you both. If I'd tried harder, there wouldn't have been a Larry."

"I forgive you." The words tumbled from Jane's lips. "Because if there was no Larry, we wouldn't be here now."

Jane clung to Gram and Carly, her mother, so tired of holding everything together. What would it be like to lay this burden down? To have someone else pick it up for her?

Noah mumbled to himself, relentless, like he'd never have another chance. Was this how he preached? She looked up through her tumbled hair to Noah's kind face, devoid of all teasing and playfulness. Beyond a friend, beyond a possible boyfriend or a soulmate. This was bigger than they were.

What would this cost her?

Not as much as it had cost God.

The anniversary clock ticked, the grandfather clock in the hallway bonged. The only other sound was the sound of four people breathing.

Pulling away from Gram and Mom, Jane put her hands in Noah's big ones. Oh, he was trembling too.

"I've forgotten how this goes."

"I haven't." Noah's face was sober, but a light danced in his blue eyes. "Jane Archer, do you believe all have sinned and fall short of the glory of God? Even you?"

"Yes."

"Do you believe Jesus Christ came to earth to take the punishment for those sins?"

"Yes."

"Do you accept him and his sacrifice and welcome him into your life?"

"Yes. Oh, yes." Tears streamed down her face again.

Noah prayed for her, his words rich with victory. She was supposed to close her eyes. She didn't. She looked up, past Noah, past this precious home where love had thrived, to a love that lasted beyond the grave.

Jane got up, moved past him, and put her arms around Gram, absorbing the older woman's strength, passing hers to Gram. Cleansed of her bitterness. Jane had never imagined feeling this light. She moved toward her mother and bent down, hugging Carly for the first time since her mother had come home, feeling the cleansing of forgiveness.

Carly only fixed her eyes like beacons at Noah. "Can I do that?"

Noah talked quietly with Carly, pointing out things in the Scriptures, Carly's face eager as she leaned forward from her nest of pillows. Gram maneuvered her walker to the window and Jane joined her, looking out at the snowy drifts and the sparkling lights.

They stood there for a moment, just being.

"Will you get counseling?" Gram asked at last.

"Probably." Jane gave a small smile. "But let's see what God does in the meantime."

"How do you feel?"

Jane considered that. "Free," she said at last.

The real work lay ahead of her. Healing, rebuilding the world that had fallen apart tonight. Being there for Gram, whose problems were only beginning. Being there for Mom. And Noah would be there for her.

"How did you ever do it?" Gram asked at last.

"I don't know, Gram. I don't know."

Eighteen years of running, even when she stood in place. Eighteen years of keeping herself distant even from her real friends. Eighteen years of shame. Eighteen years of shame taken away, all because of Jesus. He who did what her grades could not do, her achievements, her efforts. Her running in place. Perhaps God had been there for her all along.

"Everything will change now," she said.

"But it will be good change. The best change," Gram said firmly.

"Even if—" Jane couldn't voice it. Yet.

"Even if. And even when."

CHAPTER TWENTY-FIVE

Jane capped her lip gloss and turned her face from side to side. Good enough, after a half hour of fussing. Nobody would be looking at her anyway. They'd be scooping up all the fun the first night of the festival had to offer. She shouldn't care so much.

But she did. The incredible changes from that night one week ago had opened her world in ways she couldn't have imagined.

Everything was possible now, starting with a God who did love her. She wasn't alone anymore, and that gave her a new ease with the people who had loved her all along.

She and Noah had been careful around each other since that night when she and her mother opened their lives to God and his possibilities for them. Even during their last festival meeting yesterday, everything in order. Noah had turned her discipleship over to a woman from the Hilltop Church. Jane even said she'd join a Bible study with Steph and Sammi Morton.

Did Noah's avoidance due to a conflict of interest mean there was still interest on his part?

There was on hers, might as well admit it. Now that the walls had come down.

She had spent the afternoon checking on the details for the festival. Every venue, every worker was poised and ready to go. She would make her rounds of everything downtown, then take in the first night of the living nativity.

This will be the best festival ever.

Despite the fact her beloved Gram was under arrest?

Yes. Despite even that. Because Romans 8:28 belonged to Jane now too.

As Gram sat by the fireplace, Jane bent down to kiss her still-smooth cheek. "Do you want me to stay home with you and Mom?"

Gram shook her head. "No, you go. You're the chairman. You need to be out there. The point of the festival is that it's endured all these years. It's the point of, really, well, everything. We'll get past this."

"We," not "They." Gram would always identify with Hilltop, no matter what Hilltop did to her. From now on, God alone would be her safe place.

"We'll beat this, Ma." Carly looked gaunt and ashen as she lay on the couch. She was having one of her bad days, when she took a whole pain tablet and slept the afternoon away. The four words were the only words she'd said all day.

Jane looked at her mother—her *mother*—and smiled. "'Course we will. You two take care of each other, and I'll be back in a couple of hours."

Jane wanted to walk, wanted to skim down these snow-packed streets with the sheer wonder of being loved by God and having her mother home and reconciled. But she settled herself in Gram's car instead.

Jane breathed a little prayer as she drove toward Main Street. *Lord, please be with my mom. Thank you for bringing her back to us and for bringing us together again as a family.*

Thank you that we're part of your *family. Please help her through—through what's to come. Help her to die well. And please, Lord, help Gram to beat this charge.*

There were still people who pulled away from them, crossed the street to avoid them. Maybe there always would be. But Gram was right. Hilltop, the town, and the festival would survive. The truth would come out.

Lord, may justice be done.

White and colored lights gleamed from every set of eaves, trees sparkling from every parlor window. The fading afternoon felt crisp, with a peach-colored sunset just beginning to show behind Charlie's woods. It would be cold tonight. Had Noah remembered his gloves? Her cheeks warmed at the thought of him, so big but so gentle, and the way he looked at her. Would he kiss her again?

He'd asked her if she were going tonight, asked in an offhand way that didn't reveal any of his feelings. If he still had any after what they'd both spilled out.

She circled the town common three times, looking for a parking space. That's when she saw him, his golden head bare to the night air. He stood bent over, helping a small boy stir his hot chocolate. But his eyes darted around the common and darted around Main Street. Was he looking for her?

Only one way to find out.

Jane's feet had wings as she skimmed over the icy pathway. Noah's head jerked up. He patted the boy's shoulder and came toward her, his face holding all the light in the world, and she knew.

As if she hadn't before.

He tucked her under one of his big arms. "Hey, you made it."

"I'm the chairman, remember? And you're the sponsoring pastor. We have to be here."

"Might as well go together." He smiled down at her. "Where do we go first, Madame Chairman?"

So, it was this easy.

"Let's check out the nativities," she said.

As they approached the many intricate sets of nativities, they saw Bev, completely in her element, explaining the scenes and their provenance to families and couples.

Jane drew Noah toward the little olivewood set. "Bev says that will be mine—when I marry."

He nodded. "Good taste. So, Jane. How're your mom and Alice?"

"Mom's having a bad day. Gram won't leave her. But everything at home is more ... peaceful."

"That's good." Noah smiled. "Any ideas on who stole Alice's charm?"

She could trust this man. She didn't have to do this alone. Or anything else.

Jane looked around. Walls had ears, especially in the old library. "Let's walk."

They strolled Main Street, waving to friends and acquaintances.

Jane leaned closer to Noah. "We don't know who, but I've been getting notes."

Noah dodged a red-cheeked little boy chasing another red-cheeked little boy. The Parkers, being kids for once, their parents strolling hand-in-hand behind them. "Like, threatening notes? Have you shown them to Paul?"

"Yes. They're typed." Jane shrugged as they stepped back on the sidewalk. "That's not all. A few days ago, someone tried to run us off the road."

Noah stopped short, letting the crowd part around him. "Run off the *road*?"

"During that freak snowstorm. I wouldn't have cared, but I had Hayley with me. We were coming back from

Littleton. I thought it was the snow, but really, Noah, I know how to drive in this stuff. The truck came straight at us. And—and it looked like a Gregson's pickup."

Noah's eyes widened. "No way."

"And who uses a typewriter anymore?"

Then came an all-too-familiar voice. "Yo, Jane!"

Sure enough, Ryan came jogging up to them. Ryan, in faded concert T-shirt, ripped jeans, and a leather bomber jacket. Well, he wasn't pretending to be a hardware store owner today.

"Hey, Pastor. Well, this festival sure looks like something. Maybe the biggest yet." Ryan looked from Noah back to Jane. "Hey, how's it going?"

Jane might have a renewed sense of peace, but that didn't change the fact she still had a dying mother and a grandmother facing criminal charges. But Ryan was Ryan. "I'm all right. What's new with you?"

Ryan grinned down at her. "Janie, I'm out of here! Come January, I'm taking a break, going down to Nashville for the winter. I'm going to cut a few demos, see what they have to say about me." He showed them his social media page on his phone. "Look how many followers I have now. They're so excited to see me in Nashville."

She could imagine what *Greg* had to say.

"I didn't know you could play country," she said.

Ryan bit his lip. "My followers say I got the voice for it, so I'm willing to try."

"That's wonderful, Ryan." Noah shook his hand. "I know you've worked hard."

Ryan beamed.

"Is the band going with you?" Jane asked.

"Naw." Ryan allowed the briefest of frowns to mar his perfect features. "I don't want them holding me back. I'll get a new band in Nashville."

Jane tilted her head. "What about the store?"

"I have a really good assistant manager. I'll let her handle it for a couple months." Ryan sighed, making a face she didn't know Ryan Gregson was capable of making. "I think it's time I move on, ya know? See a big city, like you did. I'll miss Hayley and Steph the most, though."

Jane smiled back. Well, if Jane Archer could find God, perhaps Ryan Gregson could grow up.

"Are you driving down on your motorcycle?" Noah said.

Ryan shook his head. "Dad's gonna let me trade it in for one of his trucks for now. Gotta have somewhere to put my stuff."

Noah shook Ryan's hand again. "Then God bless you on your journey, Ryan. Feel free to keep in touch."

The way Noah said that made Jane believe he really meant it, and she admired him for it.

Ryan smiled his big smile. "Hey, thanks. Well, gotta get going. You know my band is going to play in the parade? See ya later." He still had places to go and other people to impress. He gave them a mock salute and met up with his bandmates.

Something nagged at Jane. *How could he afford this? His band couldn't be making that much money. He always did have a way of making things work, as long as they worked for him.*

Jane and Noah faced each other and spoke at the same time.

"You don't think—"

"Could Ryan have—"

But of course, he could have. Ryan, the boy who had raided the store cash register, and sometimes his mother's purse, when his generous allowance still wasn't enough. If he could find his way to get liquor in the prom, he could certainly get the combination to the safe-deposit box. He had the motives, means, and opportunity.

"As much as anybody." Jane looked up at Noah. "He was there at the school when I got the second note. He has access to the trucks and access to the Smith-Corona. He needs money, and Greg won't give it to him."

"But why approach us? Why practically confess?" She recalled the sober look in his eyes. Was it shame?

Noah crossed his arms. "Could he just not resist telling us his big plans? I mean, he went through the trouble of typing those secret threats and resorted to trying to run you off the road. Something doesn't fit."

Jane nodded. "And why go after Gram? She's always been nice to him. And why hurt me? I just asked some questions but didn't get anywhere. Why would he risk following me in that snowstorm when he could have gotten himself injured before his big break?"

"Did he know Hayley was with you?"

Jane shook her head. "No one did. But Johnnie Colarusso has a record of the accident, and Hayley was a witness."

Noah nodded. "We need to be smart about this. Tell Paul as soon as we can."

She loved the idea of a "we." She nodded.

"I'll go with you." He squeezed her hand with his own, gloved for once. "And I'll pray about it. We'll pray about it. For now, just text Paul to keep an eye out."

Jane smiled back and agreed to text Paul about Ryan. She also texted Gram.

She would pray too. That God's will would be done. Well, it had been done so far in this strangest of all Decembers.

They broke away from the crowd to enter the town hall, where children made paper chains and snowflakes under the careful supervision of adult volunteers. Shimmery gold garlands decorated the meeting room, and the adults bent over the youngest children, guiding their scissors. With no notebook to lug around this time, Jane mentally checked off "children's crafts."

They looked in at the children's cookie decorating and the Cookie Walk. Noah filled a bag for Jane, with a warning, "We're going to eat these together." He filled another for Gram and Carly. She had to drag him away from the platters of treats.

They stopped to watch one act at the coffee house and one on the mainstage at the sanctuary. She was very aware of Noah's hand at her back, Noah's deep chuckle, Noah's amazement at his first Hilltop Christmas.

But she was aware of something else, of someone's awareness of her. Was she being watched? Was she being followed? Was it Ryan? She turned once at the Masonic Temple to see a figure disappear behind the kitchen door. Was it a worker?

Should she be afraid? Tomorrow, maybe. Not tonight. She had worked too hard on the festival, waited too long to be this free to miss any of the beautiful snowy night.

They strolled around the common, admiring the good and not-so-good efforts of the skaters. They watched eager families pile into Charlie's hay wagon. Two couples claimed seats in the smaller sleigh, and Jane felt a warm blush on her cold cheeks. That wonderful sleigh ride when—

Noah bent to kiss her, right there on the common, under townspeople's and tourists' amused eyes.

There went all her doubts about his interests.

"I think we need another sleigh ride to fully enjoy the festival. What do you think, Madame Chairman?"

Jane smiled. "After the living nativity."

They hadn't had much chance to talk since the night of Jane's and Carly's conversions. Not even at their last festival meeting the day before. When they did speak, it had been in public and casual, Hilltop business. But a new kind of grace undergirded these conversations. Did she feel it too? Could she feel it in his kiss?

Noah knew something had changed. In helping three women through the darkest night of their souls, he'd found his own again.

Before he had left their house that night, Alice, sweet Alice, had taken his hand, looked into his eyes, and told him to call his family. If it wasn't too late for them, it wasn't too late for him. With God, it would never be too late.

The time away from Jane had given him clarity, clarity on what to say and how to say it. After all, he wasn't moving any more, that was for sure. Especially when Jane and her family would need him and his spiritual guidance—when Jane would start going to therapy, when Gram's trial came, when Carly's time came.

Noah might be as far from perfect as the sheep in his flock. But he knew the head shepherd.

It was enough. Whatever happened here, with Jane, with the festival, with his Hilltop pastorate, with his family, he wasn't the same Noah who had arrived here in October.

He smiled, nodded, and engaged in small talk with his parishioners. His people, at last. Despite all the craziness, Noah found himself falling in love with Hilltop more and more. And with Jane Archer most of all.

As they entered the noisy barn, he shoved away all thoughts of Ryan and the theft. He looked down into that perfect face, now shining with the light of Christ. "I'm glad we're here. Together."

"Me too." She moved a little closer. "I couldn't miss this."

Nice to be standing next to Noah in the unheated barn, their breaths coming out in white clouds, talking about nothing that was suddenly everything. She didn't know where this would go, couldn't even imagine. She couldn't even believe he had kissed her again. But they would have one perfect Christmas, here at Hilltop.

"Were you ever in the living nativity?" Noah murmured in her ear, his husky voice making her shiver.

"I played Mary one year in high school. J.P. Beaulieu was Joseph that year, but he had his iPod on under his headdress."

Noah laughed, a beautiful sound. "Well, I bet you were great."

The playgoers crowded into the wide central aisle of the barn. Three large stalls had been cleaned out and lighting set up to portray the segments of the Christmas story. The crowd parted as Mary and Joseph came into the barn. Mary rode in on the back of a live donkey with Joseph leading her to the biggest stall where they were met by an innkeeper who said they could use the stable. Joseph settled Mary on the hay. The lights dimmed, and when they came back on again, Mary was sitting up and holding a baby doll.

The high-school girl playing Mary looked down at her infant with joy and wonder, but also with the weight of what would come, the sorrow that came with being chosen to bear God's Son. Joseph, a teenage boy, looked down at her with protective tenderness.

The air in the barn chilled Jane despite her thick coat, so she moved closer to Noah who put an arm around her shoulders. How easy, how natural. She burrowed into him, and he planted a kiss on the crown of her head.

She breathed a sigh of fulfillment. *Lord, thank you for bringing this about. Thank you I don't have to go through another Christmas without you. Please be with Noah and me.*

The spotlight shifted to the second vignette, an adjacent stall where a tarp had been hung to simulate the night sky with white twinkling lights for stars. Men in rough robes mingled with real sheep. A light shone on the tarp, and the angels appeared as the men dropped back in wonder.

But Jane's gaze stayed on the stable scene, temporarily darkened, looking at Mary. *Mary.* Who had answered her Lord's call, no matter what it was going to mean. And who looked at that baby boy both as the hope of the ages and her own dear son. Mary, whose world, for this one night, centered around one little boy.

Jane's cell phone buzzed from her pocket, and she checked it to see a missed call from Gram. She threw Noah an apologetic look. "Gram tried to call. Must be important."

Stepping aside, she watched Hilltoppers and visitors enjoy the festival and checked for Ryan, but he and his band must have left to get ready for their performance.

She took off one glove and started to reply when a hard object jammed into her back, and a strong arm wrenched hers backward.

"You'll see her soon enough." said a rough voice. "Get in the car."

CHAPTER TWENTY-SIX

Noah watched as the rest of story of salvation played out before him by teens from the youth groups of his church and St. Dominic's. When love came down in the form of a newborn, who would share his people's joys and sorrows and temptations. Who was why Noah did what he did. He watched the visit from the shepherds, the visit of the three kings, and a blustering blowhard of a Herod whom they avoided on their way home. Herod, a St. Dominic's boy, delighted the crowd with his sneers and strutting.

But the space beside him remained empty.

Where was Jane? She should have at least come in to say goodbye. This wasn't like her. Was there some kind of crisis with the festival they had so meticulously planned? Was something wrong with Alice or her mother?

Noah nodded and smiled at all the right places and applauded heartily when it was done. He greeted his members and friends from the community and engaged in some small talk, encouraging the parents of the kids on stage. He met students who were home from college and retirees who flew back from Florida just for this. He checked their faces, but they all seemed genuinely happy to have him there.

As soon as he stepped outside, he found a glove on the ground, Jane's glove. *Where are you, Jane?*

Taking her glove, he sprinted to his car. Groups of people streamed from Charlie's barn, filing up the road to their own vehicles. He bit his lip as he tried to avoid them.

This can't be good.

Had she identified the thief—or had they identified her? He paged through the faces of the people he'd just been with. Beverly would still be with her nativities in the old library. But Greg was here, glad-handing and back-slapping everyone in sight. Charlie was here, in his Santa costume and greeting the guests as if he'd personally written the Christmas story. Bob Desrochers, the final board member, enjoyed the performance with his family.

Where was Anne? Toiling away at another aspect of the festival, sorting cookies for the cookie walk or brewing coffee at the coffee house? Making a last-minute repair to a costume? Why wasn't she here with her husband? If he and Jane were married, he'd want to share the living nativity with *her*.

He wanted to share it now.

Noah inched his way out of Charlie's long driveway, threw himself into his SUV, and bore down on the gas.

Jane stumbled on the back steps of Anne's Mountain Boutique as Anne shoved the gun harder into her back. "Don't try anything, Janie. I don't have a lot of time."

I knew I recognized that typeface. Anne, how could you?

They came out at the top of the narrow stairway, to a storage room filled with boxes. Anne opened a door with her free hand and jerked her head for Jane to go inside. The only light came from a small desk lamp on the jewelry counter. Jane could barely make out the antique armoire, the rack of gowns. Shadows filled the corners, and without the scented candles Anne burned during business hours, her shop smelled stale. Gram sat in her wheelchair and Mom sat bound to a metal folding chair, their pale faces standing out like moonglow.

"Kneel between them. I'm short on chairs." Anne said.

Jane ignored her and rushed to Mom who had her hands bound behind her back with stout rope. Mom, looking at the end of her endurance and no portable oxygen tank in sight. In the unheated shop, her cough racked her tiny frame.

Jane knelt to untie her hands, but stilled when Anne said, "I wouldn't, Janie. Not till we've had a chance to talk."

Gram sat erect in her wheelchair, a parka thrown over her shoulders, her own hands bound in her lap.

How could Anne have managed them both?

The way she'd managed everything else. With her famous will.

Jane squeezed Gram's cold hand and faced Anne. Anne was dressed for winter travel in a thick sweater, wool pants, and hiking boots. She had shrugged off her parka and her knit hat and gloves lay scattered on the floor. Instead of gloves, her hands were encased in bright purple plastic as she pointed a pistol at Jane's family.

"I was just on my way to the festival when I thought I'd stop by and do a little interrogating myself." She looked at Jane. "I knew you wouldn't be home, so I finally had my chance. But they knew next to nothing. Once I saw that text you sent Alice warning her about my Ryan, I had to take things to the next level."

Jane bit her lip. *Noah was right. I should have just texted Paul.*

"This is ridiculous, Anne." Gram said in the tone she had used with her fifth-graders, stern but reasonable. "It's not worth it. Do you really want two lives on your conscience?"

"I wouldn't have them on my conscience if your granddaughter had minded her own business." Anne's voice sounded as if *they* had done something to *her*. "I could have pulled this off."

Jane's voice came out small as she used her body to shield Gram and her mother, "But why?"

Anne shrugged, but kept the pistol trained on the three women. "Ryan, of course. Greg won't give him a dime. He expects him to earn his way in that dreary store, and my Ryan was meant for better things. I want him to go to Nashville and cut a demo. But the store, *my* store, isn't turning a profit. I needed to get some money for Ryan."

She made it sound reasonable, and in her mind, maybe it was.

"Anne, why me? Why did you frame me?" Gram's hands trembled, though she held her voice steady. "We were friends. We worked on Hilltop together. Your kids and Janie grew up together. I've been your long-time customer. We were in the same Bible studies. If you needed help, why not just ask me?"

Anne's shoulders sagged, her voice wavering. "Because I had to pick someone, and I knew you could handle it. You've had a hard life, and you've met every challenge. You would have come out of prison stronger than ever. I believe in you, Alice."

Alice's Victorian was dark, the front door swinging open.

It would be cold when they got back. Noah thought with the part of his brain that clung to normalcy.

If they got back.

Because they weren't at the house.

He shot past Alice's place, took a corner on two wheels, slipped on a patch of ice, and righted the car. Main Street? Too risky, too crowded with all the festival revelers. Lights blazed in front of every business and people moved in packs, ducking into the town hall or one of the libraries. Dickensian carolers on one corner, a line in front of the hot cocoa stand. Red-cheeked people laughing, unaware of what was going on in this sweet little town. No, whoever had them would avoid Main Street.

He drove down a residential street and stopped in front of a brick colonial house. Greg and Anne's place. A home of both elegance and comfort, though he could testify that wasn't always enough. And maybe not enough here.

The windows were dark. No cars sat in the driveway or under the open garage.

Was it you, Ryan? Did you take her?

Ryan. Oh, Jane knew about Ryan. The way Anne looked at him in the photos in Greg's office, in the photos at their home. The way she'd never looked at Stephanie or even her husband. Anne, and Ryan, had always taken what they wanted.

But they won't get Gram, and they won't get Mom.

"You must have other resources," Gram said. "Trust funds, family money."

Anne looked at her as though she'd grown two heads. "I need that for my clothes."

Gram's voice stayed reasonable. "You know this isn't fair, Anne. It casts a shadow on me, and a bigger one on the festival. And you're not being fair to yourself. You'll be living a lie, and I don't think you'll like it."

Anne shrugged. "I'll deal with that later. Right now, I can't afford a conscience. Anyway, this is how it's going to go down. Jane, you'll stop asking questions, and the three of you are going to pack up and leave Hilltop. Forever."

Leave Hilltop?

Gram sat up straighter. "You know the only way I'm leaving Hilltop is when I die."

Anne smiled, pointing the gun at her. "That can still be arranged."

Before Jane could react, Mom said, "I'm dyin' anyway. Don't listen to her, Jane."

"And I'm old," Gram added. "Doesn't matter to me. Janie, do the right thing."

Anne ignored them. "Yes, Jane. Do the right thing. Get your family and go. Or we can do a murder-suicide. Jane, your prints will be on the gun. You'll put Mama out of her misery, and you were really disappointed in Alice. But *you* didn't want to live any more. Right, Jane?"

No. She'd always wanted to live, even in the bleakest of times, even when Larry came to her at night. And especially now. Now that her life was coming back together. Now that she had Noah in it. Noah was right, forgiveness set her free.

Noah will find us. I just need to stall long enough. No leaving Hilltop or this earth.

Jane looked Anne in the eyes. "Don't you want to know how I figured it out?"

"Not really." Anne's features were hard and drawn, all the beauty drained away.

"It was the typeface on the notes. I worked at Greg's store in high school, and I remember the typewriter. And that you don't do computers. You had Gram take her bracelet off. And you were cleaning the counters. Anne, you never clean anything. And you were there at the school that night to put the second note in my notebook. That's how you got the charm. That's how you avoided fingerprints."

"You always were clever," Anne said. "Since Alice pulled you out of the gutter. Since your slut of a mother abandoned you." Her glance slid over Carly. "But you'll never be good enough." Anne paused for effect. "You'll always be the girl the tramp gave up."

"You will not talk that way about my child or my grandchild." Gram said, her pleasant tone beginning to ice over. "They may not be good enough for you. Really, Anne, I'm not sure anyone is. But they're good enough for God."

Yes, God had loved her now. Always had.

But there was one more thing Anne needed to hear. "You tried to run me off the road."

Gram's head snapped around. "She did what?"

Jane's gaze remained on her former friend, former mentor. "She tried to run me off the road. The night I went to Littleton to pick up that check. I didn't tell you, Gram, but that night, it was snowing. And a Gregson's pickup pushed me off the road. It was you at the wheel, wasn't it?"

"I only wanted to warn you. Not hurt you."

"You didn't just warn me. Hayley was in that car. So, I guess you warned her too."

Jane glanced at Anne's hands, shaking like the autumn leaves in a light breeze.

"I knew you were going over to Littleton. I heard about the check. I hear everything that goes on in this town. But *Hayley* was with you?"

"A last-minute ride-along. If you'd tried harder, you could have killed us both."

"I never meant—you're lying."

"Ask Stephanie about the night Hayley came home in a tow truck. Or ask Johnnie Colarusso to check his logs for that night."

Anne seemed to shrink before them. But Ryan trumped even Hayley. "Well, guess I was lucky. And you both were. But your luck is running out."

Jane smiled at Anne and found the courage to go on bluffing. "You won't get away with this, Anne. Not three of us. Paul knows it wasn't Gram. He has the notes you left me, the notes that only could have come from your typewriter. He'll figure it out soon. Really, you've made yourself the perfect suspect."

"You forget I still have the gun. I guess we'll go with murder-suicide then." Anne said, but her hands trembled. "Now, are you going to stop asking questions?"

Jane raised her head. "Could you live with yourself if I said 'yes'?"

"I'm already living with myself."

Gram sighed, putting a protective arm in front of Jane. "Anne, this isn't living."

Is this love? Jane wondered, the kind of passion that risked everything for the loved one, that was willing to hurt and steal and even kill? Was it love that gave them everything they wanted? Or love that did what was best for them?

Jane looked past Anne, to her own mother's gaunt face. Was love when you did the best thing for another person, no matter how it looked to the outside world? When you put them on a bus so they could have a better future, or a future at all? When you were less than perfect, but your heart wanted what was right?

When you made it right, even though it cost you everything?

Hadn't Noah said something similar, that Jesus gave his life so we might have true life in him? Living loved. That was really living.

"Anne, you can still turn this around." Gram, not at all afraid, and why should she be? "We won't press charges. Not for this. You'd have to pay the money back, but you'd have to anyway. Let it go. Let us help you."

Did Mom pick up on the change in her mother's voice? Jane did. She had to keep stalling. "So, Hilltop wasn't enough for you, Anne."

"For a vacation home, maybe. The skiing's good, but I never expected to be here this long."

Anne really hadn't known her husband—or not enough. Greg's blood went back five generations in these mountains. He'd never leave Hilltop.

Neither would Jane, Mom, or Gram. Not this way.

Jane heard a click. Was that the safety? No, it was Gram, twisting her bound hands to unlock the wheels on her chair and catapulting across the polished, slanted oak floor. Gram rammed into Anne who fell against the dresser with the stack of scarves, the pistol flying from her grasp.

Noah drove back through a maze of side streets, avoiding downtown, driving faster than he knew was safe. He had tried to track Jane's phone, but it must be off.

Noah tapped his car's GPS monitor to call the only one who could help him now. Paul. As soon as he picked up, Noah said, "I can't find Jane. You have to help me."

"Ok, when did you last see her?" Paul said on the other end.

"At the living nativity. I'm worried she figured out who took the money, and they took her."

"We know it wasn't Ryan." Paul said. "I've got Greg here to explain."

"Ryan was practicing that night the money went missing," Greg said. "But Anne disappeared that night. She used the truck. She never uses the truck. And she had one that Friday night Jane almost got run off the road."

"Meet us at the shop." Paul said.

"And, Noah," Greg added, "pray."

Noah forced a smile. "You got it."

Once he ended the call, he snaked around the abandoned wire factory and pulled up behind Anne's Mountain Boutique, in a bleak rear area with a dumpster and several rotting wooden pallets. The only light came from the street. He clung to the single glove in his hand. A glove he had seen on Jane's slender fingers.

God, help us.

Jane slid across the floor on her belly, grabbed the gun, and struggled to her feet. "Okay, Anne. I've got this now, and you know I know how to use it." She pointed the gun at the older woman. "Greg took me hunting when I was twelve. I bagged a deer. With a shotgun, but the skills translate."

Regaining her balance, Anne tucked her hands under her arms. "Showing up Steph and Ryan again."

Jane watched Gram and Mom from the corner of her eye. After freeing herself, Gram helped Mom out of her bindings, looking at Anne with something close to pity.

"They didn't want to learn. Anne, you've got to stop making excuses ... for Ryan, for this." Jane lowered the gun. "Plus, I know enough to know this gun isn't loaded." Jane tilted her head toward the back stairs. "But it looks like I have backup."

Anne stilled at the sound of hurrying footsteps and stared as Noah, Greg, and Paul burst into the room. "How did they—"

"It's over, Mrs. Gregson." Paul said, approaching her. "I'm sorry."

Jane handed the gun to Paul. They exchanged a quick sorrowful glance before he slipped a pair of handcuffs on Anne Harriman Gregson and began to read her her rights.

Noah turned to speak to Greg, but he was gone, leaving by a back entrance. Would Greg go home and nurse his betrayal? Anne would be in jail for a long time with the attempt at murder and kidnapping charges. And oh, yeah, embezzlement from the festival. Noah would have to talk to him tomorrow. Greg would be hurting.

An officer with a clipboard stood at the ready to take their statements.

Anne was leaving, shackled and not resisting. She was still his parishioner.

"Anne," he called.

She turned and looked at him with dead eyes. "It's too late, Pastor. Let it go."

That was that. The door slammed behind her, then the cruiser doors slammed downstairs. The officer turned toward Alice, Carly, and Jane, ready to take their statements.

Noah crossed the room to Jane, and she looked up at him with those wide green eyes. Jane. What if he'd lost her tonight?

As Gram told her side of the story, Jane disengaged herself from her mother, with a quick kiss on the woman's forehead.

Jane trembled as she turned to face him. He had to take her away. At least for a moment. He led her to the back stairs, and she leaned into him, clinging for all she was worth. He held her and let her cry.

She lifted her head to look up at him. "Poor Anne. To have that eating away at her. We should have known, should have tried to help her."

"No, Jane. She should have asked for help." He gripped her forearms. "Are you saying you forgive her?"

"It might take some time, but I want to. Forgiveness isn't just for the offender but for the one who got hurt. It's freedom, or so my small group says. Plus, she's family, isn't she? Hilltop family."

Yes, Jane carried Alice's blood, through and through. He'd never understand about the leaves, but he understood the Old Man of the Mountains, the granite-like courage that ran through these people. His people, now.

Anne Gregson was forgiven, though healing would take a while.

Could he afford to do less, be less? If Jane could forgive Anne, Noah could find the courage to finally forgive his own mother. And call his father.

"You found my glove." Jane said, bringing him back to reality.

"I knew it was some kind of signal. Jane Archer doesn't go around losing gloves."

"Only when she needs rescuing."

But she'd done most of it herself. Gram and Jane and the Lord.

Noah kissed her cheek. "You were so brave, and I'm so proud of you. Take care of your mom. I'll call you first thing in the morning, okay? And not to talk business."

"Okay, *Pastor.*" Jane grinned up at him, the green eyes dancing, the tears drying on her cheeks. "But remember, we still have a festival to run, and you have your sermon."

CHAPTER TWENTY-SEVEN

Noah let himself into the parsonage after following Anne to the police station. She hadn't wanted to talk, hadn't wanted prayer. Maybe tomorrow. And Greg hadn't shown up, but Stephanie was there, alerted by the Hilltop police. Steph would do whatever needed to be done. God only knew where Ryan was.

The parsonage was as cold as ever, and dark even after he switched on the overhead light. He hadn't decorated the house for the holidays, but it didn't matter anymore. He carried this Christmas inside him and would for the rest of his life.

With Jane? Maybe. He could hope.

Love gone wrong. The Gregsons would have a long, hard road ahead of them. Being a family was tough, there were no easy answers, but you still had to try.

Noah reached for his phone and went into the small study off the living room. His brothers had texted him they'd laid some groundwork, but it was but to him to make it happen. Dad would be the challenge. He squeezed himself into a desk chair made for a smaller man and tapped in the number he barely remembered.

God, now give me strength to forgive.

"Hastings." That was Dad, never a wasted word.

"Dad, it's me. Noah."

"Oh. Oh, well—*Noah*. What a surprise."

Noah's four words had rattled the unshakeable Richard Hastings.

"I just wanted to call to—" *Say it, Noah.* "To tell you I love you and wish you a merry Christmas."

"Oh, well, thank you, Noah. That's very—Thanks."

He could picture his father in suit and tie, even at this time of the night, or at worst in shirtsleeves and loosened tie. At a desk, at work or in his home, or coming from a meeting. Living to work instead of working to live.

"It was nice of you to call. It's good to hear from you."

Richard Hastings would never say "I love you" back, but that was okay. But Noah knew what his father really meant. Thanks to his Heavenly Father.

"It's good to hear you too. I've been talking with Ted and Jeff. They say you've been having a good year. I'm so happy for you." He took a big breath. "I wanted you to know I've been praying for you, and I forgive you. I know you've always wanted the best for me, and I truly am grateful."

There was a pause, no, was his father tearing up? "Thank you, Noah."

Noah's own eyes teared up. "You're welcome, Dad."

His dad cleared his throat. "Hey, what's it like there? Cold?"

"Brutal. We've had snow off and on since before Thanksgiving."

His father's laughter rewarded his efforts. Not sharp laughter, not cruel, but joyful. "Don't say I didn't warn you. How's the church? Those people being decent to you?"

How to describe iron-willed Alice, brilliant Paul, bighearted Greg over the phone? Even Ryan didn't seem so terrible now. How to summarize the wonder of Jane, who baked cookies and built floats and loved other people's kids and smelled when it was going to snow and looked fantastic doing all of it? Who might even love *him?*

He had to try. "Dad, I've met someone. Her name is Jane, and she teaches high school. She's great."

"Love to meet her. Bring her out here sometime, all right? I'll send the tickets."

"I'll try." Noah leaned back in the rickety chair and put his feet up on the desk. "But it may take some talking. She likes it here."

"Are you sure you don't want to go to the parade?" Jane set the tea tray on the small table between the wing chair and Carly's sofa.

"I don't think so, honey. We're still pretty shaken up from what happened." Gram glanced at her daughter, napping fitfully on the couch. "I don't want her out in the cold, and I won't leave her for that long. But I will slip out to the Christmas Eve service, if you come back for me."

Jane kissed the crown of her grandmother's head. "Always."

"Have you talked to Stephanie? Will she be there?"

"No." Jane braced herself as she tugged on a boot. "She, Hayley, and Steph's boyfriend are spending Christmas Eve with Anne. At the jail."

"Someday Anne will realize what she has in that girl." But Gram said it without rancor, and Jane could understand. Her own family was safe and whole.

Tonight was the last night of the festival. The parade came next, then the potluck, the Christmas services at

Hilltop's two churches, and Christmas itself. "I've got to go," Jane said. "I'm meeting—some people."

"He's a good boy, Janie. You can't go wrong with Noah."

Of course, Gram knew how Jane felt about him. Maybe she'd known longer than Jane had.

Jane watched as the Regional marching band played with all their heart in the parade, all sporting jaunty elf hats, followed by a harried band director trying to get them into formation. A gingerbread house rolled passed on the back of a flatbed with costumed children tumbling over it, a Nutcracker on stilts. Athletes sported their team jackets next to fragile veterans protected from the cold inside antique cars.

She waved to Sammi and Doug and their twins as they passed by.

Ryan's band stood in the back of a pickup truck tuning their guitars and practicing one of their songs. Ryan looked parade-perfect in a worn leather jacket, his hair artfully mussed.

Jane waved to him. "Hey, Ryan!"

Ryan's face creased in his patented perfect smile. "Hey, Janie! Merry Christmas!"

Did Ryan understand the sacrifice his mother had made, albeit wrongly? Did he know the sacrifice yet to come?

Ryan was Ryan.

And Greg was there, at the wheel of the flatbed truck bearing Charlie's Santa Claus. What was Greg feeling, thinking now? His expression was pleasant as he chatted through the open window with other parade participants. But he had to be hurting. Would he talk with Noah, or just pour it out to God?

Jane had seen what keeping it all in led to, saw it chip away at her and Gram's relationship, saw it eat away at her mom, saw it bring a shadow to the ever-smiling Noah, saw it explode in Anne. But now, slowly, she, Gram, and her mom were opening up to each other, learning to let the tough things go, and praying together. Yes, talking about it with loved ones and with God wasn't the thing she always believed would break her. It's what was making her whole.

She spotted Paul's tall form, made even taller by Maddy riding high on his shoulders. He maneuvered toward her with Emma at his side. "Hey, Janie. You okay?"

"I am now." It had been a long two days. "How is Anne?"

"About as good as she's going to get. She doesn't deny what she did. She's just lucky you fought back. And that the gun wasn't loaded. Should get her a lighter sentence, but we'll see."

Paul was still a protector.

Jane looked up at him. "Thank you, Paul. For being there."

He shrugged. "Hey, it's what I do. No regrets." He paused as Maddy squirmed on his shoulders. "So, Jane, will you be here for New Year's? Are you doing anything? My mom said she'd babysit ..."

Paul. Her first friend, the one who had taught her compassion. She would always be indebted to him for that, and for being Paul. But they were secondary characters in each other's stories.

"Oh, Paul. If we had anything between us, we'd have known it by now."

"Yeah, you're right." Paul grinned, and he was suddenly the boy she'd known most of her life. "Will you still help me with the kids?"

Jane tweaked the pompom on Emma's knitted hat. "Of course, I will. There's still the winter festival, and we've got to make Valentine cookies, don't we, girls?"

They turned to go their separate ways, but Paul turned back. "Janie. We made good choices, didn't we?"

Jane smiled. "Yes. Yes, we did."

"And I think you're about to make another one."

Jane tossed him a grin and scanned the crowd for the person she really wanted to see. She spotted Noah, a head above most of the crowd, his golden head bare to the chilly sunlight. Would he ever learn? She pushed past some band kids until she stood before him.

"Hey."

"Hey, yourself."

And about time. Missing her already, Noah had been looking for her since he got to the festival. He had bumped into Paul and Brad who convinced him to create a young men's Bible study open to members from both churches, proposing Father Donovan to lead the group. But as soon as Noah spotted her, he left the guys to jog toward her.

Yes, God had given him some solid friends after all.

Noah couldn't stop smiling when he stood before Jane. Beautiful, her dark hair swinging at her back, her cheeks red from the cold, her smile only for him.

He tucked her arm in his. "So, what do we do now?"

"I'd better get over to the reviewing stand. I'm filling in for Gram. They always save a seat for the chairman. And they said I could bring a date."

Noah tucked her arm more firmly in his. "I'm the sponsoring pastor, and they said *I* could bring a date."

Jane's smile widened. "Well, we'd better hurry then."

They moved through the parking lot, Noah waving to his friends, Jane waving to hers. But mostly they waved to *their* friends. A couple, a unit. Made, or about to be made one in Christ.

Near the reviewing stand, she stopped short and pulled her phone from her pocket. "It's Gram. It's a text." She frowned over the words. "Oh, no."

"What?" he asked, alert to every change in her life.

"She's at the Littleton hospital."

"Oh, Jane."

Jane shoved the phone in her pocket. "I'd better get over there."

"I'll go with you."

"No." She brushed her lips against his, clinging to him for a minute. "You need to be here. You have a parade to judge and a sermon to deliver. I'll go. If it's nothing serious I'll be back for the service, or maybe the supper. I'll text you."

She kissed him again, clung to him briefly, and she was gone, snaking her way back through the crowd.

Noah bent his head in swift, silent prayer.

The hospital operated on a skeleton staff, Christmas Eve, but the nurse at the floor station was friendly when Jane arrived. "Yes, Mrs. Merrill is here. Nice lady, I had her in school. Or she had me. She's down the hall to the right."

Jane pushed past a group of carolers and pushed open the door.

Gram was there, in the chair by Carly's bedside, her walker at the ready, an afghan draped over her knees. She looked up from her library book. "Oh, Janie."

Jane dropped to her knees and buried her face in the afghan. "I thought it was you."

Gram lifted her face. "It isn't. And it won't be me, not for a while. But your mother took a turn for the worse this afternoon, so we brought her in here."

Jane looked at Carly, high in the white hospital bed, a clear tube running from one nostril, her arms like pincushions, her mouth open in an uneasy sleep. She moved forward and took Carly's limp hand. "Mom, it's Janie. I'm here now."

"She's under sedation, honey. She won't hear you."

Jane stared at the wreck of a woman in the hospital bed. Why had it taken so long for her to love her? Why hadn't she forgiven Mom sooner, and accepted God's forgiveness for herself?

If only she could will her own strength, youth, and health into this woman. If she could skin off ten years of her life, give Carly ten more ...

No, it didn't work that way.

"She'll need more care," Gram was saying. "Hospice. Maybe a hospital bed. Better oxygen. I'm going to move her into the downstairs bedroom, just for now. For as long as it takes."

"I'll stay on the couch." It was the least Jane could do, to be there for Mom when she cried out in the night.

"No, I will. I still can't do stairs well—and, Janie, she's my daughter."

Jane looked into the old eyes and saw no denial, no fear. Gram knew what she was getting into.

"Then I'll bathe her and feed her," Jane said firmly. "We'll share this like we always have. And when it's over—"

Gram smiled softly. "We'll see her again. And my Walter. And our Lord. It will be a glorious reunion."

"I don't want to lose her." The words were true, torn from Jane for the first time in her life.

"None of us do. But, Janie, it's different now. You'll see her in Heaven. She won't hurt any more. She'll be—she'll be what Charlotte Merrill Archer was meant to be."

Jane smiled at the comforting words, the kind only Gram could give, or, maybe now, Noah as well. Jane released her mother's skeletal hand and knelt next to Gram again. Gram stroked her hair.

"You should go now. You're missing the parade, honey."

"Rather be here."

"Noah needs you. He needs to look out over that congregation, that huge congregation, and see you smiling back at him. He needs your encouragement." Gram looked into her eyes. "But I'll stay with your mom." She gestured to a heavy canvas tote bag. "I have my books, my Bible, and I grabbed a few toiletries on the way out. Won't be the first time I've sat by a hospital bed. Won't be the last."

Time to go, to be there for Noah. Gram had Mom's back. Gram had everyone's back.

Jane unfolded herself from the floor. "I'll be over tomorrow, first thing. We'll have Christmas breakfast in the cafeteria, okay?"

"That's the best thing I've heard all day. And bring Noah."

Jane kissed her mother on the forehead. *Thank you, God, for my second chance. Even if it had to be like this.*

At the door, Jane turned back. "Gram, you could have still run the Hilltop Festival with your phone and your laptop. The only things I did that were really physical were the float building and the cookie baking, and I did those on my own. Why did you rope me in? Were you trying to match-make me with Noah?"

Gram's eyes glistened. "No, honey. I was trying to match-make you with Hilltop."

CHAPTER TWENTY-EIGHT

Jane entered the Legion. The long, low frame building was filled to bursting. Bev and Mark talked quietly at a corner table, more of a couple than she'd ever seen them, with a bond that would not be shaken by death. Father Donovan filled a plate for a woman in a wheelchair. Fred Parker, his wife, and the children chatted with Bill Desrosiers as Michelle cut a piece of meat for one of the boys. Brad King held a tray for old Mrs. Barnes as she tapped her way across the dining room with her cane.

And Greg, who gave her a brief, grim nod as he set a pan of lasagna on the steam table. Nothing would derail Greg from Hilltop. Not betrayal, not loss of trust. Not the almost certain crumbling of his marriage. Would he eventually forgive Anne? It was out of all their hands.

But Hilltop, the festival and the town, would go on. Only with God's help.

Jane's heart swelled at the sight of all of them, friends and strangers. The cloud of witnesses that had never been far away.

"Pastor ain't here," Wayne MacDonald called to her. "He's over at the church."

Jane nodded. Well, what had she expected? The whole town could know she had a crush on their pastor, as long as she knew he had one back.

Her feet had wings as she ran down the street, past the deserted vendor booths and dimmed shop windows, past the library and the old library, and the skating rink at the Town Common. All dark now, hushed for the coming of the king. Her king, now. The time to play was past.

She ran up the hill, her feet sure over the packed snow. Luminarias lit the walkways, snow clung to the stone eaves. Light streamed through the stained-glass windows of Hilltop Community Church. The sanctuary tree was lit, the tall red tapers by the platform lit and wavering when she let in the cold. The room smelled of fresh greens.

And Noah was there, seated in a back pew, his golden head bent against the next pew as he prayed. As she slipped into the seat next to him, he turned and gave her that heart-stopping grin. "Hey, how's Alice?"

"She's fine. Thank God. It's my mom." She leaned her head on his shoulder. How natural, how easy it was now. "It's only a matter of time now, be we knew that. Hospice is being called in. We're making the arrangements after New Year's. Gram is with her."

"I'm so sorry, Jane." He gave her hand a reassuring squeeze. "But I can't think of any better way to spend Christmas than with my three favorite girls."

Jane would make the most of the time they had left. "I think I should be here, to help Gram. So, I'm calling the school as soon as I can." She drew a deep breath. "I talked to Bev Smith, and there's an opening in Social Studies at Regional. She said she'll recommend me. There's a good chance I'll get it, Bev says."

He grinned, picked her up and swung her until she gasped for breath. "That's great! Because I'm staying too."

"Noah! You mean it?"

"Until God calls me away. Hilltop is my home too.

He bent to kiss her, and she kissed him back, deepening their connection, a kiss of peace and hope and promise. Of what they could be together and with God. His arms tightened around her. She locked his hands around the back of his neck and pulled him closer.

"So," she said when they broke apart. "So, I think I'll stick around and see where this is going."

"I know where it's going," Noah said, his blue eyes warm with love.

She took his hand. "Come on, the nativity set is up."

She pulled him down the aisle until they stood before the manger scene that had been a part of the church since before Jane was born, probably before Gram and Walter came to Hilltop. The plaster figures stood twenty inches high with paint faded by the ages. The pieces were chipped—a little bit of a lamb's ear, the knob on a Wise Man's ornate gift box, a piece of Mary's blue veil. They weren't perfect, but neither were Noah and Jane.

"They're just like us," she whispered. "Broken but still usable."

"I would be happy to be broken alongside you." Noah dropped a kiss on her forehead. "I have to get ready for my sermon. You'll be there, right?"

"Before, during, and after." Jane smiled up at him. "Would you mind if I prayed for you before that?"

Smiling, Noah took her hands in his. "I'd love that."

Noah looked out over the congregation, his congregation. The sanctuary was standing room only, with people spilling out into the hallway. Three hundred people jammed the pews and aisles. Another two hundred watched on CCTV from the multi-purpose room.

The live tree and live garlands perfumed the sanctuary. White lights twinkled from the tree, the only adornment it had, the only one it needed. Real candles glowed on windowsills high enough that the little ones couldn't reach them. Real candles glowed from alcoves and sconces, and electric candles filled in the gaps. Plenty of light waited for the light of the world.

The antique nativity set had pride of place in the front.

During the choir performances and the children's pageant, he'd picked out faces in the crowd. Beverly Smith and Mark, for Mark's last Christmas Eve on this earth before he went to a place where Christmas was all year round. Charlie, Edith, Wayne. Greg Gregson, with his patrician features set to ward off any questions about Anne. Stephanie and Hayley would be with Anne, Ryan was who knew where.

Noah's own people mixed with the tourists who had planned their Christmas around this service. But he knew who wasn't there. Though Alice was at the hospital with her daughter, Noah felt her blessing and prayers across the miles. Alice knew where her Lord wanted her on this night of all nights. The night it all began.

And there was Jane, with the Parkers on one side of her and the McKees on the other. Little Danny Parker cuddled in her lap. Jane was at peace now, and ready to use her gifts for the Lord and his kingdom. What would the next twelve months bring?

His gaze connected with hers, and she gave him a tiny nod. *You can do it, Noah.*

Noah stepped down from the platform, ignoring the pulpit. He wasn't a pulpit kind of guy. This Christmas sermon, and the sermons to come, would be like talking with friends.

He opened his Bible. "'The light shines in the darkness, and the darkness has not overcome it. John 1:5.'" He looked at the crowd. "When I came to New England, I knew it was going to be cold. Sort of. I'd seen movies and TV shows. But even Hollywood can't give a true impression of the cold in New Hampshire or these mountains." He shuddered theatrically, and the crowd laughed. They knew their pastor by now.

"But the cold in the daytime doesn't hold a candle to the cold after dark. When the sun sets, the darkness moves in. It can swallow a person, especially one from California."

He swallowed, moved to a different part of the front. If he kept moving, maybe he could do this.

"And it's a dark world out there, people. Broken families, broken hearts, broken lives. Families in turmoil." He avoided looking at Greg. "Poverty and crime." Paul McKee gave him a nod of encouragement.

"It was a dark world for the Jews in the first century BC, living under Roman occupation and oppression. The people longed for the promised Messiah. They were a people walking in darkness, craving the light. But God used an ordinary couple with an extraordinary God to bring that light. A teenage bride and a man who made his living with his hands rode in the dark night to Bethlehem. But a star marked the sky as a sign of Jesus's coming. Angels sang of his birth.

"But the people didn't recognize the light when it came. They wanted physical freedom, but God had a better plan. A plan for spiritual freedom, to light up the dark places of our souls. A light that would spread into the world's dark places, places that would never be the same again. Jesus's disciples recognized the light. Later, they would use the Roman roads and the common language, *Koine* Greek, to spread the light to all the known world. But I wonder, do we recognize the light when he shines on us? Do we let

God's light in, purging the stain of sin and the darkness of fear? Do we seize every opportunity to shine for him?"

Noah breathed deeply. He looked at the wooden cross at the back of the church and Jane's shining face for inspiration.

"I've spent the past six weeks with 'ordinary' people doing extraordinary things. I've seen Hilltop overcome a darkness of its own, the false accusation of one of its own. And I've seen you emerge stronger. I've seen you bring the light to others, wrapping your arms around needy families with your food baskets, conducting clothing drives, showing your caring hearts. You've opened your homes and helped people find their way home."

He looked at Jane again, her green eyes glimmering with tears. "And I've seen you forgive." He fought back tears as he thought of how ever since Anne's arrest, everyone had treated Jane and her family with nothing but compassion.

"I've seen you shine the light into the dark places of the North Country. And it all began with a baby, a special baby, on a dark night two thousand years ago. So, Hilltop, keep shining brightly. I'm proud to be your pastor, and I'm proud to be your friend."

It wasn't a classic three-point sermon. Was it even a one-point? Didn't matter. The congregation surged to its feet. Noah gasped when they broke out into applause.

There was Jane, handing the Parker boy back to his mother and making her way toward the front of the church. She took both his arms as he looked down into her glowing face. "Noah. Don't you see? It's not for you. It's for God."

EPILOGUE

Jane Hastings threaded her way through the chaos of a building project. Hammers clanged and saws whined on the generous lawn of the old Victorian farmhouse. She skirted Hayley Gregson and another young teen, giggling over something as they pushed a wheelbarrow full of 2x4s, and saw the person she was looking for. The person she'd always be looking for.

Noah rounded a stack of drywall, and his face lit up at the sight of her as it always did. "Hey. How's it going?"

"Great." Jane took his hand and drew him into the shade of an ancient chestnut tree. "Everybody knows their job. It's like float-building, only in the summer."

Noah gestured toward the three-story farmhouse. "Still can't believe you talked me into keeping the porch. We could have put on a half-dozen extra rooms instead."

"Yes. But you've got to have a porch. People talk on a porch. People open up on a porch." She nodded at the farmhouse porch, a generous apron circling the old building, where Gram held the pink bundle of three-month-old Charlotte Nicole Hastings in her lap. "Great-grandmothers need to rock babies, don't they? What better place than a porch?"

Noah shrugged. "Yeah, guess you're right. Dad and the boys didn't waste any time fitting in, did they?"

Jane shaded her eyes and looked toward where Richard Hastings, a tool belt fastened over his designer jeans, bossed a floor crew. "He's in his element. And he adores Charlotte. Inviting them to help was a good move."

A good move at the end of a year of good moves. Make that a year and a half full of blessings—the gentle passing of her mother, their wedding, her job at Regional, and Gram formally acquitted of the embezzling. Jane had sold her townhouse to her very happy roommates who wished her the best. Gram had sold off one of her Littleton properties, and with much prayer, Merrill House, a children's group home, took shape.

They were in the process of being licensed by the state of New Hampshire. Fred and Melissa Parker would be the house parents with Sammi and Doug Morton as fill-ins and with Jane as the director responsible to a board including Noah and Father Phil Donovan.

Jane knew her next master's degree would be in counseling. She was most proud of how God had helped her finally make peace with what Larry had done. Even after she reported him to the police.

Now, all she could see now was what God was doing.

"Will you miss teaching?" Noah's arm tightened around her waist.

"I'll still be part-time," she said. "Social studies isn't going anywhere."

She would teach two days a week, administer Merrill House on the other three. She'd bring Charlotte to work with her and show her firsthand what a lifestyle of caring looked like. The way Gram had shown her.

Not everyone had a happy ending, or at least not yet. Greg was here, bossing the framing crew, fielding questions, and solving problems, his big laugh ringing out. Anne was still in prison, and to Jane's knowledge, Greg hadn't visited her once. Her betrayal ran wide and deep. The bank had finally put in security cameras. Ryan had disappeared right after the Christmas parade. Had he made it to Nashville, New York, LA? Hilltop didn't know. And they knew better than to ask.

But Steph stood by her, fully integrating her into her young women's Bible study.

And Paul was here, swinging a hammer while his parents watched Emma and Maddy at their home. Paul, as sturdy as the granite outcroppings. Would he find his forever woman and complete his family? He made way for a parade of Colarussos bringing lunch in foil-covered containers. She saw quips exchanged as Monique and Michelle set out desserts at the other end of a long table.

The new property had a creek for fishing and trees big enough for a treehouse. There would be an onsite library, filled with childhood classics and classics-to-be. There would be laptops and smart tablets so the children could do their homework when they weren't running about under the ancient trees.

The Parkers would have their private quarters on the third floor, while the second floor held dorm-style rooms for the little kids and semi-private rooms for the teens. Living room, dining room, library and kitchen would fill the first floor. And the basement would hold something Jane had lobbied for harder than the porch—two studio apartments for women with families down on their luck.

Carly would have been proud. Carly *was* proud.

And it had all come about through this man who loved her—and the God who loved them both.

Jane leaned into her husband. "God really does know best, doesn't he?"

"He sure does." Noah kissed the top of her head. "And I can't wait to meet our first guests."

Jane brushed his lips with her own. "I'm going to see Gram and check on Charlotte."

"Yeah, I'd better get back to work." He watched her go. "See you at lunch."

She tossed him a grin over her shoulder. "Count on it."

Despite a wet winter, Noah and Jane and their little Charlotte had enjoyed the winter carnival. An exuberant spring came followed by a lush summer. The old-growth trees leafed out over his head as he headed toward Greg's work crew. He could understand the hype of the leaf peepers now.

"Yo, Noah!"

He shaded his eyes and made out Ted and Jeff, nailing down shingles on the roof. "Hey. How's it going?"

"Okay. Next time you come to California, we're gonna put *you* to work." Jeff brushed the dirt on the knees of his jeans.

Ted followed Noah's gaze toward Jane's retreating back. "You did well, bro."

"Yeah," Jeff looked between them, "got any more like her at home?"

Noah could feel his smile stretch, feel the happiness that led him close to bursting these days. "Only child, sorry."

"That's okay." Jeff's gaze drifted to the yard below, where a dark-eyed Dumont college student had joined her mother at the refreshment table. "I'll manage."

Noah continued to watch Jane. His wife, his partner, his sister in Christ. When she was almost to the porch, he called to her. "Hey, Jane?"

"Yes?" She turned, her face aglow in the sunlight.

"Do you know you have two different socks on?"

Jane looked down at her sneakered feet, then gave a little shrug. "It's okay. I've got another pair just like them at home."

ABOUT THE AUTHOR

Kathleen Bailey is a journalist and novelist with forty years' experience in the nonfiction, newspaper, and inspirational fields. Born in 1951, she was a child in the 50s, a teen in the 60s, a young adult in the 70s and a young mom in the 80s. It's been a turbulent, colorful time to grow up, and she's enjoyed every minute of it and written about most of it.

Bailey's work includes both historical and contemporary fiction, with an underlying thread of men and women finding their way home, to Christ and each other. She has published five titles in the Western Dreams series: *Westward Hope, Settler's Hope, The Logger's Christmas Bride, The Widow's Christmas Miracle,* and *Redemption's Hope.*

In addition, she publishes local history nonfiction with Arcadia Publishing and has co-authored *Past and Present*

Exeter, New Hampshire, September 2020; *New Hampshire War Monuments: The Stories Behind the Stones,* August 2022; and *Growing Up in Concord, New Hampshire in the 50s and 60s* in 2023.

She lives in New Hampshire with her husband David. They have two grown daughters.

For more information, contact her at ampie86@comcast.net; Kathleen D. Bailey on Facebook and LinkedIn; or www.kathleendbailey.weebly.com.

Made in the USA
Middletown, DE
03 November 2023

41764557R00170